MELANIE LEAVEY

Sea Bride

THREE RAVENS
P R E S S

for my readers....your generosity keeps the words flowing

and for the women who tend – past, present and future

Contents

I

Part One

Acknowledgement

Writing is a solitary sort of thing – hours spent locked in a room, or in your own head, daydreaming, scribbling and tapping away – but it's certainly not something you do alone. It might be my name on the cover, but this book has a cast of thousands.

Well, maybe not thousands, I *am* a hermity sort after all.

Gratitude…in multitudinous abundance to:

First, last and always – my family:

My mum and dad – without whom, I wouldn't be here today. Quite literally. To my mum, especially, for knowing when to ask about 'the next book' and when not to mention it.

My husband and children who believe in me unconditionally and who know that when the door's closed and the house isn't on fire, I'm to be left in peace. Mostly, they do.

Brandt – for giving me the time and space to dream myself true

Sebastian – for living your magic out loud

and Savannah – for the world-mending conversations and wisdom beyond your young years – this one, especially, is for you and yours.

My internet family — my readers and supporters, encouragers and cheerleaders. Special thanks (in no particular order) to Helen R., Helen C., Antoinette, Trish, Ulrika, Kim N., Jayne, Indi, Nicole, Ann, Bridget, Liz G. and everyone else who's ever left a comment on my blog or sent me a lovely email. Your support means the world.

Susan Rizzo - for words and deeds too numerous to mention; for letters and tea, books and roses; for seeing me truly. *I am ever your faithful magpie.*

Karin DiBiase at Lakeside Books and Art for continued support of local, indie creators.

And to the women who inspire me - past and present, real and fictional — may I be ever worthy of my lineage.

Chapter 1

Aibhlinn

The water jug hit the frame with a crash, just as I slammed the door behind me.

"Aye! And good riddance to ye, ye cursed wench!" bellowed my da, wrenching the door open. A metal bucket clanged to the ground beside me, followed by another volley of vile curses, but I didn't look back. I just kept on running.

***

I had planned a birthday tea for myself. Seventeen is an

important age, after all. By island standards I'm practically a grown woman, only one year left under my da's thumb and then I'll be free. Most girls on Glencarragh spend the year between seventeen and eighteen finding a suitor and carrying on a year-long courtship that will end in marital bliss when she becomes officially of age. Not for me, that life; I have other plans. I've had charge of a house full of men since I was tall enough to stand at the stove and stir the soup so I've no intention of following that up with more of the same. Besides, a girl would be hard pressed to find a decent fellow on Glencarragh that doesn't stink of fish or spend weeks at a time chasing sheep or mad-eyed ponies over the moor. Not that anyone is likely to offer, anyhow, I'm not exactly looked upon as a desirable match. It's mostly my own fault - my wild ways and sharp tongue do nothing to enamour folk and, if the truth were to be told, all I want is to be left alone to get on with things myself.

Actually, what I want most is to live on my own, in a little cottage on the moor, right next to the old wood. I'm going be a healer, like my mam and Hetty, and spend my days roaming about looking for the plants I need to make tonics and medicines. That, and the veg I'll grow and the hens who lay gorgeous brown eggs for me will be enough for me to pay my own way and I won't be beholden to anyone. I'll have enough company in the creatures and I'll have no need of anything, or anyone, else. I decided all this a long while ago and it's what's kept my feet and hands moving when all I wanted to do was put down my basket of washing and walk off over the moor and never come back.

My da, though, seems to have other plans.

* * *

"I've put your name in the book," he announced, belching loudly after his third helping of treacle pudding. I'd made the pudding because it's mine and Callum's favourite, but neither of us touched it. Da had been well in his cups before staggering into the middle of our party and was only gathering speed as the whiskey bottle emptied. Callum doesn't cope well with Da at the best of times, and Da roaring drunk is enough to put him off his food. He'll be away over the moor in a minute. That's his typical response to Da's drunken theatricals.

Hetty's spoon clattered onto the table.

"What?" she said, her face draining of colour. "You did what?"

Da grinned and reached over to pat my arm. I'd frozen in the middle of bringing a fresh pot of tea to the table. His blundering touch sloshed the hot liquid onto the tablecloth as I tried to put the teapot down.

"Ye heard me, woman. I'm surprised your John didnae tell ye already. I did it just las' night - past midnight, ye ken, so's it was all official like."

"You bastard!"

"Callum!"

The table jostled as my brother shot up, reaching across to grab our da by the collar of his shirt. Alexander, who was sitting closest, rose to intervene while Duncan sat, his eyes wide and a spoonful of treacle pudding halfway to his mouth.

"Hetty?" I cried, trying to save the teapot from being

knocked to the floor in the tussle which ensued. "Surely he can't mean…"

Alexander managed to pull Callum off our da and shoved him, Callum, that is, ungently, back into his chair. "Sit down, ye daft bugger," said Alexander, breathing heavily. "What d'ye think this is? A tavern brawl? Show our Aibhlinn a bit of respect on her day, will ye? She's gone to all this trouble to make us a lovely tea and there's ye carrying on like an oaf."

Callum hung his head, rubbing his hands up and down his thighs. "Sorry, lass," he muttered. I saw him take a quick glance towards the door.

"Oy, then, what about me, aye?" shouted Da, leaning over the table.

Alexander pushed him back.

"Shut yer gob, ye drunken auld fool," he said, rounding on him, "Ye deserve every thrashing as ye'll ever get, ye heartless bastard. How could ye do such a thing?"

Alexander shot a quick look in my direction, but I averted my eyes, trying to gather control of my own emotions. What could this mean? Surely, it wasn't true. All in one scalp-prickling moment, I saw my entire future spiraling out of my control; all of my plans and dreams seemed to shimmer and fade, winking out of existence like the flame of a wind-blown candle.

I cleared my throat.

"Am I right in believing that you've put me in for the sea bride's choosing, Da?"

I forced myself to meet his gaze. His eyes were bleary and bloodshot, and he looked quickly away. Shrugging carelessly, he sloshed another glug of whiskey into his glass. Throwing it back in one swift motion, he set the glass down with a forceful clunk.

"Ye believe right," he said, slowly, staring at the empty glass. "Ye're nowt but a burden to this family, girl. Ye've brought nowt but shame and scandal and I'm tired o' listening to the village harpies tell me what ye've said or done t' bring us down. I cannae barely show me face wi'out some shrieking bitch tellin' me what a disgrace y'are. Ye make me life a living hell with yer waywardness and yer impertinence. Just the very sight o' ye brings me blood to a boil."

"Just ye shut up, Hamish MacFinlay," said Hetty, her voice quivering with emotion. "Don't ye dare say one more hateful word. I don't think ye, of all people, are in any position to be casting judgment on anyone's behaviour." She turned to me where I stood, my hands knotted in my apron to control their shaking. I felt as if all the blood had drained from my face and a hollow, gnawing, sensation churned my stomach. He wasn't saying anything he hadn't said before a hundred times, but to hear it laid out so plainly, and all at once, took my breath away.

"Aibhlinn, pet," said Hetty, reaching out to touch my arm. Her hazel eyes were brimming with tears and her chin trembled. Swallowing, she squeezed my wrist. "Don't you listen to a word he says, *mo leanbh*," she whispered. "'Tis naught but spiteful lies."

I shook my head and withdrew from her grasp.

"It might be spiteful, Hetty, but it isn't all lies and well you know it," I said, turning to face my da where he sat, smiling triumphantly at my admission. "But it *would* be lying to say that I'm sorry for any of it."

The grin disappeared off my da's face in an instant, replaced by a scowl. The reaction spurred me on. I was long past caring.

"Whatever I am, I'm not one bit sorry. And if you think, even for a minute, that trying to marry me off to the sea will change me, then you couldn't be more wrong. There's nothing on this earth that will make me into something I'm not and that goes for your hatefulness and spite as well."

"Ye'll sit down and hold your tongue, girl, if ye've any mind as to what's good for ye," said my da, rage choking his words. He pushed himself up from the table, leaning heavily on it to support his swaying frame.

I took a step towards the door and he lunged at me.

"Oh no you don't, ye feckless wretch. There'll be nae more gallivanting across the moors whenever ye fancy. Ye belong to the folk of Glencarragh now and ye'll behave as such."

I took advantage of his lurching step to slip back around the other way. Callum stood up and shielded me as I ran past, blocking our da long enough for me to get to the back door.

I paused, long enough to look back at my da's struggling form. Callum had him by the arms and Duncan had stirred himself to stand, inconveniently, between our da and the door.

"If you know what's good for *you*, Da," I called back, breathless with anger and fright. "You'll never take me, or what I am, for granted. There's far more to me than you'll ever be bothered to notice and even more than you'll ever understand, because if you did, you wouldn't believe that handing me over to the sea would stop me from carrying on making your life a living hell."

Chapter 2

I ran until my lungs ached, reveling in the sharpness of the wind against my bare skin. I knew exactly where I was going and the thought of getting there dulled the stitch in my side and the ache in my heart.

I'd come away without my coat, wearing only an apron over my clothes. Under it was one of Callum's old jumpers, much darned and still smelling faintly of sheep and pipe tobacco. I prefer to wear old jumpers with my skirts, rather than bother to iron blouses or starch jacket collars. Which is just one of the many reasons people think I'm wild and unkempt. It's just that I can't quite see the point of being *presentable* when my days consist mostly of scrubbing floors and carrying armloads of peat. And when I'm not keeping house for my da and brothers, I'm scrambling about over the moors and tramping in the old woods, sometimes just for the sake of it but mostly I'm collecting plants and herbs for Hetty, pastimes which call even less for tidiness and proper behaviour. And then there's my secret place.

About a year ago, when I was out collecting early greens for our tea, I stumbled across the loveliest, most rundown and bedraggled little croft, tucked right up against the western edge of the old wood. It was like it was put there exactly for me. I don't know who it might have belonged to - probably one of the pony-men - because most of the shepherd's crofts are deeper into the moor. Not that it matters because it was quite obvious that no-one had lived there for a very long time. Right then and there I decided it was going to be mine. I was going to fix it up and make it even more perfect and then at the stroke of midnight when I was eighteen, I'd pack myself a bag and go and live there. Since then, I've been spending any free time I have tending to it; giving it a good scrubbing and sweeping and mending. I had planned to keep it a secret but then I'd asked Callum so many questions about how to fix holes in stonework and how to secure loose roof tiles that he pestered me until I had to tell him. He's been sworn to secrecy though, and I trust him to keep it. He has his own bolt-hole out on the moor so I think he imagines that's what I'm keeping it for. I haven't told him otherwise. That's a secret I'll be holding close.

I slowed to a walk when the croft came in sight, right by what I call the Sentries - a stand of ancient and impossible trees that lean in the direction of the prevailing wind. I breathed in deep lungfuls of air then stopped for a moment, bending over, one hand on my knee, the other pressed against my side against the stab of the stitch. Straightening after a moment, I closed my eyes and soaked in the vast, empty quiet.

The expanse of the moor frees me. I feel as if nothing can confine me, as long as I can feel the wind off the sea, sharp with salt, and see the grass and heather rippling all around me. I took another deep breath and exhaled, feeling the last of my anger blowing away on the breeze. Wrapping my arms around myself, I sat down in the shelter of a gnarled and ragged old apple tree and pressed my cheek against the familiar roughness of the bark. It was everything and enough to be here and to be able to see my little cottage in the distance.

I've always sought refuge in the wild places. Even from being very small, I've thought of the moor as a place that welcomes me. I draw a steadying sort of comfort from the undulating landscape that, despite appearances, is far less bleak and barren once you grow familiar with it. The hills burn red and gold one minute, then disappear under rolling mists the next; it changes in an instant and it's never wise to grow complacent. Glencarragh is fierce and sometimes savage; it gives life and livelihood if you know where to look but will just as easily snatch it away and I love it with all of my heart and soul. I like to pretend that it understands me, that it recognizes me as one of its own.

People of the mainland can't understand why anyone would live here and dismiss it as a place for wanderers and lost souls. Hetty always says that those are the only sort of folk who can survive here; those who know something of struggle and what it is to be an outcast. After the first folk came the Norsemen and shipwrecked raiders from Ireland; then came the holy men and pilgrims from the north and west of England and Ireland, looking for a place to find their god and live in quiet and peace. The land was enough of a challenge that there was no room for petty grievances between folk and eventually everyone intermingled so there was no telling where one clan ended and another began. "Mongrels," my da used to laugh, on the days when he remembered what it was to be civil. "We're all just a pack of scrappy auld mongrels as no place else has use for."

The bark of the old apple pressed roughly into my cheek as I leaned into it, hugging myself to its crooked solidity and feeling the unlikely warmth that radiated from it. Sighing, I closed my eyes and let the peace of it wash over me; I could feel the spirit of the island filling me up, washing away my troubles.

As a child, I learned the secrets of the creatures who dwell here. I would lie on my belly, pressed into the heather for hours, watching fox-kits roll and tumble, delighting at their antics. I ran behind the herd of red deer that roams over the north side of the island, pretending I was one of them, wishing, with all of my childish heart, that they'd adopt me into the herd. In the old wood - the impossible wood that most folk give a wide berth, for fear of what might live there - I would scramble up the limbs of indulgent beech and ash trees; I would burrow into the hazel thicket, looking for bird's nests and complimenting them for their fine work, tearing my clothes and snagging my unruly hair on twigs and thorns. I felt comfortable, as if I could breathe freely; there wasn't anyone shouting or throwing things, no-one complaining or criticizing. The birds didn't care that my hair wasn't tidy, and the badgers cared nothing for crisp, white, blouses or shining boots. I was myself and that was enough.

And now it could all be taken from me; the idea of losing my freedom is bad enough, but losing my sanctuary is unbearable.

Chapter 3

Winter Solstice

Hetty sighed heavily as she lifted the tray of ale onto her shoulder and made her way towards the men's side of the tavern. I never understood how a woman so small and slight could bear the weight of her trade. Then again, she's been hefting pints of ale since she was a young girl, having inherited the tavern from her mother. The tavern is one of the only things that passes down the female line on Glencarragh and it's withstood numerous male challenges to that tradition. I knew I ought to offer to help, but I was filled with nervous excitement which sat in uneasy combination with the burden of dread that clung to me as well. The chatter from the next room was loud and slightly shrill. Not that I'd had occasion to discuss it with them, but I supposed the other girls were feeling much the same as I was. It wasn't every day that a girl faced marriage to the sea.

From my perch in the tavern kitchen, I watched as Hetty passed out frothing mugs to the tables full of loud, boisterous men. She laughed easily at something one of them said and patted the sleeve of one of the others. Hetty can talk to anyone about anything, even coarse fishermen and sly pony-men, she's just that sort of person, but I know how much it drains her to mingle among the patrons of the tavern. I think she'd have been quite happy to permanently hand over her apron to her husband, John, and devote herself fully to her midwifery and her herbs. But tradition demands that a woman run the tavern, which seems to me to be just as confining as not being allowed to. Either way, she upholds her duty and always does it with a gentle smile and a kind word.

In addition to all of that, she's also stood watch over these gatherings of women for more years than she'll put a number to - soothing ragged nerves and giving out encouraging smiles and compliments to mothers and daughters alike. The choosing time is the only occasion where it's deemed appropriate for women to be present in the tavern so I suppose it just stands to reason that Hetty would look after the women. But how the Avis' have inherited the task of supervising the actual drawing of the name and fulfilling the subsequent obligations, no-one quite knows, it's just the way it is. I suspect it has everything to do with John and not Hetty, who, despite her calm exterior, never seems to be quite at ease around the choosing time. Still, to live on Glencarragh means to leave plenty of things to the realms of mystery and given that no-one particularly likes to discuss the details of the sea bride, it isn't hard to maintain a veil of secrecy around the whole thing. Watching her now, as she winds her way back towards me, I saw her raise her eyes and I knew that she was listening for the sound of Father Ewan pacing across the floor of the room upstairs. He's just one more aggravation that I'm sure she doesn't need.

"D'you need any help, Hetty? I'm ever so fed up with the waiting."

She gave me a warm smile and then an assessing look. At her raised eyebrow I self-consciously put a hand to my head, trying to tuck a wayward strand of hair back into my kerchief. It was also entirely possible that there was a smudge of dirt on my cheek. I'd found a series of snares up on the moor, on my way across to the tavern, and I'd stopped to spring them. I knew I'd probably be robbing someone of their dinner, but snares are a particularly cruel way to die and no-one on Glencarragh has ever gone hungry for the want of food. The islanders look after each other that way. It's only right that someone looks after the creatures just as well. I blushed and smoothed my hair again. That wild MacFinlay girl; that's what everyone thinks of me. I know they speak of me that way, and not in affectionate terms, but I've never let it bother me. Too much and not enough, that's me; bound to shock and disappoint in turn. Still, I don't ever like to be found wanting in Hetty's eyes.

"Ye look fine, lass, dinna fuss. There's no competition for ye in loveliness, I'll say that for a true thing."

I blushed again.

"Well, you'll be the only one thinking that, Hetty," I replied, "and even if it were true, there's no value in it if it can't keep me from being put up for auction like a prize ewe."

Hetty's face clouded over and her lips compressed.

"Now ye just mind yer tongue, young lady. Ye know as well as anyone else here that it's not like that at all. There's lasses here that think of this as a great honour, to be able to do something so brave and good for the island folk. And for some of them, it's their best chance at making a good match for themselves."

"But what if a person has no interest at all in making any sort of match, Hetty? And what if the island folk have been nothing but horrible to a person their whole life?"

While seventeen is the minimum age, it's rarely thought of to put down the name of a girl so young for the choosing. It's generally left to the older girls, the ones not yet claimed, that it might increase their fortune and marriageability. Like Hetty said, to marry the sea is supposedly a great honour and the girls that come out of that union are much admired when all is said and done. They're supposed to carry some sort of good luck with them and most of the island menfolk are so caught up in the superstition of it all that any guarantee of good fishing and fertile ewes is worth marrying for. Which, to my mind, is exactly what I said it was: like being put up for auction like prize livestock. That said, it's still a task best suited to respectable types — the ones who keep their hair tidy and their fingernails clean. Not for girls like me, who nurse orphaned fox cubs and cut down the rabbit snares out on the moor. Not for the first time, I wondered if that's why my father put my name down - to increase my chances of finding a husband who might put a stop to my general disagreeableness. Mostly, though, I think he did it out of spite.

Hetty sighed, passing a hand over her face.

"Och, lass. We're not having that one again, are we?" she said, with a tired smile. "There's no sense arguing with ye, I know. Ye're determined not to see sense, nor the truth o' what's right in front of ye."

I said nothing, biting my lip and keeping my head down. I could hear the weariness in Hetty's voice and immediately felt badly for adding to her burden.

"Go on, pet," she said, "Save me a trip and bring along that tray of bread and cheese to the womenfolk will ye? There might be some as have a bit of an appetite."

I giggled.

"Yes, Morag's looking a bit peaky," I said, peering through the pass-through at the round-faced, pale-haired, girl.

Hetty stifled a chuckle.

"Now, then. 'Tisn't charitable to say such things. Morag cannae help but be how she is."

"Oh, Hetty!' I said, hoisting the laden tray. "Has someone been forcing her to sit about on her backside all day instead of doing a day's work? And I know, because our Duncan has delivered more than a box or two, the Dunn's get an awful lot of cakes and sweet things in from the mainland."

Hetty shook her head and pushed back through the swinging door into the main room of the tavern to collect the fresh tray of ale that John had pulled, with me following close behind.

The room was a haze of smoke. The honeyed scent of beeswax from the profusion of candles, brought out especially for the occasion, mingled with the tang of forest and peat that emanated from the fire and from the boughs of pine brought in to decorate the room. The overlay of pipe tobacco lay rich and fragrant and stirred faint memories of happier childhood moments, before my father fell so hard for the whiskey. The mix of it all is such a lovely, homey, sort of smell. It's like having the outdoors on the inside; it lets me imagine I'm outside, even when I'm forced to be in.

I've always loved spending time in the tavern with Hetty, which is yet another black mark against my name, that a girl of my age would be frequenting a drinking establishment and acting like a common barmaid. It doesn't seem to matter to the wagging tongues that I spend all of my time in her kitchen, absorbing the bits of knowledge that seem to ooze from Hetty's every pore. The great pots and ovens are always bubbling and baking – sometimes with food, sometimes with the herbs that Hetty uses in her medicines. Given the choice, I'll always choose an afternoon gathering herbs with Hetty or watching her in her kitchen, over one spent with the sewing-circle or the Island Ladies Meeting, that awful gathering conjured up by Isabelle Dunn. Unlike the majority of the island women, neither of those appeal to me in the slightest, which goes a long way to explaining why I spend most of my time alone. Hetty has the mantle of herbwyfe to protect her from the scorn of the Glencarragh women; I'm just the feckless wild thing, the living contradiction to proper womanly behavior.

"Ah, Hetty!" exclaimed the odious Isabelle Dunn. "How very kind to think of refreshments."

I bit my lip and looked away as Hetty darted a sharp look in my direction.

Isabelle Dunn is widely known for taking on airs. No-one ever mentions it, though, as it's her husband, Frederick, who acts as agent for Lord Pennorth. Without Lord Pennorth's good graces, the folk of Glencarragh would be left without a place to sell their fish and fleece, and, as dark rumour has it, ponies. It must be a sore point altogether that it's come to putting their daughter, Morag, down for the choosing. If influence and fortune can't attract a husband, it's a desperate leap indeed to have to marry her to the sea in the hopes of making her a more attractive prospect. And it's one of my many failings that I feel I should point out these sorts of things to Isabelle and anyone else that would listen.

"Ye've got to stop saying the first thing that ever comes into that wild head of yours," Hetty has told me time and again. "Ye're no' a wee lassie anymore and folk won't go looking past things as they did when ye were just a bairn."

"But Hetty," I'd argued. "Aren't I just telling the truth of things? How can that be wrong?"

"Folk dinna always like to have the truth shoved in their faces, lass," Hetty had replied. "Some things are best left unsaid, aye?"

I always try to remember Hetty's advice, I really do. But it's a struggle.

Clearing my throat, I smiled brightly at Mrs. Dunn. "Doesn't Hetty just think of everything, Mrs. Dunn? I was just saying to her that your Morag looked a bit peaky and might do with a bit of sustenance to see her through the vigil. It's a terrible strain, isn't it? All this waiting around in hope of a husband, like we are!"

Hetty made a choking noise, which she quickly converted into a cough. She made a point of putting the tray of ale down with a clatter.

Isabelle frowned. I took it as a successful jibe that she seemed unsure if she was being ridiculed.

Morag, however, blushed furiously and looked away as the rest of the women and girls gathered to take mugs of ale and plates of Hetty's coarse bread and sheep's cheese.

Content with how that had been received, I took myself off to sit at a table by the window, pressing my forehead against the cold glass, to stare out into the darkness.

***

"Mind if I sit with you for a spell, lass?" asked Hetty, approaching my little corner, rubbing a reddened hand across her face.

"You work too hard, Hetty," I said, reaching over to pat the older woman on the arm. "You really should try and have a proper rest once this..." I waved a hand around the room full of women. "...business is over."

Hetty smiled, wearily, revealing a mouth full of surprisingly straight and white teeth.

"Och, pet. I wish with all my heart that it'd be over."

I sighed and closed my eyes.

"Do you think that if I wish hard enough, we could go backwards in time to when there was no such thing as sea brides?"

Hetty chuckled.

"Ye'd have to go back an awful long way for that, lass."

Opening my eyes, I looked around the room. The women had splintered off into family groups. Some of the girls had their entire female family around them - mother, sisters, aunts, grandmothers. Others were there with just their mother. I was the only one who sat alone.

I wasn't alone, I reminded myself, I have Hetty; Hetty who has always stood in for my absent mother, who's shielded me, I'm sure, from the worst of what my father would have done had no-one been paying attention.

Hetty caught me looking around at the other girls.

"It doesnae matter in the end, pet," she said softly.

"Hm?" I said, startled from my musing.

"In the end it doesnae matter how many of your womenfolk you've gathered around ye."

She glanced around the room at the huddles of women, talking softly among themselves; hands touching, arms reaching around shoulders in a show of quiet support and solidarity against what had been laid at their feet.

"In the end it's just you. You and the sea."

Chapter 4

"Can I get you ladies anything else?" I asked, with as much sweetness as I could muster.

I stood with a hand on one hip, a tray full of empty pint pots and plates balanced on the other. Much to Hetty's exasperation, it really did amuse me to play the insolent barmaid.

Isabelle Dunn scowled before quickly adjusting her features into an air of indifference.

"Thank you, no," she said, smoothing her hands over her dress. "If you could be so kind as to remove the plates, that would be sufficient."

She reached over to Morag and made a point of adjusting the jeweled shawl pin that held together the folds of the richly woven cloth. The Dunns never wore homespun or knitted garments, it was one of the many things that Isabelle did to quietly set them apart from the rest of the island women. The gems on the pin glinted in the flickering candlelight. Clearly, I was meant to notice the pin so made a point of scrutinizing it closely. Morag shifted in her seat under my exaggerated interest.

"Is that a new pin, Morag?" I asked, fully aware that I was meant to ask the question. "It's very lovely."

"Yes, it is," interrupted Isabelle, as Morag opened her mouth to reply. She snapped it shut, a gesture which, with her wide, round, face, gave her the look of a frog having just caught a fly.

The vision of Morag-as-frog required me to pinch my lips together to suppress a smile.

"I'm sorry, Morag. What was that you said?" I asked, ignoring Isabelle's imperious glare. "I couldn't hear you over your mother."

Morag blushed. "Yes, erm...yes, it's new. It was a gift..."

"From Lord Pennorth, himself," said Isabelle, loudly enough for everyone sitting nearby to hear. "A token of luck, he said. To wish our Morag good fortune in the choosing."

"Is that right?" I said, widening my eyes in a show of surprise. I raised my voice to equal Isabelle's. "Wouldn't it be better luck altogether if he were just to offer marriage, Morag? Surely that would be a quicker thing? Him being such a fine gentleman, and not entirely ancient, as these things go...."

"Well!" exclaimed Isabelle, her hands fluttering like frantic butterflies around her face. "What an impertinent creature! Not that it's any surprise, mind you. Faery-begot and raised by coarse fishermen..."

I could feel a rush of heat rising to my face. I slammed my tray down on the table, making Morag squeal in shock at the rattle and clink of empty glasses.

"Now you listen here, you bloated harpy..."

"Aibhlinn!"

Hetty marched over to the table and caught me by the elbow, steering me away from the red-faced, blustering figure of Isabelle. She called over her shoulder, "I'm terribly sorry, Isabelle. Ye know how it is with the lasses on a night like tonight. They're all full o' the nerves and not themselves at all."

She marched me back to the kitchen and pushed me into a chair.

"What in the blazes are ye thinking of child? Stirring up trouble like that!"

"Oh, Hetty. You can't mean to say I'm wrong! Surely hasn't everyone been saying just the same things for months now? For all the boasting Isabelle Dunn throws about, you would think Lord Pennorth was moments away from going onto bended knee..."

"Heaven help me, lass! How many times have we to go over this? Ye make life hard on yerself when ye go on so. It doesn't do to aggravate the likes of Isabelle Dunn. She can make life terrible hard on yer da, yer brothers and the other menfolk. One word from her and suddenly her man is turning away catches and buying someone elses fleeces."

I snorted and turned away in the chair to look out of the darkened window in the kitchen. "As if my da ever gave a second thought to me," I muttered.

Hetty reached over and took my chin in her hand, turning my face to her own. "Then think of Alexander and Duncan and Callum, aye? Yer brothers do as well by ye as they're able. And besides, it's cruel of ye to take on so wi' poor Morag, just to get at her mother. Did ye ever think on that?"

I blushed.

"Aye, just as I thought." Hetty started to move around the kitchen, piling the dirty plates into the stone sink. "That's yer trouble all over again, though, isn't it? Ye just dinna think. Honestly, lass, I don't know what to do with ye sometimes. Heaven knows I've tried my level best to do right by yer mam... "

"I'm sorry, Hetty," I said in a small voice.

I sat with my head bowed, hiding my face so that Hetty couldn't see my eyes filling with tears. I'd promised myself many years ago that I wasn't going to be the sort of girl who cried. Crying was for weak-minded people, and I was determined not to be weak or helpless. Not ever. I swallowed hard and blinked furiously until I was sure they'd retreated, back to the tightly defended borders where I kept my emotions. I keep myself going by being strong; I can ignore the taunts and worse, the whispers behind hands, if I believe that I don't need anyone's help or approval. And I absolutely don't. I've survived this long going my own way and that isn't about to change now that my fate has been handed over to the terms of some old and time-forgotten bargain. There are very few people that I can count on and Hetty is one of them. Her good opinion is the only thing standing between me and a life of complete scandal, I'm sure. If not for Hetty - and Callum, I suppose - I would've given myself over to the moors long before now. Still, when it comes down to it, I know that her idea of what my life ought to be is very different from my own view on things. And as for Callum, he's spending more and more time on the moor rather than at home and it's only a matter of time before he just stops coming back altogether. No, I'm far better looking after myself; doing everything on my own is the only guarantee it'll be done the way that's best.

Hetty paused in her tidying and sighed.

"Aw, pet. Dinna take a bit of notice of me. I'm running away at the mouth like a right auld harpy, aren't I? It's this bloody business as gets right into me...."

She shook her head and left the sentence unfinished when I raised my head questioningly.

Hetty shook her head again and smiled a weary smile. "Tell ye what. Put the kettle on and take a cuppa up to Father Ewan, will ye? It'll give us all something to do, and I'm sure he's gasping for a nice cup of tea by now. They allus want to ply the poor sod with ale and he never touches a drop of it."

I jumped to my feet, glad of the diversion, and relieved that Hetty wasn't going to continue the litany of my bad behavior. I can't bear it when she sees the faults in me. I also couldn't help but pick up on the undercurrent of worry in Hetty's voice and her unfinished sentences, which made me even more cross with myself for adding to my friend's burden.

I squeezed Hetty's hand as I walked past her to the sink.

"I'm sorry," I said, again, pausing while I filled the kettle from the pump. "I know I'm a terrible chore sometimes. I just can't seem to help being so contrary. People like the Dunns just rub me all the wrong way, always throwing their weight around and lording it over the rest of us." I set the kettle on the hob and turned back to face Hetty with my arms folded. "It could just as easily have been anyone that got the job as agent for Lord Pennorth, you know. Our Alexander would've done a much better job and been a better friend to the menfolk than weasely old Frederick Dunn. If it weren't for Da being such a..."

"That's enough, Aibhlinn," said Hetty, flapping a tea towel

at me. "Whatever yer da may be, he's still your da and ye'd better mind and pay him some respect."

I scowled.

"Aye," I muttered under my breath. "I'll pay him as much respect as he deserves."

Chapter 5

I knocked loudly on the door. The narrow hall of the upstairs is barely wide enough for me to walk with the tray holding the teapot and a plate of bannock, so I had to stand at a rather awkward angle to reach it. Not quickly enough for my comfort, I heard a scuffling sound from within and the sound of a chair scraping. The door opened with a rush and Father Ewan stood, red-faced and wide-eyed.

"Yes? What is it? Is it time?" he asked, his voice tremulous. "Oh, Aibhlinn. My apologies, child. I thought it was perhaps... ". He trailed off, waving a hand in a vague gesture of apology.

"No, Father. It's nothing any more exciting than a nice cup of tea," I said, brightly. I always feel at odds with myself in the presence of the old priest. He has an air of constant disapproval about him and always manages to make me feel grubby and somehow wanting. Although, in all fairness, I usually *am* grubby and wanting.

"Hetty thought you might prefer it over the ale that was provided."

I tilted my head and smiled, trying to resist the urge to apologize for being there.

"Oh, quite. Yes. That's lovely, thank you," said Father Ewan, stepping back from the door. "Would you be so kind as to bring it in and set it on the table."

I squeezed past him into the room. The heat was stifling, and the sickly-sweet smell of his pipe competed with what I like to refer to, in the quiet of my own thoughts, as the smell of stuffy old priest.

"It's warm in here," I commented, placing the tray gently onto the small table beside the armchair then retreating back to stand by the door. "Shall I open the window a bit? Let some fresh air in?"

"Hm? Yes, it is, rather," said Father Ewan, ignoring my question and narrowing his eyes at me. I made a point of standing as tall as my small stature would allow, my back straight, and forced my eyes to meet his - despite their general preference for avoiding his accusing gaze.

"Tell me, child," he began, walking over to the teapot and pouring himself a cup. "Am I correct to understand that your name was placed in the, er, book, this season?"

I nodded. "Yes, Father. My da...my father wrote my name down right on my seventeenth birthday."

"I see."

He stirred two spoons of sugar and a dollop of milk around the cup, frowning as he did so.

"And how do you feel about that, my dear?"

He raised that dreadful glance to me, his rheumy eyes blinking slowly in question.

He looks like a bloody cod when he does that, I thought, traitorously close to breaching all of my promises of good behavior to Hetty. A great blinking stupid fish.

"How do I feel?" I echoed, making a show of pretending I didn't understand what he was getting at. "Do you mean, how do I feel about having my name written down? Or how do I feel about marriage to the sea? Because, as to the first, there's not much I can do about that, is there now? My da does whatever he likes and if he wants to write my name down in a book he's well entitled to do so. Him being my da and me not being of an age to have any say in it...."

"Insolent child!" snapped Father Ewan. "I might have expected as much, though. Foolish of me to imagine you could respond in a civilized manner. You are a feckless piece, that is quite obvious. No surprise there, given your upbringing, or lack thereof as the case may be."

Once again, the heat of anger rushed up to my face.

"How dare..." I began, quite unable to abide by Hetty's sage advice of keeping my mouth shut.

Father Ewan held up a hand to silence me. His fingers are long and thin, a large signet ring glinting on his bony little finger.

Cod, I fumed, my fists clenching and unclenching. Sneaking, sniveling, codfish.

"I've no wish to engage in argument, child. I understand you've a penchant for that as well." He put down his mug and spread his arms in what I imagine he intended as a benevolent gesture, as if the sharp, angry words hadn't been uttered. He smiled widely, revealing crooked, tobacco-stained teeth. "My sole interest, as it has always been, is simply a wish to offer a chance for redemption, a chance to walk away from this travesty of heathen superstition."

I took a deep breath and forced my expression into one of what I hoped to be penitent submission. Slumping my shoulders, I hung my head meekly and folded my hands in front of me, using the few seconds to rein in my indignation. Gritting my teeth, I could hear the priest's triumphant intake of breath.

I took another deep breath of my own and raised my head. Reaching behind me, I placed one hand on the doorknob.

"Father Ewan?"

"Yes, my child?"

"If you were the last chance of redemption, this side of heaven, I'd throw my lot in with the sea devils and be a far sight happier for their brief company over the thought of an eternity with the likes of you."

I spun around quickly and slammed out of the room, laughing to myself all the way down the narrow hallway. If only I'd stayed long enough, I'm sure I'd have enjoyed the vision of him sputtering like the land-locked cod he so closely resembled.

Chapter 6

Callum

I hate the sea.

When I was ten years old, I watched two of my brothers swept overboard during a terrible storm, the kind that've been the plague of the sea around Glencarragh for as long as anyone remembers. One minute they were there, hauling ropes as they tried to stop our nets from being torn away, the next minute they were gone. They've never been found and only two small stones at the fisherman's cemetery stand to mark their passing. It was a long time until I could visit them there. I used to think the stones were an empty gesture, with no feeling of their lives having mattered. I thought that if you've no body to bury, how can you be sure they're gone?

Anyway, it was after they were lost, that our mother changed. Even as a young lad I knew that she was different from the other women on the island – fine-boned and delicate looking, but with an uncanny strength to her. Too beautiful, the women always said of her. Far too beautiful to be a fisherman's wife. Especially when that fisherman was Hamish MacFinlay. It was Alexander who'd told me that was the reason the story started of her being a selkie-woman, and that our da only held her because he'd found her skin and buried it somewhere she'd never find it. I thought it a grand story in a way – not the bit about our da holding her captive, though it's something I'd believe of him – but the idea that our mam was a faery-woman; beautiful and strange and loved by everyone. Alexander said even the jealous women couldn't help but be taken by her kindness and happy spirit.

Her name was Anwen – which means "very fair". She'd bright blue eyes, as merry as a summer sky, and golden hair like the sun that shone in it. She was the person folk'd come to in a crisis; she'd make them one of her plant brews and carve up a slice of warm bread and slather it with honey while she helped them find some peace of mind. There was always some wayward soul or other wandering in and out of our kitchen. All were welcome and she never turned anyone away as was in genuine need of help.

After my brothers were taken by the sea, she took to walking the cliff edges for hours at a time. I would often walk with her. We rarely spoke, but if we did, it was about strange things; things that my ten-year-old self didn't quite understand, and even now, my grown self struggles to get my mind around. She would tell me stories about the faery creatures of the sea and the long-ago days when the people of Glencarragh lived in harmony with the otherworldly folk known as the Old Ones. As a child, I thought them just that - stories - but as I got older and saw things that didn't reckon in the usual ways, I began to wonder that maybe there was a truth to them. That's why I made a point of telling it all to our Aibhlinn. Our da didn't allow that sort of talk in the house, so I would take her out onto the moors, from being a very young bairn, and tell her all about our mam and the stories she'd told me during those strange days on the cliff path. It likely sounds a bit mad, but I'd a feeling our mam was telling me those tales precisely so as I'd tell our wee lass when she was grown enough to hear them.

Not long after those walking days, it was discovered that she was pregnant again. From the very first, she'd confided in me that the baby was a girl because she'd spun the magic of the sea to give her the girl-child that she'd always longed for. Not that she didn't love her boys, she'd assured me, for she loved us with all her heart, but she needed this child to be a girl. It was important, she said, for the island itself. She swore me to keep it a secret, saying that our da would never forgive her what she'd done. When I'd asked her what it was that she'd done that was so terrible she would only smile and run her hands over her swelling belly, her eyes far-looking and her hair wild from the salt breeze.

When our Aibhlinn was only a few days old, our mam nursed her one last time, tucked her into the wee cradle at the foot of the bed and told our da she was going for a walk, for a bit of fresh air. She never came back. Two days later, one of the searchers found her nightgown, sodden with spray, tangled in one of the old hawthorns at the cliff edge.

I'd thought I'd go mad with sorrow. If it weren't for that wee bairn, red-faced and squalling as she was, we might've all just walked around in a daze, so stunned were we at yet another loss.

Without her to hold us together, we were scattered, adrift. Hetty was fond of telling me that our mam had been the bright spark in a house of hard-bitten men, a beautiful thing in a world of sharp lines and cold edges. Hetty said she'd softened us all, made us gentler and prone to small kindness.

If that were true, it all ended when she left us. My older brothers became coarse and uncaring and our da, lost without his heart's love, became cruel. He was especially foul to our Aibhlinn, poor wee thing, blaming her for the loss of his wife. He'd never a kind word, never a fondness for the tiny bairn, no matter what she did to try and please him. He treated her like a scullery maid, and she was always the one to bear the brunt of his drunken rages. I think that's why she went a bit wild, to get away from all that. She found the wind and foxes to be better company than her own menfolk and I'm ashamed to admit I were as much to blame for that back then as the others. Even now, I know I should be helping Aibhlinn, shielding her from our da but the truth is, all I want is to be away from it all.

Anyhow, it was after our mam died that I began to really hate the sea. I blamed the sea, not our Aibhlinn, for her loss. I believed, in my childish heart, that there was foul magic at play; that she'd made some terrible bargain with the creatures of the sea for her longed-for daughter. Even now, as a grown man, I hold a lingering hatred for anything to do with the fickle ocean and its deadly whims.

When I was eighteen, and had a say in things, I told our da that I wouldn't be going out on the fishing boat anymore. With my savings from years of mending nets, I bought myself a small flock of sheep and set about scraping my own living from the moors. The less I have to do with the hateful ocean, the happier I am.

But there's no getting away from the sea and its wickedness entirely. I've as much to lose from not going down to the water's edge, each winter solstice, as the fishermen. It's bad enough having to give up a good sheep every year, but the sea bride years are the worst of all. And it's especially bad this time, knowing my own sister's name is among those in the woven basket lying at John Avis' feet.

* * *

"Are ye ready, then?" asked John, his breath coming in frosty clouds. A low murmur from the crowd of men indicated that they were. "Right. Alfie?"

Alfie, a small, bushy-haired man, dressed in a heavily embroidered waistcoat, typical of the pony-men, stepped forward. The pony-men, more than most, have reason to fear the sea and what comes out of it. He nodded and began to tap a slow rhythm on the drum he cradled under one arm. Four more drums followed time, the sound carrying on the sea air. The haunting melody from two sets of pipes joined in, settling into a steady, rising, song.

"Know this, men of Glencarragh!" began John, his voice clear and pitched to reach to the large group that gathered at the water's edge. "Know that we stand together, as we've stood for centuries past. That we honor the bargains of old and act in the faith of our ancestors to protect and deliver us from the perils of land and sea. Know that this thrice-gone year, we heed the call and make an offering of our most valued prize - our womenfolk - in a show of faith and partnership with those to whom we are indebted for the continued bounty of our harvest and the health of our flocks."

"Hear, hear!" came the response. The sound of the drums grew louder, rising to a battlefield beat. Out past the edge of the sea, the waves began to foam and crash. A low-pitched hum erupted from somewhere beyond the reach of the naked eye.

"There it is!" someone shouted from near the back.

Slowly, a dark shape appeared within view of the lanterns. Shapeless and black it came closer with each advance of the tide. The men took a collective step back from the edge of the water, leaving only Alfie and John and his basket standing alone. The drums kept a steady rhythm, the faces of the drummers tight with concentration. The drums are a summons but also a protection. Like the coloured thread and charms sewn into the pony-men's waistcoats, the drums shield us mortal folk from the worst of what comes out of the sea.

I stepped away from my da and brothers and moved to stand next to John. Alexander reached out to grab my sleeve, but I shook it off and he let me go, not wanting to venture any nearer.

The dark outline began to take shape as it got closer. A massive-shouldered horse, black as the deepest parts of the sea, its mane, a foaming mass of kelp, streamed with saltwater as it emerged from the waves and stepped into the shallows. Someone near the front of the group moaned.

Another shape separated from the outline of the water horse and an impossibly tall and slender woman slid from its back and stood facing us. She wore a long, flowing dress of shimmering, iridescent fish scales and her black hair was woven through with small bones and shells, lying in ropy strands almost to her waist. Her face was beautiful, in a cold, emotionless sort of way; her eyes, particularly, seemed to have no light in them.

My nose wrinkled involuntarily, and I had to resist the urge to cover my mouth and nose. The creature stank of fish and the rotted remains of something long-dead. It turned a black eye towards John and I, as we were standing closest, its nostrils flaring red. Its muscled neck lengthened as it reached towards us, giving the impression of a predator, scenting the air. It blew softly through its nose and lifted its lips to show a row of pointed teeth. I shuddered.

"Well met, my old friend," said John, to the water horse, his hands open in welcome. "My lady." He touched a finger to his forehead in the old way of respect. "I'm honoured that we meet again."

The water horse dipped its pointed head, blinking slowly. The woman smiled, showing gleaming, white, teeth, but said nothing. She just stared with those strange green eyes.

"I have the names here, of our pledges for this thrice-gone year."

The creature stood, unmoving, the sea curling around its hooves while the woman stroked its massive neck with long, thin, fingers.

"Do I have your promise, my lady Lira? That we bargain in good faith and with deference to the terms set out by our ancestors?"

I felt a clenching somewhere in my chest. There was a shuffle of feet on wet sand behind us. The drums continued. The beat had shifted now; it echoed the rhythm of the sea.

With an almost invisible gesture from the faery-woman, the water horse lowered its head and stepped closer towards us. I couldn't help but move back, so repulsed was I by the size and stink of the beast. John held his ground, though, and reached out a hand to touch the dripping muzzle. How easily, I thought, could the creature tear John's arm from his body. I shivered in the damp breeze and willed my knees to stop trembling. This was the closest I'd ever stood to a water horse, preferring, as I did in the past, to be as far back in the group as to not have to look at it. But I'd promised myself, for our Aibhlinn, to face what stood before me.

John nodded and removed his hand. The creature stepped back into the surf.

"You may choose," said the faery-woman, her voice low and slightly musical.

"Callum?" said John, unexpectedly.

I started.

"Would ye do the honours then?"

John picked up the basket and held it towards me.

I held up my hands in protest, taking another step back. That wasn't why I'd come.

"No, John. I couldn't. Don't ye have to..."

John shook his head.

"No, lad. I've the task to hold the names and call forth the creatures, but the choosing goes to any that's willing." He shrugged, wearily. "Better it's not me, anyhow. Some folk like to talk if it doesnae go their way, aye?"

"But, I can't be the one," I stammered. "I don't even...."

I felt myself being shoved forwards.

"Do it!" came the harsh voice of my da from right behind me. "Just choose the bloody name, ye dithering fool. Enough of the sentimental nonsense. If ye dinna do it, I will."

Our da went to push himself forwards, but John held up a warning hand. "No, Hamish. Not you," He said, quietly, "Callum?"

"Right, then."

Swallowing hard and making a point of not looking at the waiting creature, I reached a shaking hand out to the basket.

"Please, let it not be her," I muttered under my breath. My fingers closed around a folded piece of parchment. I paused, taking a deep breath and let that one go, rummaging around for another. Finding one, I pulled it out and handed it to John. I closed my eyes at the sound of the paper being unfolded.

John cleared his throat noisily.

"By the rights of my ancestors and the rights of those dwelling upon this land; by the rights of bargains struck and faith held fast, of promises made and upheld. 'Tis the task fallen to me to name and shelter the bride of the sea, and to deliver her, as is custom, at the turn of the spring tide to be wed to the sea and in return, on faith of that union, that for the span of three years, the luck and bounty of the harvest shall be ours, whence another bride shall be chosen."

A cold sweat prickled under my collar and my heart thundered in my ears.

John paused, letting the pipes and drums rise to a peak before suddenly falling silent. Only the sound of the sea, whispering over the sand could be heard.

"Aibhlinn MacFinlay."

There was a ringing in my ears and I staggered slightly.

Alexander and Duncan appeared beside me, each taking an arm so as to prop me up as our da walked forwards to shake John's hand.

Eventually, I looked up, seeking out the flat, cold, gaze of the faery-woman. She smiled again, an odd mixture of menace and sorrow. Nodding, she effortlessly mounted the massive water horse. It opened its ragged mouth and hissed softly, before turning and walking out to sea.

Chapter 7

Aibhlinn

The air in the tavern is thick with smoke and laughter. The men on one side, toasting my da with large, frothing mugs of ale, and the women on the other in chattering clusters in the comfortable chairs by the roaring fire. Hetty is run off her feet, carrying platters of bread and meat and cheese while John stands behind the bar pulling pint after pint of his finest brew. The aftermath of the choosing is always one of relieved frivolity - as the held-breath of anticipation becomes an exhale of sprung tension.

I glance over at the women, no doubt proclaiming their relief, despite the secret hopes of unwed daughters, but the men are more concerned with the near certainty of calmer seas and successful lambings. They shout and laugh with the boisterous arrogance of those who never doubted it could be otherwise, just so long as they hold their part of the bargain. Whether that's a few sheep or someone's daughter seems not to matter. No-one is speaking of the trials not yet faced, and no-one will. The choosing and the continued good graces of the sea folk – and relative safety from the marauding water horses – are all they need to hold them from the edges of despair.

And despite being the focus of their celebrations, here I sit, mutinous, in a corner with only Callum and my other two brothers.

"I don't see why I have to sit here like a pariah," I said, when they'd steered me into a seat and placed a mug of strong tea in front of me. "Aren't I supposed to be mingling about with my subjects?"

"That's enough o' yer cheek, lassie," Alexander retorted, "And that's exactly why ye're sittin' here." As the eldest, he's the closest in temperament to our da, but with enough of our mam to smooth away the edge of cruelty.

"Dinna be so sharp with the bairn," Duncan said. "She's a right to be a wee bit tetchy given the state o' things, aye?"

"I'm not a bairn, Duncan," I replied, haughtily. "Aren't I just about to be wed?" I forced my tone to be merry, but I was dangerously close to tears. "And to the sea of all things? Why, I'm surprised I've not got the whole of Glencarragh trying to curry favour."

My voice broke and I clamped my lips tightly closed. I wasn't about to let them know how truly terrified I was; terrified, and also furious. I've lived with a great degree of freedom and unrestraint that few girls ever experience on Glencarragh – to the disapproval of just about everyone – but now, all of a sudden, my movements are to be monitored and I'm to be "kept and sheltered", whatever that means.

We sat in silence then, each of us preoccupied with our own thoughts. My brothers slowly sipping their ale, waving away the offers of more; me, pretending to drink my tea and avoiding everyone's gaze.

"Callum?" I said, after a while. He'd been strangely silent since the men came back from the shore, even more so than usual.

"Hm?"

"Why are you so quiet? Don't you have anything to say about the whole thing?"

Callum shifted in his chair, keeping his eyes down, his calloused fingers cradling his pint pot.

"You know how I feel about it, Aibhlinn, lass. And I've even less inclination to be happy now."

"But aren't I doing a good thing for us all, though, Callum? Isn't the whole thing just a marvel?" I didn't want him to worry. I'm also trying to convince myself. If I don't find a way to make this right in my mind, it's entirely likely that I'm going to go mad.

Callum slammed down his pot, sloshing ale over the pitted surface of the table. He stood up abruptly and leaned in towards me.

"There's naught good, ever, to be had from dealings with those...those creatures," he said, his voice low and bitter. "A bargain struck with the sea is no bargain at all." With that, he shoved his chair in with a clatter and pushed his way through the crowd and out the door.

I made to follow him, but a large hand clamped down on my shoulder, holding me firmly in my seat.

"Now, then, lass," said my da, his fingers biting tightly into my flesh. "Let's not start this off wi' any o' yer displays. Why not try and act like ye've an ounce of manners in ye, instead o' showing yersel' up for a harridan, aye?"

"I suppose you've been chatting with Mrs. Dunn, then?" I replied through gritted teeth. His grip was painful, but I wouldn't let him see. "Speaking of harridans, that is."

I sucked in my breath to quell a cry as his hand clenched deeper before suddenly letting go.

"Father Ewan!" boomed da, genially. His mood turning as quickly as the tide. "Can I offer ye a mug of ale? Must be a terrible thirst ye'd have, up there praying for our souls all this time."

Father Ewan smiled thinly.

"Hamish," he said, nodding. "It's no chore to me to engage in such worthy conversation with Our Lord."

"Aye, I'll warrant the two o' ye have many a chin-wag over our heathenish ways," said my da, tilting sideways as he swung an arm to encompass the gathering of folk. He was well on his way by now, no doubt having had an early start in the day.

"Come on, Da," muttered Duncan, getting up from his chair. "I think mebbe it's time we were heading off home, aye?"

He took our da by the elbow and guided him away from the table. "My apologies, Father Ewan," he said as they walked past. "It's been a long sort of night."

"Indeed," said the Father, moving aside to let the two men past. My da clapped him heartily on the back on his way by.

"Never ye mind, Father, now," he said, loudly. "Our Aibhlinn'll do us right proud on the night. She's allus been a wild one so she's well-suited to the company o' the sea devils. I reckon she'll give 'em a right good romp for...."

Whatever else he thought was thankfully lost in the press of the crowd.

I sat with my hands folded in my lap, rage and shame competing once again in my heart, both bursting for expression.

I settled on rage and gave Father Ewan the benefit of my brightest, merriest, smile.

"Well, then, Father. Imagine that, eh? So, tell me, have you any biblical insights as to the appropriate deportment of the virgin bride to her demon consort?"

Chapter 8

I've never felt so loved in all my life.

Even as a small girl I sensed the hostility that my da had for me. Alexander and Duncan, kind enough in their way, were never much for great shows of feeling and neither had much time for a disobedient, tearaway of a younger sister. It was Callum who'd taken time with me, telling me imaginative tales about his flock of sheep and showing me badger setts and the best places to watch the puffin nesting grounds without disturbing them. He told me about our mam, repeating things no matter how often I asked, spinning stories of the merry-eyed, soft-spoken woman who'd somehow coaxed love from our iron-hearted father.

Besides Callum, I've had Hetty to love me. Hetty had been very fond of my mam; she said my mam had taught her more about the healing plants of Glencarragh than even her own mam and that she knew all sorts of medicines - the kinds to heal body and soul. More than that, though, Hetty loved my mam's spirit – her kindness and the way she found joy in the smallest of things.

I'm sure Hetty knew how things were for me at home; she knew my da could be hateful and unkind and that my brothers were too caught up in their own troubles to notice much of the time, so she took me under her wing and tried to coax some of the wildness out of me. With her help and guidance, I managed to become self-sufficient and run my household of coarse men while still having the freedom to roam the moors. I know it worried her, my wildness and my delight in causing disapproval, and I was sorry for it. But I also think she understood why I escaped to the fens and braes, why I felt the need for the company of ravens and hares instead of folk. Besides, I always brought her back the herbs she needed and entertained her with my stories of fox families and deer sightings.

But other than those two, I'm almost universally despised. At the very least, I elicit scorn and criticism. I'm too contrary, too untidy, too outspoken. I'm too much of most things and not enough of the rest. Mostly, though, I'm not bothered by it. After all, I've been able to take care of myself – and my family – without anyone elses help. I had Callum and Hetty, and, when they weren't preoccupied with the tides or weather, Duncan and Alexander. They're all I've ever needed, and, if I'm honest, not all that often. There's been a few times when I've thought it might be nice to have the company of a friend – perhaps another girl with whom I could talk about private things, share confidences and such. But that would require me to be someone I'm not and I've no intentions of changing my ways to suit anyone. From a very early age, I learned that the only person I can really depend on is myself and I happily resigned myself to a life of noble and martyred loneliness and have been entirely content.

But then Callum pulled my name from the basket and now everything's changed. Suddenly, I've become the recipient of a bewilderingly huge outpouring of kindness and consideration. It's been such an outpour that I feel very unsettled by it all. Of course, I know it's not genuine; it's not as if all of a sudden my past behaviour has been forgiven and now everyone is my friend. No, I'm fully aware that it's everything to do with making sure I don't run off or refuse to participate in the upcoming ceremony. It's about making sure I do as I'm told for once.

Still, for a few, precious fleeting moments, I felt as if I belonged and that my being here actually matters.

* * *

"Hold still, child."

Hetty is behind me with her mouth full of pins. She collects the linen dress in soft gathers, poking a pin here and there before lacing up the fitted bodice.

"Not a pick on ye, lassie," she tutted. "I don't know as I'm going to be able to take this in enough to fit without ye looking like ye've been strung in a tatie sack."

"Do I have to wear it, Hetty? It's a bit ancient, and I'm not terribly keen on the smell of it."

49

"Whisht now! That's Isabelle Dunn's lavender posies it's been packed away in. She has that lavender brought in from the mainland, you know. Costs a small fortune, as I hear. Keeps the moths away, aye?"

"Keeps everything away," I muttered. "I don't like it. It smells too pointy."

"Never mind that rubbish. And aye, ye have to wear it. It's the tradition."

Hetty moved around to view her handiwork. She shook her head and bent down to fuss with the hem.

"Why is everyone being so kind to me all of a sudden, Hetty?" I asked. "Even Isabelle Dunn came 'round the other night with a fish pie for our tea. I thought da was going to keel over at the surprise of it."

Hetty smiled.

"Aw, pet. They're just doing their bit to make sure ye're well looked after, that's all. It's as much of the tradition as the dress. Ye're to be celebrated like."

"Well, they've never given two hoots for me before now," I replied. "I don't see...." I stopped suddenly, a chill prickling over my scalp as a sudden thought occurred to me.

"Am I," my voice cracked, and I had to clear my throat before I croaked out in a whisper, "Am I going to die, Hetty? Those creatures.... the sheep... Callum said...."

Hetty leaned back on her heels and looked up at me, no doubt seeing the worry on my face. She grinned and rose creakily to her feet.

"Nay, lass. At least, not likely 'til ye're auld and grey, the good Lord willing." She frowned and pursed her lips, as if considering something. "What else did Callum tell ye, lass? Has he ever spoke to ye of the way of things?"

"What things?" I asked, frowning as I tried to decipher her question. "Do you mean the water horses?"

"Well, aye. But what I meant was, in the way of the marriage. And where they figure in all that business."

I flushed with embarrassment.

"Hetty! I've been out to help Callum on the moors more than once. I've seen the ram...". My eyes widened in horror at my next thought. "You can't mean the water horse...oh my god!"

Hetty threw back her head and laughed, a deep, throaty chuckle that rose from her toes.

"No, lass. Nowt like that! There's nowt like that expected of ye at all."

She held out her hand and helped me down from the up-turned crate on which I was standing.

"Come on, pet. Let's put the kettle on. There's a thing or two ye'll need to know afore the night."

* * *

I took the long way home.

The cliff path winds around the edge of the north marsh before one fork branches off to its descent to the beach. The other fork keeps alongside the edge of the cliff, up the hills to a little copse of trees before wending its way back around the marsh. I paused at the fork, tempted to keep walking down to the shore, even though I'd been forbidden by Hetty to go anywhere near the water's edge until the spring tides turned.

But I always feel closest to my mam down on the sands, and I'd a great need to feel close to her just then. Listening to the ancient, murmured, conversation between the sea and the land, I fancy I can hear my mother's voice. I can close my eyes and imagine the face I'd never seen – a face sewn together in my mind's eye from the scraps of other people's memories. I imagine it smiling down at me with great love.

Callum has an old photograph of our mam, tucked into the inside lining of his overcoat. Our da forbade us any reminders of her, but Callum kept the old picture and brings it out to show me any time I ask. It's an old daguerreotype – strangely posed and formal – taken when they were first wed; da with his hand clamped firmly on mam's shoulder and her looking off to the left of the camera. She wasn't smiling but her eyes were soft, and her expression was solemn but peaceful. When I was younger, I would imagine that our mam was thinking of her future children in that picture, especially of her daughter.

* * *

The wind buffeted me as I stood, undecided. My long, fair hair was unbound and flew in a wild halo around my face. I closed my eyes and spread wide my arms, letting the salty air flow around me as I often liked to do. I felt like I could feel the whole earth when I stood like that – taking it all in, welcoming the whole of it into my being.

The tang of winter still hangs in the wind; the emerging

warmth of the spring breezes still have a knife-edge of cold to them. I fancy I could smell the first of the spring blossoms, ghosts of things yet to be. I find myself musing that even though the sea makes me think of my mam and its own voice is as steady in my ear as my own heartbeat, I'm much more at home on the land than the sea. Still, I feel torn as to whether to go further up the path, to the hills and out onto the moor to visit my little croft, or down to the forbidden shore. What I ought to have done was go straight home and get the tea ready. I waited for the wind to tell me.

* * *

"Sometimes, I think I could fly," I told Callum, one afternoon as we'd stood in the exact same spot on the cliff path. We were on our way out to check on his flock but had decided to take the long route so we could walk by the sea. "I feel like the wind would just pick me up and let me ride on it, if I let it."

"Is that so, lassie? And why d'ye suppose it doesn't just carry ye off then? Is it such a polite thing to wait for permission, like?"

"Oh, you'd have to believe in it, before it would happen," I'd explained, quite seriously. "The trouble with most folk is that they'd rather things stay simple and easy to explain. They'd never entertain the notion that the wind might like to let you ride on it, or that a tree would fancy a chat."

* * *

"Would you take me now, then?" I murmured to the snapping wind. "Would you lift me up and carry me away from all of this nonsense? I wouldn't mind it a bit."

I waited for a reply, then dropped my arms to my sides and grinned. Throwing my head back, I shouted, "Fine then! Off with you, contrary creature!"

Still laughing, I decided that the wind wanted me to take the path down to the beach after all. Tea would wait, I reasoned. Besides, someone was bound to have come along with some sausages or a bit of cheese pie while I'd been with Hetty and, as consolation, I promised myself to not go near the sea. Surely that wasn't breaking any rules.

I skipped, as sure-footed as one of Callum's sheep, down the steep path to the sand below. The wind tugged at the scrubby grasses and swirled tiny dervishes of sand along the incline. When I finally reached the bottom, the force of the wind subsided as I stood in the shelter of the cliff wall.

The tide was out and so it was easy to keep my promise and stay far from the water's edge. The beach was littered with the remnants of the winter storms. Soon, the women would make their way down to the sand and salvage what they could of timber and kelp. Not yet though. Until the ceremony took place, it wasn't safe to be too close to the shore. I wandered along, keeping my eyes down in search of sea glass or the smooth rocks with holes through the middle that Hetty called witch stones. I picked up a crooked stick with which to poke at the clumps of kelp and turn over the various bits of gnarled driftwood.

"You're not supposed to be down here, Aibhlinn MacFinlay," came an imperious voice from behind me.

Chapter 9

I started guiltily and dropped my stick. Whirling around, I came face to face with the pale, sweating countenance of Morag Dunn. Morag stood with her arms folded across her ample bosom, her hair wrapped in modest plaits and covered by a multi-coloured kerchief.

"Neither are you," I retorted.

"I just followed *you*," snapped back Morag.

"So? How does that make it better? You're still here, aren't you?"

Morag faltered. Her small, pale eyes darting nervously to the water's edge.

"I won't tell if you won't," I said, grinning mischievously.

Morag managed a reluctant smile and nodded primly.

"Still," she said. "You should go. It's worse that you're here. Nobody would really care if I got carried off by a water horse. But it'd be the end of the world if they got to you before...."

I stared at Morag, whose eyes brimmed suddenly with tears. Her lower lip trembled, and she wrapped her arms more tightly around herself.

"Morag?" I said, surprised by her sudden display of emotion. "Are you alright? Do you need to sit down or something?"

Without waiting for a reply, I steered her over to a rocky outcropping near the cliff wall. There were several smaller boulders on the outside of the cluster and so I hefted Morag onto the nearest one before clambering up beside her.

"There now," I said, trying to jolly Morag out of her bewildering state of sniffles. "No chance of a sea beastie getting hold of us up here. I'm told they can't jump very high."

I gave Morag one of my best and most merry smiles, but it seemed to have no effect.

"Morag?"

No answer, just a quiet sniffle. I looked out to sea. The water was calm, the waves rolling gently in the distance. Sighing, I rummaged in my coat pocket for my hanky. It was clean and crisply starched, courtesy of Molly Flanagan who'd come to do the washing and ironing two days past.

"Can I at least offer you a hanky?" I asked, passing it down over Morag's shoulder. She reached up and took it, turning to smile weakly.

"Ta, Aibhlinn."

We sat in silence for a while. I thought it best to let Morag gather herself without my interference. She blew her nose noisily. I waved away the proffered hanky.

"Keep it," I said. "I imagine there'll be another pile of clean ones waiting for me when I get home. Right next to two fish pies, a brambleberry crumble and a tureen of potato soup."

A pair of gulls called raucously from their roost, higher up the cliff face. One of them lifted off and glided out towards the sea, flying low over the undulating surface. Lucky things, I thought, absently.

"What did you mean, anyway?" I asked, by way of an effort to drown out the ongoing and uncomfortable silence. "When you said no-one would care if you got carried off? Surely aren't you the treasure of the island? Everyone dotes on you. Your mam and da think the world of you, aren't they always going on..."

"I'm no such thing," said Morag, her voice clipped and bitter. "And that's just what they say in front of other people. I'm nothing but a tremendous disappointment to them, really. And the only reason people are nice to me is because they're afraid of my da and what he might say to Lord Pennorth."

Most people would instinctively deny those sorts of unpleasant proclamations, rushing in to placate and reassure, but I wasn't most people. I knew I ought to do those things, that there was some sort of unwritten rule of polite society to do so, but I just couldn't, in good conscience deny what was obviously true. So, I sat quietly, thinking over what Morag had said.

"Well," I said, finally. "I can see the bit about folk being scared of what your da might say to Lord Pennorth, because he is a bit of a tyrant. Your da, that is," I added quickly. "Not Lord Pennorth."

Morag narrowed her eyes.

"Well! He is!" I said, "Anyway, I don't see what that has to do with you being a disappointment. Aren't you the model of good behaviour and deportment? Aren't I always being held up to your shining example?"

"You really don't understand any of this, do you?" asked Morag, a familiar exasperation in her tone. "You roam about the place, wild as one of your brother's smelly sheep, without a care in the world. You're all sharp-tongue and mockery, poking fun at the well-meant efforts of your neighbours. But did it ever occur to you that some of us would have actually been *honoured* to be chosen for this? That maybe it might have been a chance to do something good, something worthy, a chance to be something more than just a burden?"

My mouth hung open.

Morag had barely said three words in my presence as long as I'd known her. Oh, she had plenty to say about me behind my back and made no secret of her quiet loathing of me, but, of course, it would never have been considered proper to engage with me in actual verbal warfare.

"What? You can't be serious, Morag," I said, unwilling to believe a word of what I was hearing. Who in their right mind would actually *want* to be in my shoes? Especially after what Hetty had just told me. It was on the tip of my tongue to let Morag know precisely what she was missing, just to see the look of horror on her bland, sheep's face, but I bit it back. Hetty had sworn me to secrecy and, for once, I was going to do what I was told.

Morag just stared at me; pale blue eyes swimming with fear and seething fury.

"But why?" I persisted. "Why on earth would it matter to you? Everyone knows Lord Pennorth is going to offer for you. Won't the two of you be perfectly suited?"

Lord Pennorth was twenty years Morag's senior. A tall, foppish, but kindly gentleman, it was rumoured he preferred the company of handsome, young boys. But even if that were so, he was obligated to marry at some point. Morag seemed to be everyone's logical choice.

"Lord Pennorth has no intention of marrying me," replied Morag softly, looking away and out towards the sea.

"Is it about the boys?" I said, quickly and without thinking. "Because I'm sure that's just a rumour started by some bad-tempered fisherman."

"No, it isn't about the boys. And it's not just a rumour, by the way. None of it matters anyway. Lord Pennorth has made it quite clear to me that he has no interest in marrying me whatsoever. And it's excruciatingly painful for me to see the lengths to which everyone seems to go to convince us both otherwise."

"Oh," I said, quite unsure how to respond.

"Not that you'd have any experience of this at all, but there's nothing worse than knowing you're not wanted while everyone tries to convince you that you are."

I snorted in a most unladylike fashion. Morag pursed her lips and wrinkled her nose.

"That, Morag Dunn," I said, emphatically, "is one thing I happen to know better than anyone."

* * *

"What do you suppose it would be like to be able to do whatever we wanted?" I asked, chewing thoughtfully.

Morag had found some toffee wrapped in a bit of brown paper at the bottom of her apron pocket. It was old and a bit stale, but nothing a bit of extra chewing effort couldn't overcome.

She grunted; her mouth too full to respond.

"Well, I think it would be a marvel altogether. I'd never marry and live in a tiny cottage on the edge of the moor. I'd come and go as I pleased, and no-one could tell me to tie up my hair or iron my hankies. I'd have my own pony and a few hens, and a cat named Philippe."

"Philippe?" said Morag, swallowing her lump of toffee with a cough. "What sort of name is that for a cat? Besides, you'll never be able to do any of that. Especially not now."

"Oh?" I said, frowning down at her. "How's that, then?"

"Everyone knows that once a sea bride, always a sea bride. You'll have no choice but to get married, your da'll be over-run with offers for you. There won't be a bachelor on all the island that won't be setting his sights on you."

"And who decided that my da should have a say in who I marry?" I said, "Aren't I my own person? And who says I'd want to marry any of the poxy fishermen on this island anyway?"

It was Morag's turn to snort.

"You'd best get yourself clear of any notion of choice, Aibhlinn," she said, with a hint of malice. "That disappeared the minute your da wrote your name in the book."

"And you'd best get yourself clear of any notion of hope that you'll ever find anyone stupid or desperate enough to marry *you*, Morag Dunn!"

I jumped down off the rock and spun to face the startled Morag, my hands on my hips. I'd tried to be nice to her, I really had, but she'd crossed an uncrossable line.

"You hateful little beast!" shrieked Morag, sliding and bumping from the boulder. She landed in an ungraceful heap, her feet sliding in the sand in front of me.

I bent down and picked up a handful of kelp from the ridge of high-tide mark.

"Go on!" I shouted at Morag, my hair whipping a fury around my face. "Be off with you, you great, sweating, lump! And don't you ever tell me what I can or can't do! Nobody tells me what to do. Not ever!"

I drew back my arm as if to throw the kelp.

Morag let out a squeal and scrambled back, running clumsily in the slippery sand. When she was out of arm's reach, she turned and shouted back, "Just you wait, Aibhlinn MacFinlay! You'll not know what hit you in a week or so. It'll be the end of all your flitting about on the moors, chasing deer. It'll be over, do you hear me?"

I roared and hurled handful after handful of sodden kelp at Morag's retreating figure before standing, slump-shouldered and worn out.

"Now then, young lass. Why is that ye're throwing about good kelp? It's all these auld bones can manage to get across the sand without ye hurling it back in t' the blessed sea."

For the second time that day, I jumped, guiltily dropping the kelp I still held.

"What are you doing down here?" I asked, then winced at my own rudeness. "Sorry, that didn't come out right. It's just the women don't usually come down here before...."

"Before the sea takes its bride?" said the old woman to whom the voice belonged. She was bent almost double with age and leaned her slight frame on a long stick for support.

"Well, yes. Although I've never quite heard it put that way," I confided, quite liking her turn of phrase.

"Aye, I dinna imagine ye have an' that," muttered the old woman. "Yer lot are all about what ye imagine ye give, not what gets taken."

"What's the difference?" I asked, genuinely puzzled by the vague distinction.

"Everything," replied the woman. "It's all the difference in the world. Here," she passed me a large wicker basket. "Fetch me that full o' kelp and I'll tell it ye."

Chapter 10

"Ye have it all wrong," said the old woman, lowering herself gingerly onto a large, driftwood log. She rummaged in the pocket of her patched overcoat and pulled out a clay pipe. I sat impatiently at her feet while she painstakingly tapped out the old tobacco and filled it anew. Her fingers were long and bony, stained brownish-yellow at the tips.

"Oh?" I said, trying to prod her along.

"Aye," said the woman, puffing experimentally at her pipe. A spiral of sweet-scented smoke curled up around her head. It smelled of pine and heather and the salt-breeze.

An eternity passed by as we sat in silence. I fidgeted and glanced at the dimming horizon. I could already envision the look on my father's face when I got home. Also, there was no doubt in my mind that Morag would have run straight to her mother to tell yet another tale of my shocking behavior.

Isabelle Dunn was probably already knocking on our door.

"Ye know what yer trouble is, lass?" said the old woman, jabbing the stem of her pipe at me.

"Well, it depends who you ask," I replied, grinning. "Most people have an opinion on that one, so it's no surprise to me that you have as well. Even though I don't think we've ever met."

The old woman cackled.

"Aye, well. That's two troubles, then. Impatience and impertinence."

I shrugged.

"That about sums it up, I'd say. Variations on those themes, anyway."

"Whisht now! Has no-one ever tellt ye to think afore ye open yer great gob?"

I blinked, surprised at her words. Yet again, her turn of phrase delighted me.

"Actually, yes. Although, again, not quite in those terms." I folded my arms around my knees. "Do you suppose you might tell me how we've got it all wrong? I need to get back home, you see. Not to mention, I'm really not supposed to be down here." I tilted my head and smiled in my customarily winning way, quite sure of the extent of my current infamy. "I imagine you know who I am?"

The old woman scowled and spat over her shoulder in way of reply.

"Are you from across the moor, then?" I asked, sure I'd remember such an irreverent person had I come across them before.

"Aye, summat like that," said the old woman. "Why are ye down here if ye aren't supposed to be?"

"I could ask you the same thing," I replied, tartly. "None of the women are meant to come here before, well, before the sea takes its bride, as you put it."

"D'ye allus answer a question with a question?"

"Do you?"

We both erupted into laughter. It echoed off the cliff face and bounced out to sea, carried by the breeze.

"I'm here exactly because I'm not supposed to be," I said, finally, having honestly considered the question.

The old woman nodded. "So I thought."

"Then why did you ask?"

"Because I needed ye to say it."

"Who are you, really?" I asked. "Because you're not from around here, are you?"

The old woman nodded inconclusively.

"I'm from here, and not," she said. "Of here, and not."

I frowned.

"Are you one of the faery then?" I said, in for a penny and all that.

The old woman raised a spidery eyebrow.

"Are ye one for believing in the Good Folk?" she asked, a twinkle in her blue eyes.

I snorted, in my unladylike manner again.

"Aren't I well known to be faery-begot?" I said, with a wry smile. "Isn't that just common knowledge?"

"And if ye were?" asked the old woman.

I shrugged.

"If I am, then I am," I replied. "I don't see how it matters."

I couldn't admit, even to this strange old woman who was probably as welcome among folk as was I, that it had always been my secret, childhood wish that I really *was* faery-begot.

Because that could account for my other-ness, rather than it being my own failings that excluded me from everything.

The old woman grinned a toothless grin.

"Ah, but lassie. Ye'll find it matters a great deal."

***

"Back in the days afore the churchmen were such a number," the old woman began. "It were that the women knew the way o' things. It were the women who saw to the land and to the keeping of it. It were the women who kept the old festivals; who lit the fires and spoke with the spirits o' the land on behalf o' the people. They were sure to keep the balance - to never take more than was needed and to give back, in kind, for what was taken."

I closed my eyes. The wind had warmed considerably as we'd sat, and the sea's gentle hum and roar rose and fell with the cadence of the old woman's story.

"It was right for it to be that way," she continued, "seeing as how it's women as carries the gift of creation their own selves."

"Do you mean because we bear children?" I asked, very much enjoying the notion of women tending to the land as being an important thing.

"Exactly, lass. And because it's women whose lives run in time to the moon; to the tides and to the rise and fall of the seasons."

67

"Callum always says his ewes like it best when I'm there for the lambing," I said. "He says they're more settled when I'm there."

"Of course they would, lass. A sheep's no' so stupid as to no' recognize one o' her own when she's on her birthing time."

I nodded; my own quiet thoughts having been confirmed.

"Anyhow," said the crone. "Eventually it was that the churchmen came to the land and started retelling the old stories to suit their own selves. Soon the women lost the trust o' the people and fear took over where respect once lived."

The crone paused to relight her pipe. The sun had slid lower on the horizon and a fiery orange glow burned out across the sea. I wasn't thinking about the tea, or Isabelle Dunn, or my da anymore. I felt, quite suddenly, at home there on the edge of the world. I studied the face of the old woman in the dying light and plumes of fragrant smoke. The creases that had etched the weathered skin had softened in the kind light. Blinking contentedly, I hugged my knees more tightly.

"How could they let that happen?" I asked. "Why didn't the women fight?"

The crone shook her head.

"I've no notion o' that, lass. I suppose it were done so carefully, like. The land isn't gentle sometimes, aye? Harvests fail, lambs die, and the sea is as fickle a creature as there ever was. The churchmen knew well how t' use fear o' those things - all natural and necessary things, mind ye - to twist the minds o' simple folk. And the gift o' creation itself is a powerful thing. It's something the men cannae ever have, ye ken? And what some men dinna understand, they ha' to control."

She glanced sideways at me, watching, I suppose, at how I was taking it all in. Could she have known the effect of her words over me? With them, she'd spun the world into a pattern I recognized at once, from somewhere deeper than just in my mind.

"You mean like giving us over to the sea?" I asked, realization dawning on me.

"Aye, lass. It's all been turned around, see? By striking a bargain that gives away the most valuable thing the human folk have, they've damned ye all."

I felt myself shiver, despite the sudden warmth of the breeze.

"How do we stop it, then?" I asked. "Because we have to, don't we? That's what you're telling me."

The old woman tilted her head and smiled sadly.

"It's no' my place to tell ye, lass. Me being here is as much a breaking o' the rules as it is for ye and I've talked long enough for now."

"So why are you here, then?" I said, feeling cheated. "If not to tell me what to do next? Surely you can't just leave me hanging like that. Aren't you going to finish the story?"

The crone chuckled and rose to her feet. She stood straighter than when she'd sat down.

I followed her, brushing sand off my skirt.

"It's time I was getting on, lass," said the crone, picking up her basket. "Spring is in the air, cannae ye feel it on the breeze? Me auld bones is ready for a rest. Besides, mebbe the story isn't mine to finish."

She turned to go, shuffling away into the lengthening shadows, without a backward glance.

"Wait!" I called after her, struggling to see her in the rising darkness. "What am I supposed to do? Why won't you help me?"

I ran towards the place that I'd last seen the silhouette of the old woman, but there was no sign of her. "Are you still there?"

"Just remember, lass," came a voice from behind me.

I spun around but there was no-one there.

"Remember what ye are."

Chapter 11

It was just as I had predicted.

Isabelle Dunn stood, arms folded and toe tapping at the bottom of the path that led to our cottage.

Instinctively, I glanced up the road in the direction of the tavern but there was no sign of my da.

"No, he's not here," said Isabelle, her voice smooth and superior. "For once it is to your advantage that your father is a drunken sot."

I bristled. I don't have all that much that's nice to say about my da, but he is my da and someone like Isabelle Dunn has no right to comment on him. I opened my mouth to retort but she held up an imperious hand.

"Listen very carefully, young lady," she began, her eyes like two pieces of glittering black stone. "My Morag has told me that she saw you down on the beach..."

I narrowed my eyes, noting the phrasing. Clearly Morag

didn't mention that she, too, was on the beach. I started to point it out then, for some inexplicable reason, changed my mind. I gritted my teeth and said nothing.

"...and I don't think you need me to tell you all that you're risking with this careless and selfish behaviour."

She regarded me for an instant, tilting her head like a cat, just before it pounces on a mouse.

"Then again, perhaps you do need me to remind you." She smoothed her hands down her fine silk dress, the fabric shushing and rustling with the touch. The gesture wasn't lost on me. I was supposed to be reminded of her great wealth and influence. I left my expression carefully blank.

She scowled and leaned in. Her breath smelled of onions. I did my very best not to recoil.

"You are, perhaps, aware that my husband is to take a meeting with Lord Pennorth next month? To establish the quotas and inventory for the season?"

I nodded. Of course I was aware. It was the only thing being discussed around our table at mealtimes. Both Callum and Alexander, who handled the business end of his and Duncan's fishing boat, depended on the renewal of their contracts.

"And it would be a terrible shame to think that Lord Pennorth may not require quite as much from Glencarragh as in times past," She paused to examine her perfectly clean and sculpted fingernails. "Apparently he can acquire comparable goods at a lesser price on the mainland."

A cold sweat prickled up my spine. Surely that was a lie. Lord Pennorth had always prized Glencarragh wool over any other and those who fished off the mainland didn't have access to the same territories and catches as the island fishermen and they certainly didn't understand the fickle tides and tempestuous weather.

"Of course, my husband is doing his absolute best to convince Lord Pennorth otherwise. He always has the best interests of the island people at heart, you see. But should it come down to it, sacrifices may have to be made. And I don't imagine it would be hard to decide who would be cut off, should the chosen sea bride bring shame to her family and, even worse, potential danger to the community with her willful and disregarding behaviour."

My face burned and I was genuinely afraid I would grind my teeth to powder. I knotted my fingers into my skirts and took a deep, steadying breath and exhaled slowly.

"I would never put my family at risk," I said, "Not ever."

"And your community?"

I hesitated. What had my community ever done for me? Who among them, other than Hetty, had ever extended a hand in aid? I couldn't bring myself to say anything so just nodded, leaving the interpretation open.

"Excellent," she purred, "Just as I'd hoped. Now then, you will proceed, from this day, in a deportment fitting the honour which has been bestowed upon you. I haven't worked…. *we* haven't worked this diligently as a community to protect our land and our livelihoods from unholy influences simply to have that cast aside by some feckless scrap of a half-breed. And if you cannot behave yourself, rest assured, matters will be taken out of your hands."

Before I could even respond, she was off down the path towards the village, her skirts billowing around her in the rising wind.

I hope you get blown off the cliff, I thought, viciously, as I stamped into the house.

* * *

Nobody cared that the tea was late, probably because they didn't notice.

Da came storming in, just as I was taking the warmed fish pie out of the oven (thoughtfully provided by Eileen Thomas, someone who never had a kind word to say about any of us before now). Obviously, word had got out that I'd been down to the beach. Alexander and Duncan came in a few minutes later and I listened to them all rant and rave and argue for over half an hour, as the pie turned cold again. Callum didn't even bother coming home. I suspect he'd got himself a bowl of stew from Hetty and gone straight to his croft. If he could avoid an argument, he would. Not that I could really blame him. Still, it would have been nice to have someone on my side.

Eventually, the bluster died down and I was able to quietly slip out the back door as they finally sat down to their dinner. As long as their bellies were getting filled, they wouldn't notice I was even gone.

The evenings were slowly getting lighter, but it was still growing dark by the time I made my way to my own little sanctuary on the moor.

It isn't much to look at from the outside, at least, not yet. I have plenty of ideas to rebuild the little stone wall of the kitchen garden and I've a lot of work to do clearing away the brambles and snarls of honeysuckle. Still, though, the sight of it always fills me with the most comfortable, warm feeling as if there were already a fire burning in the grate and the lamps all lit against the night. I fight my way through the thicket of heather and bracken - I don't want to clear a proper path just yet, in case a passing someone should think someone was living there and want to investigate. It's far better that it stays looking rundown and uninhabitable. The door is a bit crooked and sticks a little but with the right lift and push it creaks open and I slide through. Even though it's almost fully dark I know exactly where to go to find the lamp and matches and soon there's a gentle yellow glow chasing the shadows from the corners.

I make a small fire of twigs and scraps of peat under the billy can that I found in a rubbish heap behind one of the boat sheds. It's dented and leaks, but only a bit and not enough to stop it brewing. I keep a jar of herbal tea on a shelf by the chipped stone sink and soon I'm sitting on the prickly and balding horsehair settee, breathing in the fragrant fumes of my brew.

For the thousandth time, I find myself daydreaming of what it'll be like when I'm living here all of the time. I can see, so clearly, how the cottage will look and feel and there are times when my heart aches for the wanting of it. I just know that I can make it happen, I just need everyone to leave me alone to get on with it. Even Hetty, who I love with all of my heart, doesn't think it's going to work - me living on my own and making my own way. She says that no-one will take me seriously as an herbwyfe unless I'm respectably married. Something to do with old superstitions and fears around witchcraft and some such nonsense. There are times when I wonder whose side Hetty's on - she's so clever but at the same time she goes along with the stuffy ways of the rest of the islanders. Callum says it's because she has to keep on everyone's good side, because of the tavern, but I think it goes beyond that. Anyway, it doesn't matter because I'm going to do whatever I need to, and I don't much care what anyone else thinks. And if going along with this sea bride business will give me some sort of status, then that's what I'll do. No-one will argue with a bride of the sea if she says she's going to live alone on the edge of the moor, will they? After all, by doing this thing for the island - and that's exactly how I'm looking at it, I'm doing it for the *island* and not the hateful traditions of the people who've put me in this position — I'll have earned the right to go my own way. In fact, I think that I'm going to pack myself a little bag and stay right here until I'm expected to turn up for my impending nuptials. My brothers have enough people to help feed and keep them tidy. No-one will even notice I'm gone.

I'm distracted from my plotting by the sound of the wind whistling softly through the gaps around the windows. It gently wafts the curtains that I've hung there and for a moment it sounds like someone humming. I close my eyes and imagine that it's my mother, singing me one of the faery lullabies that Callum taught me when I was little. I take a sip of my tea, close my eyes and lose myself in one of my favourite daydreams — the one where a strange and beautiful woman knocks on the door of my tidy little cottage and says she's looking for her long-lost daughter and that she's sure it's me.

Chapter 12

Hetty

I love her like she's my own, I always have. It was me whose hands first held her, as she slid, squalling before she'd barely landed earthside, in a gush of blood and saltwater from her mother. I already knew that beautiful Anwen wouldn't be with us for much longer and I'd promised that I'd care for her bairn as she would've done herself and that's exactly what I've done. And now, knowing what the child is facing and how ill-equipped I feel to help her, I can't help but wonder if her mother would regret her choice in me.

***

There were all manner of tales that followed the tall, fair-haired woman around, from the very first day she arrived all those years ago, seemingly out of the mist from the moor. The most commonly held belief was that she was a selkie - how else could a man like Hamish MacFinlay claim such a beautiful bride but to have stolen her skin and hidden it? But no matter what was whispered behind hands in kitchens and over pints of ale, it could never be said that she didn't blend into island life just as if she'd been born here. And, if you want to split hairs over it, she was more a part of Glencarragh than any of the rest of us had claim to and that I know for a fact.

Five strapping lads she'd borne that hard-eyed husband of hers, though he'd been softer then, kind, even. She had that effect on folk — you couldn't help but want to be a better person when she was around. It was like she expected it of you, and you didn't want to disappoint her. Anyway, it was when her two eldest boys were lost to the sea that she started to change. Her eyes seemed always to be on some distant horizon and even though she never wavered in her care of her folk, she spent more time walking the cliff edges and down on the shore than ever before, her hair wild and uncombed and her dresses wrinkled and stained. People whispered that the darkness was on her, and she was slowly going mad. I half-believed it and am ashamed of that even now.

I knew she'd always wanted a girl-child, she'd said as much often enough, but she came ever more insistent that it needed to come about. She spent hours scouring the moors and fens for particular plants and even more time singing strange sounding songs to the wind and the sea. When at last she fell pregnant again, she seemed to settle, in the way that many womenfolk do when they're in a family way. She combed her hair and ironed her dresses, tended her garden, fed her menfolk and went back to singing the songs with words that you could understand.

Three days before she went into labour, she came to visit me at the tavern. I hadn't seen her for a few weeks as we'd been so busy with the sheep shearing, extra men brought in from the mainland meant food and beds to provide. I was shocked to see her looking so pale. Her eyes were smudged under with dark, and her skin had lost that pregnancy glow. She must have noticed my shock because she was quick to reassure me.

"Worry not, Hetty my dear," she said, in her soft, sing-song voice. "I'm faring just as well as I should be right now and shall only improve." She ran a hand over her swollen belly and smiled, her gaze shifting to that far-off place that it often did. "My precious girl will be here soon and there's something I would ask of you."

I nodded, happy to do anything she would ask, and led her to a stool in the kitchen, so that she could rest her legs.

"This child of mine is such a blessing," she mused, accepting the steaming cup of brew I handed to her. "To think, after five handsome boys and all this time, I should be gifted with a girl."

"Well," I said, not wanting her to get her hopes up. "There's always the chance it'll be another boy, ye know. 'Tis just chance, after all."

She shook her head, her mouth quirking up at the corners.

"No, Hetty. There's been no chance taken this time, I've made sure of it."

I shifted uncomfortably in my seat and glanced around, but there was no-one else within earshot. Such talk wasn't the wisest thing, there were still those on the island that lived with superstitious fear of unsavoury practices and wouldn't hesitate to make accusations. Despite her general popularity, Anwen MacFinlay still had her detractors.

Her laugh was like the sound of water bubbling over rocks.

"Don't fret, Hetty," she exclaimed, reaching over to pat my arm. Her fingers were ice cold. "I haven't done anything untoward, although there are those who would think it thus. No," she paused to rub her belly again, "no, the worst that I have done is to break a promise that I ought never have made."

I frowned, confused. Anwen sometimes had the habit of speaking in riddles and this seemed to be one of those times.

She waved a hand, as if to clear something from the air.

"Never mind all that," she said, her voice becoming brisk and business-like. "Of course, you will attend me when my time comes,"

I nodded. I'd been trained as a midwife since I was a girl, following in my mother's and grandmother's footsteps and had attended the births of all of Anwen's children.

"And I would ask you now to promise me, that should anything go wrong - and you and I both know that at my age, that could easily happen - that you will do everything in your power to give shelter and aid to my girl."

She said the last part with deep seriousness, leaning towards me with her eyes boring into mine. I had no choice but to nod, speechless. Anwen had always seemed to defy the passage of time, she looked as fresh and youthful as she had when she first arrived on Glencarragh. I hardly considered her a risk for childbirth. Still, if it would ease her mind, I would gladly agree.

"Excellent," she said, leaning back in her chair. She regarded me with a thoughtful look.

"There is another thing, Hetty my dearest friend, upon which I would have you give your word."

There was something in her tone and her eyes that suddenly made my mouth go dry. I swallowed and nodded, gripping my mug lest my hands tremble and betray me.

She tilted her head and smiled at me, her face radiant, despite the paleness and dark smudges under her eyes.

"I know that you know what I am," she said, softly and without guile. "And I know that you've always defended me from the vicious gossips and those who would spin lies about my people, about who and what we are." She held up a hand as I opened my mouth to protest.

"It's no use, Hetty, darling heart. I may have not let it show, but I wasn't entirely oblivious to the hateful stares and the suspicion. I cannot blame them – they're so steeped in superstition and fear that they're simply unable to see the truth of things. But that's of no importance to us now. Time is growing short, and I will have debts to pay before long."

"Debts?" I croaked, uneasily thinking of her cliff walking and strange songs.

"Oh yes, my friend. This wee girl comes with a price, you see."

She smiled, her hand resting lightly on her belly, though there were tears in her eyes.

"And you shall help me pay it."

* * *

What happened next, I daren't say. The workings of the faery folk are strange, and I don't understand their ideas of fair bargaining. But what I can say is that it's not true what they said about Hamish MacFinlay holding Anwen to the land against her will. She came of her own choosing and stayed for the joy of her children and her life on the island. I think, though, that the loss of her boys was more than she could bear. Mortal life is an incomprehensible concept to the long-lived ones, and I think perhaps the pain of it broke her heart beyond repair. I was sworn to secrecy about my true part in it all - and I will honour that promise made - so when the story was passed around that three days after her bairn was born, Anwen MacFinlay finally succumbed to the darkness and threw herself into the sea and was drowned, I did nothing to dispel the rumour.

Chapter 13

Spring Equinox

Aibhlinn

"I can find my own way there, Callum," I said, linking arms with my brother. "I hardly think I need an escort, considering where I'm going to be, this time tomorrow. Or are they all still thinking I'm going to do a last-minute bunk?"

I plucked his sleeve, trying to coax a smile from his troubled features.

"I wish ye wouldn't take so lightly with the whole thing, Leeny," said Callum, frowning. "It's a terrible serious business. Ye'd do well to have a bit o' fear in ye, I think."

"Who says I haven't?" I said, meaning it.

Callum stopped and tugged me around to face him. He placed his hands on my shoulders and bent low to look me in the eyes.

"I wish with all my heart it wasn't ye having to do this, Leeny. I'd give up my right arm to those foul creatures if it meant sparing ye."

I smiled, reaching up my own small hand and put it over my brother's large one.

"I know, Callum," I said softly. "I know."

Linking his arm again, I tugged him along. "But I tell you what would make it easier for me," I teased. "If you would stop being so dire and gloomy so that I didn't have to worry about you."

Callum gave me a small smile. "Aye, go on, then," he said. "I'll try my best."

"Good! Now, why don't you tell me again about the day our mam told you I was coming. And how the sea itself sparkled like a million gems whenever she would walk the shore with me all tucked up in her belly. Oh! And don't forget the bit how she sang me into world on the edge of the cliff."

Callum looked down into my smiling face. I know he could see past my smiles and jests to the very real fear I felt in my heart. I could never fool Callum; he, and Hetty, are the two people who I think might really see me. So I hope it meant that, along with my terror, he could see my courage. And my defiance for what the whole thing meant.

He shook his head, as if perhaps to clear the unpleasant thoughts, just as I'd asked him. Then, for the hundredth time since the solstice, he cursed our father's name.

* * *

I never did get to escape to my cottage.

I slept there, the night after all of the fuss about me going down to the beach, then went back to the house in the early morning. It wasn't the first time I'd done that - I often did it when I knew that da was going to be late getting up after a heavy night of the drink - and I knew that as long as I was back in time to get the fire going and the breakfast started, no-one would be any the wiser. I hadn't counted on Isabelle Dunn, though. She was lying in wait for me and after yet another lecture, she promised me I'd be far too busy for gallivanting from that time on. She wasn't exaggerating. I've been pestered constantly with requests to tea and generally having my presence required in places. There's not a minute in the day that some woman or other isn't turning up wanting me to go and do this, that or the other or to help me with my washing or mending. I know what they're up to, making sure I don't go off and do a runner. I suppose they can't understand why I haven't. Which shows them how much they underestimate the sort of person I am. Anyway, it'll all be over soon, and I can do what I want. I just keep that thought in my head when I think I might go mad with the frustration of it all. And there's Hetty and Callum to think of too. I don't want to make this any harder for them than it already is.

* * *

"Here she is, then, Hetty," said Callum, as we walked into the empty tavern. It was early; the fishermen were still out with the morning tides and with lambing time drawing near, the shepherds were bringing the flocks down from the moors. Hetty would have a large pot of stew bubbling away on the stove and I could already smell the bread baking.

"Aren't I the luckiest one?" I asked, brightly. "To have the most handsome shepherd on Glencarragh to escort me to my nuptials?"

Callum tried to smile but it more closely resembled a grimace. Hetty patted his arm.

"Will ye have a mug o' something, pet?" she asked. "I've just put the tea on to steep." She eyed his worried face. "Or mebbe something a bit stronger?"

Callum shook his head.

"No, thanks anyway, Hetty. I have to get back to the moor. I've got Mick Flanagan helping me bring the ewes down and I dinna like to keep him waiting."

"Right, lad. Of course. Oh! Hang on a minute, pet." She disappeared into the kitchen and returned a few minutes later with a cloth-wrapped parcel.

"Just a bit o' ham and egg pie," she said, tucking it into his overcoat pocket. "And a lump o' me best cheese. For you and Mick, aye? Keep the wolf from the door, right?"

She grinned, but I could see that it was forced and the worry in her eyes matched my brother's. I fancied an unspoken agreement passed between them in that glance and suddenly their moods shifted.

Callum rubbed his hands together.

"Brilliant! Ta very much, Hetty. That'll go down right well at the end of a long morning. I'll not have to pay auld Mick now!"

The two of them chuckled companionably as Hetty walked him back to the door. "Pour yersel' a cuppa, Aibhlinn, love. I'll be in in a minute," she called back over her shoulder.

"Dinna worry, pet," I heard her murmur to Callum as they stood in the doorway of the tavern. I inched closer to them, pretending to be taking in the view out of the front window. The morning sky was dotted with wispy clouds and a sharp breeze blew up from the shore. "She'll be alright. She's a strong wee thing and they've a way o' kindness about them. It doesnae serve them to hurt the lasses. They need them just as much as we do."

"D'you really believe that Hetty?" said Callum, his mask of cheerfulness slipping now that he thought me out of range. "Because I cannae get my head around it. Any of it. And nobody'll talk about it."

Hetty smiled. "There's some things as the menfolk cannae understand, and neither is it their place to. Give us that much, at least, aye? Dinna worry. She'll not come to harm."

"I'll take your word at it, Hetty. For all our sakes, you'd best be right."

* * *

I sat in the vast feather bed, a brightly coloured patchwork quilt wrapped around me. There was a small fire crackling in the grate, chasing away the chill of the early-spring evening. Hetty sat in a rocking chair beside the fire, knotting strips of material into a mat.

"Are you going to sit there all night?" I asked, "I'm not going to do a runner, if that's what you're thinking."

Hetty smiled widely.

"Nay, lass. I know you're not the type to run away. Although there's some as has." She paused to snap a thread. "I did."

My mouth hung open.

"You?" I said, my voice incredulous. "You were a sea bride once?"

"Aye, pet. Just the once." Hetty smirked. "Once was plenty."

I opened my mouth and then shut it again, stopping the questions that bubbled there.

I studied Hetty, who had gone back to her clippy mat, apparently not intending on elaborating further. The older woman was small and fine-boned, like me, but with a wiry strength that made her appear bigger than she was.

Hetty had always said that this island bred hard women – strong and fearless. Eking a life out of the fickle sea and a changeable landscape left little room for softness. And Hetty had been raised in a time when things were even more harsh than they were now. Still, I found it hard to imagine Hetty as a young woman.

"Afore ye ask," began Hetty, not looking up. "No, I won't tell ye about it. Just that I was terrified and so I ran away. The men brought me back, though. And I got the tannin' o' me life for going."

"Why do they do it?" I asked, my voice barely above a

whisper and my gaze on the flickering fire. "Why do they suppose they have the right over us?"

Hetty snorted.

"Isn't that the question we all want answered? Still, it's a funny old thing. Back in the long-ago days, 't'were the women that took a Year King for the land. The women were the ones as had the rule o' such things."

"That's what the old woman told me," I said, then immediately blushed. I hadn't told anyone about my encounter down at the beach. Folk had been quite occupied enough with my blatant defiance of the rules by just being there.

Hetty narrowed her eyes.

"What woman, pet?" she asked quietly.

"Oh. Just a batty old creature I met out on the moor, one afternoon," I lied. "I think she must be from across the north side of the island. I didn't recognize her."

"Hmph," Hetty frowned. "And what else did she have to say, then?"

I shrugged.

"Oh, she just told me about the old ways and, like you just said, how it was women who took care of the land until the churchmen came and twisted it all around."

"Aye, well. I don't know as we can lay it all at the feet o' the churchmen. They were a canny lot back in my time. Not like your one there, Father Ewan. Now he's a pinch-faced ogre if ever there was one."

"Hetty!" I put the back of my hand to my forehead in a gesture of shock and horror. "I'm scandalized!"

Hetty chuckled.

"'Tis naught but the truth. And it were men like *him* who turned it all around, and there were just as many o' them were lay-people. Greedy, grasping men who wanted more than was their due. They'd have turned in their own grannies if they thought they'd come out better for it."

"That's what they did, though, isn't it? Only not their grannies, their own daughters?"

"Aye, lass. They thought to meddle wi' things not their place to touch. The land, and the sea, and all that it gives and takes, is the rightful business o' women. That's just the natural fact o' things."

Hetty shook her head. "Eeh! Would ye listen to me go on? Dinna pay any mind to me, pet. It's just the old one coming back as got me turning things over as best left alone. What's done is done and all we've to do now is make the best o' things."

She stood up from her rocking chair and set her handwork down into a basket. She prodded the fire and put on another lump of peat. Sparks flew at the disturbance and then settled into a bright glow.

"Right, my lamb. Let's get ye snugged in tight. Ye've an early start, aye?"

She fussed around the bed, tucking the quilt snugly around me. "Ye look a pea on a drum in that big bed," she remarked, smiling. She reached over and pushed a strand of hair behind my ear. "Sleep well, lovely one. And I'll see ye with a nice cuppa, first thing."

I nodded, my eyes never leaving Hetty's face.

As Hetty turned to go, I spoke.

"Who was she, Hetty? You just called her 'the old one'. Do you know who she is?"

Hetty paused in the doorway, her back to me. The light from the oil lamp cast a flickering shadow around her.

"She's the oldest of us all, lass. And if she's come to ye, then it means hard times ahead."

Chapter 14

I woke to the sound of drums.

Dawn had barely seeped around the edge of the curtains, so I burrowed more deeply under the thick quilt. The bed was gloriously enveloping, and despite everything, I couldn't remember when last I'd enjoyed such a deep and restful sleep.

Groaning loudly, I pulled the quilt higher over my ears, trying to muffle the drums. I sent a stream of silent profanity at the men who I knew must be standing on the nearby cliff edge, banging away and disturbing the morning's peace.

Just then, the door swung wide and Hetty bustled in carrying a tray with a large teapot and a plate piled high with fried potatoes, mushrooms and rashers of bacon. She set the tray down and lit the oil lamp, humming merrily as she did so. Next came the fire - prodded back into life and fed with a sizable lump of peat.

"I know ye're awake, lass," she said, flinging the curtains open. "I don't see how anyone could sleep past the racket that lot is making out there."

"Why are they bothering with the drumming at this hour?" I muttered, sitting up. "Do they suppose it conjures up the good spirits, or what?"

Hetty chuckled.

"I imagine they fancy it sounds manly or some such. Makes them feel like they're doing something useful, at any rate."

I nodded.

"I thought as much. I will say this, though," I said, reaching to take the mug of tea that Hetty was offering. "It does lend a certain solemnity to the occasion. All very to-the-gallows-with-you."

Hetty grinned and winked.

"It does, aye." She paused to peer out of the bleary window. "It'd spoil their fun if we told 'em the truth, though."

She turned to look at me. I obliged her with a big smile and wink from behind my mug.

"Poor souls," I said. "Let them have their bit of ceremony. We all know who matters in the end, and it's not a crowd of smelly pony-men and their stupid drums, playing at druids."

Hetty shook her head.

"Ye're the first lass in a long while as makes me think there's a hope for us all."

She turned back to the fire and started tidying the hearth. When she spoke again it was in a voice barely above a whisper. "Like mayhaps the suffering of us all gone before ye doesnae have to be for naught."

"Well, it doesn't, Hetty," I said, getting out of bed and going over to wrap my arms around my friend. "It's just not right that people don't know the extent of it. They think it's all a tidy business and no-one ever gets hurt."

"Not as anyone sees, anyway," said Hetty. "It's all in here, aye?" She pointed to her chest.

"Those are the greatest hurts of all," I said, knowing it to be the truth.

"Aye, pet. That they are."

* * *

For a long time after Hetty had left the room, I sat in the chair by the hearth, and just stared into the fire. Hetty had draped a shawl around my shoulders and instructed me to eat some breakfast, saying she'd be back before long to help me get dressed.

The old linen dress hung on a knob on the back of the door. Hetty had carefully sewn the hem and tucked in the bodice to fit my small frame.

"Exactly how old is this dress?" I'd asked, during one of the many fittings.

Hetty had sat back on her heels and frowned, removing the pins that she held tightly between her lips.

"Well, I'll say as I don't rightly know, lass. It's been around at least since my own great-grandmother's time, and likely much longer than that."

I whistled softly.

"How can it still be in one piece? After all the adjusting and sewing and taking to bits?"

Hetty had smiled.

"Tis the weaving, aye? 'Tis faery-spun, to be sure. Nothing made by mortal hands could've withstood the saltwater and the mending this long."

* * *

The door creaked open, and I turned from my study of the flames. The tavern's elderly, one-eyed cat, Humphrey, snaked through the legs of the chairs and came to sit, purring, on the hearth rug.

"Taking advantage, are you?" I asked, reaching down to smooth his orange-striped fur. "Best not let Hetty find you in here. Aren't you supposed to be out in the storerooms catching mice or something useful like that?"

Humphrey responded to my question by purring even more loudly and settling himself into a comfortable ball, his tail curled tidily around his paws.

"I know. We can't always do what's expected can we?"

I pulled my knees up to my chin and wrapped the shawl tightly around myself. "Once we know there's other options, how can we possibly?"

Chapter 15

"Now, then," said Hetty, tucking the end of a ribbon into the long braids hanging on either side of my face. "Only John and the pony-man will be with you at the last. None else of us are allowed down at the water's edge."

"Not even you? Or Callum?" I said, unable to hide my fear.

I'd been perfectly fine until I'd felt the dress slip over my head. A strange feeling had come over me, then. The dress felt warm against my skin, as if it had a life, a heartbeat, all of its own. The plain, unassuming linen seemed transformed into something richer, more sumptuous, certainly not like anything I'd ever worn before. When I moved, it rippled about me with a whispering susurration that at once soothed and agitated. I had to resist the urge to rip it off and fling it far away.

"It has that effect, lass," said Hetty when she saw the

expression on my face. "It'll pass in time."

"But it never did that before," I said, shrinking inside it. My instinct was to get my skin as far from it as possible. "I've had it on lots of times before now, why is it all strange now?"

"Tis all to do with the turn of the season, lass. The spring tide is turning, and the water horses are just offshore now."

No-one had dared to tread the beaches for several days, even the men. No fishing boats had gone out, nor would they for the next nine days. The sea around Glencarragh was full of water horses, come in with the spring tide to hunt. Supposedly, it was only the bargain of the sea bride that kept them from coming ashore to take what they could from the land, be that someone's best ewe or a wayward child. The water horses were lightning fast and vicious, they could drag a burly fisherman into the sea and tear him limb from limb in a matter of minutes. Nothing left but red-tinged foam and an occasional boot, or so the stories went because I'd certainly never heard of anyone who was quite so foolish as to venture down to the shore so close to the turning of the spring.

I felt myself shudder, waves of nausea rolling up from my belly.

Hetty frowned, narrowing her eyes.

"Did you eat your breakfast, lass?"

I shook my head. "I wasn't hungry."

Hetty sighed.

"Well, it wouldnae be ye if ye didnae make it harder on yerself. Breathe in deep through your nose and blow it out gently. It'll calm yer belly a bit."

"What is it?" I asked, swallowing a mouthful of queasiness.

"It's the faery magic, in the dress, pet. It unsettles a body. Although not usually as badly as this. Must be as ye didn't eat anything to cushion it.”

“Eating is your answer to everything, Hetty,” said a voice behind us. “Did you pack our lass a picnic to take as well, like?”

“Callum!”

I flung my arms around my brother and buried my face in his neck. Breathing in deeply, I inhaled the peat-smell of the moors and the damp lanolin of sheep on his skin and clothes. “I’m so glad you came,” I said into the tangle of his hair. And I was. Even with Hetty looking after me, I was feeling very much alone.

“Now, then, lass,” he said, pulling my arms from around his neck and pushing me gently backwards. “Let’s have a look at ye.”

He held me at arm’s length and drank me in. His face was tight with strain, but he managed a big smile and a wink.

“She’s a picture, eh, Hetty? Ye’ve done us all proud.” His voice faltered at the look on my face.

I’d seen myself in the glass and knew I was pale and drawn; my eyes were full of worry and my chin was trembling traitorously.

“It’s ever so strange all of a sudden, Callum,” I said. “The dress...”

I stopped and closed my eyes briefly, taking a shaky breath.

I opened my eyes and forced a little laugh.

“Oh, never mind me,” I said, waving a hand. I reached over and smoothed down the lapels of his overcoat. “Hetty said I ought to have eaten breakfast, and she was right, of course. I’m just a bit light-headed with nerves, that’s all. It’ll pass.”

Callum frowned but nodded his head. He turned to look at Hetty who avoided his gaze.

“Right, well,” he said, clearing his throat loudly as he turned back to me. "I just came te give ye this. For luck, like." He reached into a pocket of his overcoat and drew out a pendant hung on a long silver chain. "It were our mam's," he explained, unnecessarily, as I took it from him with thin, trembling, fingers. "She gave it me, long afore ye were even born – as soon as she knew ye were coming, actually – and said I were to give it ye when the time was right. She said I'd know when."

My eyes filled with tears.

"And you knew this was the right time?"

Callum's mouth crooked into a small smile.

"Whatever other time could it be, lass?"

He took it from my hands and motioned to me to turn around. He undid the clasp and put it over my head. The pendant, a strange, knotted shape resembling tangled fronds of kelp settled warmly against my skin.

I let out a small gasp.

"What it is, Leeny?" he asked, turning me around again. "Are ye feelin' poorly again?"

"No, not at all, Callum," I said, all traces of nausea gone. "I feel perfectly fine, actually."

I put my hand up to touch the pendant and took a deep breath.

"I feel absolutely fine."

Chapter 16

Hetty

Aibhlinn stood shivering between John Avis and Alfie McKinnon, the old pony-man who came to do the drumming.

I had put the shawl around her when they'd been waiting, but removed it as the two men came to take her down the path to the sea.

"This is as far as I can go, lass," I'd said as I took the shawl from her thin shoulders. "And the shawl has done all it can for ye by now."

Aibhlinn had raised an eyebrow at that, but I just smiled and kissed her on both cheeks.

"The women have their own magic, lass," I whispered into

Aibhlinn's ear. "And they've all had a hand in weaving it into this shawl. It'll be here waiting for ye, when ye come back to us."

"Right, enough o' that," muttered John, impatiently. He's a placid, taciturn body, is my man, but the strain was showing, and his features were pinched and scowling. A brief pang of sympathy washed over me, but I brushed it away. What the men felt was nothing to what the women of this island have endured for centuries. "Ye know there's naught to be any chatter between ye."

I pointedly ignored him and turned away. I walked back to where Callum stood, alone, just outside the tavern. Hamish hadn't come, nor had Alexander or Duncan. No surprise there, I thought, irritably.

I reached out and took hold of Callum's hand. He squeezed mine in response and we stood, not speaking, as Aibhlinn disappeared down the ridge of the cliff, towards the sea.

* * *

"Oh, sweet Jesus," I muttered as we walked into the tavern.

Father Ewan stood near the open fire, his back to us.

"Quite right, my dear lady. To invoke the name of the Saviour at such a time," he said, without turning. "Would that it might help you."

I pulled a face behind him and headed towards the kitchen. "I'll get some tea, shall I?" I called back, not waiting for an answer as I pushed through the swinging door. I spooned tea into the pot and filled it with boiled water from the kettle on the hob. Putting mugs onto a tray, along with a pot of honey and a jug of milk, I carried it back through.

"Father Ewan," nodded Callum. "'Tis good of ye to come,"

He stood with his cap in his hands, twisting it awkwardly. The waves of worry were coming off him, but I made a point of not bothering to acknowledge it. As fond as I am of the lad, he's not deserving of my sympathy either. He's had plenty of opportunity to do right by our Aibhlinn and he's let her down time and again. Gadding off over the moors when he should've been standing up to that brutal lout of a father. Pulling her name from the basket was the final betrayal, as I see it. I put the tray of mugs on the table with a clatter.

"I know we're likely as not deserving," began Callum, walking towards the old priest as he turned around. Father Ewan tilted his head, encouragingly. "Seeing as how we're in this up past our eyebrows, like."

His lips pressed primly together, Father Ewan nodded.

"But I were wondering if there were a chance as ye'd say a word for our Aibhlinn, to hold her safe as it were."

He stumbled over the words, uneasy, as we all were, in the priest's gaze.

"I've already done so, son," said Father Ewan. "And I'll continue until she's returned to us. Why else do you think I'm here? Surely not because I'm welcome."

Callum shrugged.

Father Ewan sighed heavily and pulled two chairs from where they'd been tucked under the table nearest the fire.

"Sit and have a mug of tea with me, lad," said the priest. "I'm not the enemy, despite what you all prefer to think. I'll be in and out of this place for the next nine days, holding vigil, just as I have done every sea bride year since I came to this blessed heap of rock. Much to our good landlady's irritation," he smiled thinly at me. I snorted, in fine Aibhlinn fashion, having gone to retrieve the teapot and a plate of currant biscuits.

"She's never forgiven me, you see," said Father Ewan, smiling, sadly, at Callum.

I scowled and poured the tea into three large pot mugs.

"For what?" said Callum, a look of shock and surprise on his face.

"For not ending it when he had the chance," I retorted.

Chapter 17

Aibhlinn

The familiar path down to the sea is a meandering one. I'm used to running and skipping down it, using the steep decline as momentum, thrilling in the feel of the wind buffeting me as I go. This time, though, I'm having to walk quietly behind John and Alfie. Alfie went first and considering he's about three hundred years old and with a limp from being half-killed by one of his own ponies *and* having to drum as he walks, it's an infuriatingly slow descent indeed.

I suppressed my irritation, instead trying to hold the memory of the journey in my mind. I want to absorb every detail; I rehearsed how I'd tell myself, afterwards, what it was like to walk down to the sea that day. I would know every vivid detail so that I could tell the tale like it was just happening.

I had to do it – because Hetty had told me that I'd forget.

***

"It won't stay with ye, lass," she'd told me, that day of the first dress fitting, before I'd met the old woman down at the sea edge. "None of it. Ye'll have it for a short spell afterwards, but then it disappears. The memory fades like it never was and soon enough ye wonder had it happened at all."

Then she'd laughed, a bitter sort of laugh.

"Unless there's a bairn, o' course. Then it'll haunt ye forever."

"A child?" I asked, wide-eyed and slightly afraid at the implication. "How can that be? I mean, I know..."

I broke off, blushing straight up to the roots of my hair.

Hetty chuckled, the bitterness receding.

"Aye, sometimes it happens. Thankfully, not that often. The faery folk aren't the most, well, fertile lot, as it were. They don't often have their own, which is one of the reasons why they take ours."

I swallowed hard, not believing what I was hearing. I had so many questions, all tripping over themselves in my head, wanting to get out.

Hetty must have seen the expression on my face because she sighed, a sigh that was heavy with the weight of something like sorrow.

"Sit ye down, lass," she said, "Ye may as well know the truth of it."

And so she told me all of it — how part of the bargain that had been struck with the sea folk involved the right to claim the child borne of any union of the sea bride marriage. How the child had to be handed over within nine days of its birth so that the taint of the land wouldn't bind itself and how refusing to do so threatened to raise such storms as even Glencarragh had never seen before, not to mention the terror of marauding water horses.

"But what about the sea bride, the mother?" I'd asked, horrified. I could only think of my own mother and how Callum had told me how much she loved us. To have to hand your own baby over to the sea folk seemed a terrible thing to face.

Hetty had shrugged.

"Most women would rather not be raising a half-breed," she said, her voice raspy. "The child of a sea bride carries with it some faery magic and that can make things, well, complicated. 'Tis not an easy thing to be different on Glencarragh, as ye well know. And besides, for all the talk of honour and glory, there's not many who truly believe it's such a grand thing after all. All they want is a peaceful life and so they're happy to forget the whole thing and be done with it."

"But not you," I said, watching her face as she fought to keep the tears from spilling over.

"No, lass," she said, quietly, "Not me."

* * *

After what seemed like an eternity, we reached the bottom and stepped out onto the open sand. The air was damp and smelled strongly of the sea - an iron-tang of salt and seaweed and something else, some unnameable thing that prickled the inside of my nose. The dampness of the spray clung to my hair and sent it curling into ringlets. Reaching up, I pulled out the ties that held the braids in place and shook my hair free of its tethers.

John raised an eyebrow and opened his mouth as if to say something, but I glared at him, defying him to comment and he closed it again, shaking his head.

I smiled grimly to myself and touched the pendant where it hung above my breasts, reassuring myself that it was there. The dress whispered and blew in swirling folds around my legs as the wind gusted, but I was no longer troubled by its strange effect.

The beach was deserted.

"Isn't anyone here?" I asked. I think I'd expected a gathering of the sea-folk or something, some evidence of this as a grand occasion. Alfie's drum came to a sudden stop. The silence was filled with the crash of waves against the rocky outcropping further along the beach. We were in the exact spot where Morag and I had argued and where I'd met the strange old woman.

"Hush, lass," said John, his voice a strained whisper. His eyes were darting along the water's edge, and he clenched and unclenched his hands where they hung by his sides.

He's frightened, I thought. I looked over at Alfie whose face was the picture of abject misery.

Bloody hell, all they have to do is deliver me here. What about me?

"Soon, now," murmured Alfie, hitching his drum under his arm. "I can allus feel it in me bones when the bastards get close by."

"Hmmm. Good to know," I said, smiling winningly at the old pony-man. It gave me a small fizz of pleasure to see him flinch at my gaze before he lowered his eyes and shuffled his feet in the sand.

"Here!" said John, taking me by the elbow. "It's coming."

I stared out at the roiling waves; they became a foaming crest before folding in on themselves and spilling onto the shore. The sun was still low on the horizon, leaving a trail of gold and silver across the surface of the sea.

"I don't see...."

And then I did.

Chapter 18

Hetty

Callum wrapped his work-rough fingers around the large mug, making it look no bigger than one of my thimbles. A thin, curl of steam spiraled upwards from the untouched tea, disappearing into the cool air. I'd built up the fire and the three of us sat huddled against the chill of the spring morning. Each of us bound up in our own thoughts, not a word between us since I'd spoken of the Father's failure.

I could see Callum wanted to ask, bless his heart, but he'd have picked up the tension between myself and the old priest. I knew the lad well enough to know he'd too much consideration to stir up any old unpleasantness with his prying. Knowing him, he was already torturing himself with visions of what might be taking place down at the water's edge; I doubted he'd want to burden himself with the facts of the thing, so I said nothing. Part of me thinks the men have no right to know anyway.

"I was a young man when I arrived here," said Father Ewan, breaking the silence. "I was full of the fervour and enthusiasm of the newly-ordained. I flattered myself to think that the bishop saw something in me, that he'd chosen me especially, to come here to Glencarragh. There'd been rumours, of course, that the folk here were insistent on keeping many of the old, heathen, ways of their forebears, but I imagined it would be a simple task of showing the way."

I grunted and folded my arms.

"I know now the arrogance of my younger self. Who among us isn't burdened by the sin of pride, eh?"

Callum chuckled politely.

"Anyway, it wasn't long before I was made aware of how things are here — and how impossible a task it would be to lead the folk of Glencarragh away from the...heathenish ways."

"Aye, but ye had the chance once, didn't ye? And ye were too much the coward to take it," I spat, the memory as fresh as if it'd been yesterday; how I'd gone to him, terrified and desperate only to be turned away with feeble excuses of bishops and church law.

I don't know as I'd ever been so angry since the day itself. If the look on poor Callum's face was anything to go by, I'd worked myself into a state. I took a deep breath and tried to rein it in, but there was no quelling my rage.

Father Ewan set his mug down on the table and rubbed his hands on the thighs of his trousers. He was dressed much as any of the other men of Glencarragh - thick trousers, woven from a heavy tweed and a knitted vest over a collarless linen shirt. I wondered at the lack of his clerical collar.

"You know as well as I, Hetty, that my intervention wouldn't have made a difference. And even if it had, I'm bound by the laws of my faith, just as you're bound by the godforsaken agreement you've made with those devils in the sea."

I snorted again, unfolding and refolding my arms, against the urge to reach across and slap him.

"It weren't any agreement of mine, priest. That were the work of men. There's no woman on this island - now, or in the long ago - that would ever have dealt with such wickedness. No woman would put herself in the place where she'd to give up a bairn...."

My voice broke and I stopped abruptly, turning my face to the fire. I used the edge of my apron to dab at my eyes. As much as I'd wished to remind the priest of his wrongdoing, it wouldn't do to give Callum cause to worry about our Aibhlinn.

Father Ewan sighed heavily, lifting a shaking hand to scrub over his face.

"So ye agree it's wicked, Hetty?" asked Callum, setting down his own mug. "Ye sent our own wee girl into it, believing as ye do?"

Father Ewan reached over to grasp Callum's wrist.

"Mind Hetty now, laddie. She's been in this longer than any of us and there's no man who should stand in judgment of her."

"Never mind that, Father," I said, quietly. "Callum, pet, it all comes down to the choices we make. We can only do the best we can with what we're given at the time. It's the way it was in my own time as well. I shouldn't be so harsh with the Father, aye? We're each a prisoner of our own conscience in the end."

"Aye," said Callum, thinking, I'm sure of it, of his part in the drawing of Aibhlinn's name. "I suppose I know a bit of something about that. But what happened that ye take on so wi' the Father here?"

I frowned down at my hands, which were busily knotting and unknotting the strings of my apron. Father Ewan squeezed my shoulder and I reached back and awkwardly patted his hand.

"'Tis a rare thing," I said, my voice pitched low. "But once in every generation or so, the sea bride bears a child. The child represents a powerful magic — it bridges the worlds, ye ken? Not of the mortals and not of the faery folk, but a part of each."

I paused, swallowing, unsure if I could carry on.

Father Ewan stepped in.

"Our Hetty bore a child, Callum."

"To the faery creatures?" asked Callum, his face traveling between awe and repulsion.

I nodded, silently.

"What happened to the bairn then?"

"Same as allus happens," I said.

Callum looked to Father Ewan, who grimaced and smoothed a hand over his vest.

"To keep the terms of the ancient bargain," he said. "The child must be given to the sea."

Chapter 19

Aibhlinn

I stood, rooted to the spot.

John and Alfie took hurried steps back as the water horse rose out of the churning surf.

"Thanks ever so much, my valiant escorts," I muttered, gripping handfuls of my dress to stop my hands from shaking. John grunted.

"There's nowt we can do for ye now, lassie. It's all up to ye," I answered him with a grunt of my own.

"Hasn't it always been?" I said, not expecting an answer. "What happens now, then? An exchange of pleasantries?"

"Ye'd do well to watch yer lip, lass," said Alfie, his breath coming in a wheeze. "Ye've far too many opinions, I warrant."

"Oh, why don't you two just sod off!" I snapped, finally at the end of my patience with the entire ridiculous ceremony. I turned to look at the two men, who stood with wide eyes and mouths agape. I made a shooing gesture with my hands. "Go on, you useless gits. Bugger off and leave me be!"

"Well, I never..." sputtered John, torn, I'm sure, between defending his pride and being quite happy to do as I said.

"No," I murmured, turning my back on them. "I don't suppose you have."

Without a further glance, I gathered up the hem of my dress and walked to the water's edge.

* * *

The creature had risen like malevolent darkness from the foaming surf. Its coat, streaming with rivulets of seawater, was the black of midnight. Its mane hung with kelp and was tangled through with shells and shards of bone; it hung in knotted ropes over heavily muscled shoulders, reaching down to the massive, feathered hooves.

I trembled where I stood, at the edge of the water. I could have reached out a hand and touched the glistening neck, but fear of the razor teeth and the rumoured fondness of flesh kept me gripping handfuls of my dress.

For a brief, lunatic, moment, I wondered if I ought to curtsy. I suppressed a hysterical giggle at the thought.

"You may curtsy if it would amuse you," said a soft, laughing, voice. "Although a gentle hand upon my brow would suffice as greeting."

I almost jumped out of my skin. I turned around but John and Alfie were standing where I'd left them, grim-faced and tight-lipped, no doubt observing some intricacy of the ceremony which required them to see me off. I turned back to the water horse, which was quietly watching me, the slanted eyes blinking slowly. It blew softly through narrow nostrils, tilting its serpentine head sideways.

"Is that you?" I whispered, feeling a bit silly for asking as I leaned towards the creature. The sharp tang of ocean made me want to shrink away, but I held firm, quelling the urge to wrinkle my nose in disgust.

The water horse inclined its head.

"There is no need to speak aloud, my lady. I can hear your thoughts, as you can, mine."

"Lady?" I giggled. "Can't say as I've ever been called that before. At least not in the intended fashion."

"There's the girl, then!" shouted John. "By the terms of the ancient bargain, and by the trust placed on the line of my forefathers, I give her to the sea for nine days. We'll be back at sundown on the ninth day and woe betide you should any harm befall her."

"Can't get away fast enough, can they?" I said aloud. "No fancy end to the ceremony then? Just a 'here you are and off you go'. Typical."

The water horse shook its long mane, scattering droplets of water, then made to step towards the two men.

Alfie uttered an extremely unmanly shriek and turned to run, his awkward, limping gait making him look like a lame chicken. His tweed cap flew off, but he didn't stop to pick it up. John shuffled backwards several paces, probably trying to decide between saving his honour and following his instincts. His instincts won out and he ran after Alfie.

I heard a burbling chuckle inside my head.

I took a deep breath and reached out a trembling hand, placing it nervously on the forehead of the water horse. It stood quietly, head lowered to receive my gesture. Despite being sodden with seawater, it felt surprisingly warm under my touch.

"Why is it that I can hear your voice in my head?" I asked.

"The dress you're wearing," said the water horse, "is made of faery cloth. It holds apart the veil between our worlds. It lets each of us view one another through direct contact of thought, without the need for languages that neither of us understand."

I smoothed my hands down the rumpled skirt of the dress, viewing what had once been tired old linen with a different eye.

"It will also prevent me from killing you."

Chapter 20

Callum

I stared, in utter disbelief, into the pale, lined face of Father Ewan. The old priest held my gaze, his watery, blue eyes meeting my own.

"So, you see now, my son, the extent of my sin? And why I must do penance here, every bride-year, for the rest of my days."

"Ye mean ye went along with it?" I croaked. "Ye let them throw a newborn babe into the bloody sea for them faery savages?"

Hetty spoke up, her voice reaching across an echoing in my head. My vision swam and I had to hold the table to stop myself from swaying. I'd never heard such a thing in all my days.

"It isnae like that, pet. Well, not quite," she glanced at Father Ewan who wouldn't meet her gaze.

"They don't kill the babe," he said. "At least, so the stories go."

I made a choking sound, trying to put it all together in my mind. What's our Aibhlinn in for? I always knew it was a horror of a thing, but I'd no idea how much.

"It's said that they take the child and raise it as one of their own," continued the Father.

He waved a hand at the question he knew must be coming next. "Of course, there must be some vile faery conjuring at play, so the child can survive the sea. Although, it being a half-caste, I imagine that provides some protection."

"But why?" My voice came out as a rasp. "Why in the name of all that's holy would they want a human child?"

"Not entirely human, Callum, love," reminded Hetty. "The child is half-faery."

"And half human!" I retorted. "Don't forget that bit!"

"I'm not likely to," said Hetty, rising to prod the dwindling fire. "That's the bit they're after. The one that's in charge of it all - that nasty piece, Lira she calls herself - well, the story goes she lost her only daughter to the Good Folk of the land or some such bad business long ago. The tales tell it that this is her way of punishing mortal folk, because she can't directly get at her own kind. She thinks the land-dwelling fae have thrown in their lot and sided with us, like." She gave the fire a vicious prod. "It's one of the ways she has to get at us, anyhow," she added, darkly.

"Well, that's their bloody problem, not ours!" I said, pounding my fist onto the table, making the mugs, and Father Ewan, jump.

He placed a hand on my shoulder, but I shrugged it off. He wasn't going to get away with trying to coddle me into quiet like he did with everyone else.

"And ye! Ye two-faced druid! How can ye dare be all fire and brimstone ower what goes on and then quietly let them give the bairns to those...things!"

That caught him. He winced and shrank back, like I'd just smacked him.

"I deserve your anger, Callum. I know how this all must look to you. But you must understand, that by all the holy laws of the church, these creatures do not even exist. I sought to intercede and was refused - by your kinfolk and by Rome, the very first season I was here. I'm bound, both physically and spiritually, from intervening in any way beyond trying to convince you all to stop the whole ruddy mess."

"That's not good enough, Father," I said, dismissing him as useless. "Nowhere near good enough at all."

I turned to Hetty.

"I don't even understand how any of this is possible, any of it. I mean, they're...." I paused, blushing with the effort of putting the vision out of my mind, "horses."

Hetty smiled.

"No, lad. Not really. 'Tis just the shape they take when they're hunting, aye? It's a glamour of a sort, nothing more."

"So, what're ye saying, then? If that's just a glamour, what do they really look like?"

Hetty shook her head.

"I cannae tell ye that, pet. I wish I could, but I barely remember. They're not much different from us, really. Taller, mebbe. And with a painful sort of beauty to them," she shrugged. "I'm told that they take the memory so's we don't go mad with it," She shot a cold glare at Father Ewan, "But I suspect it's more to do wi' the mortal menfolk not wanting to come up short in our eyes. Ye cannae be among their kind and not be changed by and by. Ye remember that there's stories of men going right out o' their heads for wanting to be back among them, such a wondrous marvel is their world. All I can tell ye is that it weren't terrible, not at all. My own faery bridegroom was kind in his way, and I know that I'd a great love for him. I bear them no ill will as I reckon they're just as much puppets to Lira as we all are."

She shook her head again and put the poker back in its place with a loud clatter.

"No, my laddie. It were all a grand adventure for a young lass such as meself. And I know it'll be the same for our Aibhlinn. It weren't 'til they sent me back to me own folk that things started to go horrible wrong."

She glared at Father Ewan again before starting to gather up the tea things.

"Right. I've a breakfast to cook. John and Alfie will be back shortly, and I'd best have something ready to settle their nerves."

I stood up, scraping back my chair, feeling as if I'd aged ten years over the course of the morning.

I heaved a heavy sigh, full of the weight of the whole awful mess, and ran a hand through my hair, sure that I looked as rough as I felt.

Hetty gave a small smile.

"Be easy in yer mind, laddie. 'Tis a rare, rare, thing that there's a bairn from it. My wee boy was the first in more'n fifty years. She'll be back among us in nine days and none the worse for it. Just think on that, aye?"

"Hetty, I cannae imagine thinking on anything else. I'll go mad otherwise."

I nodded curtly to Father Ewan and strode to the door, sidestepping John and Alfie as they bustled in.

"Alright, Callum?" said John, his face red with exertion.

"Sod off, John," I muttered, and headed out towards the peace of the moors.

Chapter 21

Aibhlinn

I removed my hand and quickly stepped back.

"You what?"

The burbling chuckle reverberated through my mind again. The water horse bowed its head and also took a step back.

"Apologies, my lady. My skill with words is not as it should be. The dress is protection for you, from me, that is true. I am not quite myself in this form. We surrender our higher, civilized, thoughts when we take to the hunting grounds. Without the dress, and with no-one to drum for you, you would be nothing more to me than a possible meal."

"And *with* the dress?" I whispered, suddenly feeling less

than confident with my position. It had all seemed a bit of good fun up until this last revelation.

"You are quite safe."

The faery creature stood quietly. It watched me without expression. I tried to wrap my thoughts around the situation. What now? I sneaked a look at the water horse. It was a thing of monstrous beauty.

I can't believe I'm standing here talking to everyone's worst nightmare, I thought.

"Do you believe me, my lady?"

I blinked, jolted from my thoughts.

"I don't suppose I'm in any position to *not* believe you, am I?" I said, holding my mother's pendant in one hand and continuing to smooth the dress with the other.

That was the plain truth of it. I was essentially helpless, completely without control over what happened next. I didn't much care for that, having spent most of my life living quite the opposite. It was confronting, to say the least.

"Indeed," said the creature, bowing its head again. "Perhaps a display of mutual trust and goodwill is in order?"

"Oh?" I said, "What did you have in mind?"

The water horse moved closer. I had to resist the urge to step away. I took a deep breath and then regretted it; the stench of the creature was truly abhorrent.

"Will you climb upon my back?"

I laughed, a silly, high-pitched and nervous laugh.

"Oh! I think I know how this one goes," I said. "Every child of Glencarragh learns the kelpie stories. I'm supposed to climb on your back so you can carry me away to your underwater kingdom, is that it?"

"Quite," agreed the water horse. "That is precisely what I'm asking of you."

My mouth hung open.

"But, but I won't be able to breathe...." I began. "How..."

"That is where the trust comes in," replied the creature. "In return, I will be able to reveal to you my true form. The change leaves me vulnerable for a spell. I would be at your mercy. Especially as you are wearing that."

It gestured towards the pendant hanging around my neck, its expression was a mix of curiosity and wariness.

I frowned, a new thought suddenly occurring to me; one which both comforted and disappointed me.

"This is the way it's meant to go, isn't it?" I asked. "It's all planned out. This is how it happens every time. For all of us."

The creature nodded.

"I see you already have something of an understanding, then?"

It paused, looking at me closely. "Nor are you truly afraid. Not really."

I shrugged.

"Would it matter if I was?"

Without waiting for an answer, I stepped quickly forwards, knotted my hands into its mane and scrambled awkwardly onto its broad back.

It felt surprisingly warm beneath me – I think I'd expected it to be cold. It shifted slightly, settling me more firmly into place.

"Ready?" it said.

"As I'll ever be," I replied, this time, speaking only inside my head.

With one powerful movement, the water horse spun on its haunches and plunged into the waves, with me, clinging like a limpet to its back.

I felt its feet leave the bottom and soon we were swimming. I held tightly to the mane, my fingers ached with the wet and the cold, but I daren't have let go for fear of being left adrift in the sea.

"And now we go under," said the water horse. "You may wish to hold more tightly."

I swallowed a whimper and folded myself down low over its mane, wrapping my arms around the thick neck.

I took a deep breath and felt the water close over my head.

* * *

The water was frigid, but it didn't make me feel cold. Nor did I drown, which was, I reflected, the only part that mattered. Personal discomfort was a secondary element.

I don't know how long we swam. I was still clinging like a barnacle to the creature's back as it took me further and further from the surface. I wondered, more than once, what might happen if I did let go — would I lose my ability to breathe underwater, would I be able to reach the surface before my lungs exploded? I doubted it very much.

Not that it mattered, I wasn't planning on letting go. In for a penny, as Hetty would say.

The water was a strange shade of blue-green; I had expected darkness. And numbing cold. It was neither. It felt like a caress against my skin, like fingers trailing gently over me, lifting my hair and playing it out behind me. It was wonderful and terrifying in equal parts. I opened my mouth and laughed aloud, delighting in the bubbles that erupted from my lips.

The burbling murmur of the water horse's laughter echoed through my head.

"Do you have a name?" I asked, suddenly wondering whether faery monsters bothered with familiarity between themselves.

"Fingal," came the answer. "I was named Fingal, once. And so I am still."

"What do you mean, once?"

The creature shook its head.

"We're nearing our destination now,"

"You didn't answer my question."

"No," it replied, slowing down and banking to the left. "I didn't."

* * *

We came to a stop in front of what looked like the entrance to a cave. A wall of rock rose up from the ocean floor, stretching towards the surface. The opening, shielded from view by a scattering of boulders, was just large enough for me to walk into without stooping. I slid down from the creature's back, marveling that I didn't immediately begin floating. It was an odd sensation - what my eyes could see, and what my brain thought it knew, didn't match the actual physical feeling. It was very disorienting, and I actually stumbled a little as I tried to get my balance.

The water horse gestured towards the entrance of the cave. I hesitated slightly, unsure if I should continue. The horrible details of every cautionary tale concerning faeries ran through my mind.

"I will enter first, if that is your preference, my lady," said Fingal.

"No. No need," I said, not wanting to offend him with such obvious mistrust. He'd been impeccably polite and mannerly up to that point, surely he wasn't going to turn on me the moment I stepped into his lair?

"I was just wondering at the similarity to a rock formation on the beach, you know, back up there," I gestured upwards, assuming that's where the beach was, although I was no longer entirely certain of my whereabouts.

Fingal nodded.

"Not an accident, I assure you," he said. "The lines between here and there are somewhat complicated at this point."

Still marveling at the fact I could take a deep breath, I did so, and walked inside.

* * *

Not a cramped cave, but an impossibly large cavern. The walls soared higher than I could see, disappearing into an infinite darkness above me. They were lit with a soft, green light that seemed to glow from all around rather than from a single source. The floor sparkled with white sand and was inexplicably dry underfoot.

I looked down at the dress — I was expecting it to be clinging to my body, wet from the journey through the water, but it hung lightly about me, swaying with its whispering motion that did not require a breath of wind.

I spun around, expecting to find Fingal standing behind me, but there was only more sand and more cavern walls.

Trying to quell a rising panic in my throat I called out to the dark heights of the cavern's ceiling, "Fingal! Are you here?"

"I am," came a voice behind me.

I turned to the voice but staggered back in surprise.

"I'm sorry, my lady," he said, bowing his head. "Perhaps I ought to have warned you?"

Where once had stood the massive, black, water horse, now stood a tall, black-haired man. His hair was long and knotted in the same fashion as the water horse's mane. Broad-shouldered and pale-skinned, he was dressed in simple, coarse-linen trousers and a white shirt, open at the collar. If not for his slightly slanted, barely-blue eyes and extraordinary height, he could've been any of the fishermen of Glencarragh. I narrowed my eyes and scowled.

"Is this a glamour as well?" I asked. "Because I don't have a preference for stinking fishermen."

Fingal threw back his head and laughed. His teeth were small and white and came to a slight point.

"No, my lady. I don't suppose you do."

He spread out his hands in a gesture of ambivalence.

"This is my truest aspect," he said, tilting his head in a gesture that echoed that of his water horse form.

Remembering why I had sought him in the first place, I asked, "Are we still not in the sea? My dress," I felt my head, "my hair, they're dry. And the sand...."

Fingal shook his head.

"No, my lady. This cave, like its mirror on the beach, is a portal to my world, nothing more. We need not have traveled the sea to get here. It was simply a test of trust between us that I suggested it."

"Oh."

"And I also sensed that, at the very least, you expected to be taken into the sea."

He smiled at my quizzical look.

"For appearances, of course. So as not to disappoint your friends, land-side."

His mouth quirked upward, and a mischievous glint appeared in his strange, transparent eyes.

I grinned.

"No, we couldn't have that, could we? Hundreds of years of dramatics and ceremony would be sorely disappointed."

Our laughter echoed through the cavern, bouncing from wall to wall and up into the endless heights.

Chapter 22

I do not know how long we stayed in the cavern.

Fingal built a fire and produced a loaf of delicious bread. A hedge-loaf, he called it. Baked from the seeds and berries of an ancient hedgerow that borders his world and mine. It was meant to be a symbol of our worlds coming together. There was a bottle of honey-sweet summer wine which we drank out of goblets that had been forged by dwarves under mountains whose summits had never been reached.

Those were the tales he told me, anyway - painting beautiful, elaborate pictures of a world so full of wonder and magic that I wanted nothing more than to go there, immediately, and never return.

In the end, I suppose they were just that - tales. Tales designed to enchant and enthrall; tales meant to distract frightened young women from the true purpose of their time there. For my part, I was willingly enraptured, I wanted nothing more than the escape and the chance to live a different life. So I couldn't possibly bear him any ill-will for his part in what came about, because I've since learned that the bargains struck were built on deceit on both sides of the arrangement; there were no innocent parties. Fingal, himself, and every other faery bridegroom before him, was as much a pawn as I was. At some point during our time in the cave, whatever ideas I may've had about being a sea bride fell away and I began to see it all very differently.

Right from the beginning, he treated me kindly and with utmost respect and consideration, far more than I've ever received in my own world. Well, other than perhaps from Hetty and Callum, of course. Oh, they love me and care deeply for me, I've no doubt about that, but this was different, somehow. I felt treasured; as if my being there was the most important thing and that my thoughts and opinions were worthy of notice and consideration, not correction or guidance.

Yes, it was a different sort of feeling altogether, something entirely unexpected and unplanned for. I always knew that I was there out of duty - a strange and difficult thing because I cared very little for the yearly catch and less for the price of wool; whether the island folk prospered or struggled was of no consequence to me. It's a shameful thing to admit, I know, but that was the truth of it. I'd been held at arm's length my entire life; tolerated when necessary, but mostly excluded and usually avoided. When it came down to it, I knew that the only person I could really depend upon was myself. Even dearest Hetty is too afraid of Isabelle Dunn and her influence over everything to ever really stand up to her. And so because of that, I've never felt much connection with the folk of Glencarragh.

But I do care about the moors and the fens and the wild

things that live there. I care for my brother's sheep and the herds of deer; I care that they're safe and protected and so I think that's why I didn't fuss and refuse to go along as the sea bride as I imagine everyone expected I would. If marriage to the sea meant harmony between the Otherworld and my beloved island, then I was willing to play my part. The land has always given me a sense of worthiness and belongingness that I rarely feel among people. I believed that if going along with the marriage could help repay that blessing, then I was willing to do what was required of me, including spending nine days with a faery creature. That, and the firm belief that I would finally have some standing in the community, that I would be permitted to go my own way after all. So I drank in his tales of wonder and allowed him to convince me to follow him wherever he'd have me go. I fully expected there to be an element of faery trickery to it all and I didn't much care.

But I hadn't expected to love him.

Chapter 23

I spent nine days by my own world's reckoning with Fingal, but entire seasons passed for us in his.

It might have been a week, or a day, or even an hour, but eventually we left the sea cavern, following a narrow corridor at the back of the cave which, upon turning a particular bend, became a corridor of trees.

To enter into his world was like emerging from a dark and muted place into one of bright sunlight, so much was the contrast between the world I'd known and the world I would come to know. Everything in his world was bright and full of colour; no more sea-washed blues and greys, ominous skies and slicing winds. There were trees such as I'd never seen and flowers and birds that were like something from a storybook. My harsh and ragged moors, so beloved to me, were soon upstaged by meadows of fragrant flowers and by sun-dappled woods.

Oh, how we traveled! Time moved in strange ways in his world, as did distance, for no journey was ever too long or too arduous; it seemed as if every new destination was just around the next bend or through a gap in a hedge. He took me to the dwarves' mountains and showed me the Valley of the Bees where the honey for the summer wine was harvested. We climbed trees with branches wide enough to host a dance and daydreamed by streams that ran with musical, silver-strung, water. We dined with sprites and dryads and danced in the Revels of the Seelie court.

Everywhere we went I was fêted. I was given gifts of jewels and cloth and had flowers woven into my hair. I felt loved and wanted. I felt important.

And oh, how we talked! We spoke of many things - of my tempestuous moors and the sea, of every dream and possibility that I'd ever dared hold in my heart but never revealed. I told him about my little croft, and we laughed over the petty foolishness of Isabelle Dunn. He became my friend, my confidante, and, in a time of my own choosing, he became my lover. Hetty had impressed upon me that consummation of the marriage was not expected nor required, the union was only meant to be symbolic, and I'd had every intention before I met him, to refuse that part of the situation. But to have done so would have been to rebel against my own desires. He was my perfect match in all things, and I could not have asked for a more wonderful companion.

All in all, it was simply an incredible adventure. To be sure, it wasn't always safe, and perhaps we courted peril more than necessary - the world of Faery does not come by its reputation of danger without good reason - but I reasoned that if I was to be there, I ought to experience it to the fullest. Not everyone was glad that I was there, either, nor was Fingal always treated well. I asked him, several times, about that, but he would never answer and eventually I learned that he preferred to keep his past as just that, the past.

***

When we weren't off adventuring, we lived in a tiny cottage by the side of the musical silver stream. Each night, as the sun began to slide down the sky, Fingal would ask me to promise to stay indoors for the night. I don't know where he went, but he never stayed with me. I slept in the vast and comfortable bed alone, but he was always there at dawn, his long body curled around mine, his strange eyes watching me as I awoke.

After a while, I stopped thinking of home; I didn't spare a thought for Callum or Hetty and certainly not my father. I didn't care if I ever went back.

***

"Have you been happy here, my lady?" Fingal asked, one late summer's evening. We had roamed the forest all day, chasing wood-nymphs in a merry game of hide-and-seek. Tired, I leaned my head against his shoulder and sighed. I took his long-fingered hand in mine and squeezed it gently.

"Why do you still insist on calling me that? Are we not friends after all this time?" I asked, taking delight in watching him blush.

He shrugged. "I suppose it's because this particular moment is one of a more formal nature."

"Oh?" I sat up at the serious tone of his voice.

He smiled down at me. "Are you going to answer my question?"

It was my turn to shrug.

"I don't even know how you can ask it," I replied, waving a hand out towards the forest that surrounded the tiny cottage. "Haven't you shown me all the wonders of your world? Aren't I just filled with love and the magic of it every moment? Aren't I just never wanting to go back to my own?"

He lowered his eyes.

"Oh," I said again, suddenly understanding. My stomach lurched and I felt a clench of something like fear in my chest. I reached up to touch my mother's pendant that still lay against my skin.

"The time grows near when you must return, my....my Aibhlinn," his voice faltered as he spoke my name. I had never noticed the strange accent of his speech until he said my name. He drew it out, like the held note of a song. A shiver ran up my spine.

I cleared my throat.

"And if I don't wish to go back? What then?"

He stood up, holding onto my fingers until his height pulled them gently from my grasp. I let my hand fall onto my lap, smoothing over the grimy folds of my dress. Upon his instruction, I never took it off, not even when I went down to the stream to bathe. As a result, I had a constant look of grubbiness about me. That, at least, was consistent between both worlds.

"You know that cannot be," he said, facing away from me. His head was down, and his hands clenched and unclenched into fists.

"Fingal," I began, rising to stand.

"No!" he said, turning back to face me, his face a mask of cold fury.

I had never seen him angry, and I took a step back, widening the space between us, but then closing it by reaching out my hand.

His expression altered, grief and anger and something else flickered in his eyes and he pressed his lips firmly together, taking a deep, shuddering breath.

"I understand that the effect of our time here would convince you that staying was an acceptable, and possibly desirable option," his tone had become polite and formal, like it had been when first we'd met on the shore so long ago. "However, I need not remind you of the terms of the bargain between your world and mine. Nine of your days and then I am to deliver you back to your people. You've already been here far longer than most. I don't know why..."

"But we've been here much, much longer than nine days," I exclaimed, interrupting, unwilling to face the unwavering truth of that. "It's been months, maybe more than a year, hasn't it? Yes, this is the second summer season surely. Why not just let the time drift onward? We can make nine days last a lifetime. You can send me back when I'm a doddering old lady and you can't bear the wrinkled sight of me!" I tried to coax a smile from him. My voice wobbled and I felt dangerously close to crying. I wouldn't cry. I wouldn't. Not now.

He didn't say anything. He didn't have to, his face said all I never wanted to know.

"I won't go," I said, folding my arms like a recalcitrant child.

He stepped towards me, his hands outstretched. I unfolded my arms and reached my hands out to him. He drew me in and wrapped me in his warmth. I let myself melt into him, breathing in the scent of moss and warm honey.

"Aibhlinn, *m'anam*," he breathed into my hair. "You must... ."

"No," I whispered, pulling back and placing a finger to his lips. "Just, no."

I replaced my finger with my lips and willed the world to fall away.

Chapter 24

On the last night, he stayed.

The fire cast a flickering orange glow on the walls of the corner of the cottage that served as our bedroom. A slight breeze drifted in through the open window; it held an edge of coolness to it and carried the scent of gorse blossom.

I shivered and pulled the eiderdown more tightly around me. Fingal lay beside me, his sharp features softened by sleep. The black tangle of his hair pooled in knotted ropes on the pillow, and it was all I could do to not reach out and straighten them. But I didn't want to wake him. I didn't want to remind him that he was supposed to leave me. I couldn't bear it. If it was to be the last of our time together, then I wasn't going to squander a single moment.

I think I spent hours just watching him sleep, I vowed to commit his every feature to heart. I relived everything we'd done, everywhere we'd been, everything we'd talked about, to burn it all so deeply into my memory that even the strongest of charms couldn't take it from me.

* * *

"Why do you take away the memories?" I'd asked him once. We'd been walking for hours, talking of nonsensical things. It was the sort of conversation that you'd likely not remember anyway, but I wanted to keep them all.

He'd shrugged and reached out to lace his fingers into mine.

"It wasn't always the way," he'd said, after a while. "And it was your folk who asked that they be taken."

"Whyever would they do such a thing? How cruel!" I'd said, outraged at such an idea. "Isn't it terrible enough that we're packed off like sacrificial lambs to serve as faery broodmares..."

I clapped a hand over my mouth, mortified at what I'd just said. I was afraid to look at him in case I'd caused offense.

But he was smiling.

"Faery broodmares?" he asked, raising a thin, black eyebrow in mock surprise. "Is that how you see it, then?"

I blushed furiously.

"Of course not! Well, not now, anyway. But don't you see? It's knowing that it can be like this," I flung my arms wide at the expanse of the wildflower meadow through which we were walking, "that would make up for being treated as such by our own people. If every girl was to know the joy and wonder of what was possible here, then it would save a lot of fear and heartache."

He pulled me around to face him, gently holding my arms to my sides.

"Perhaps that is so," he replied, searching my eyes with his own. "But what of when you return? How would you hold the memory of such a place, such a time, when you were back in your own harsh world? What place has the memory of this," he'd broken his gaze to look at the meadow, "when the rain is sleeting down and the cold seeps under the doorway? Would you smile with the remembered beauty of it? Or would you grieve for what can never, ever, be?"

"That's just nonsense!" I snapped, unwilling to accept the possible truth of it.

He let go of my arms and started to walk again.

"You may be right," he'd said. "But then, so might I. And I would save you a life of empty longing."

* * *

I must have dozed off eventually, because the next thing I remember was waking to the sound of the kettle whistling. The morning sun filtered in through the window, dappling the eiderdown. I reached out my arm to touch Fingal and found the bed was empty.

I sat bolt upright.

"Fingal!"

There was no answer. My heart sank. Surely, he wouldn't just leave.

I scrambled out of bed, pulling on a thick woolen cardigan over my grimy dress. I tucked my feet into a pair of soft, felted slippers that had mysteriously appeared several days ago when the weather had turned chilly. I padded over the stone floor into the main area that was kitchen and sitting room all at once. The kettle was whistling furiously so I took it off the hob and set it down on the trivet on the small wooden table. I turned to see Fingal sitting by the window, his back to me, looking out over the silver stream and fields beyond.

"You didn't leave," I said, without thinking. To see him sitting there was an immeasurable relief.

"I'd every intention of doing so," he said without turning around. "It's not...permitted, for us to stay."

"Us?"

He turned to me, his face concealed by shadow.

"I'm not what you think I am, Aibhlinn," he said, his voice low and full of weariness.

"Oh? And what do I think you are, then?"

"I'm not sure. Some sort of faery noble, perhaps? Some elevated personage of high birth and privilege?"

I giggled. We had often made fun of the Court faeries, those who frequented the Revels and fancied themselves grand schemers and dabblers in intrigue.

"Well, aren't you? After all, who else would be considered a worthy consort of an elevated personage of high birth and privilege such as myself?"

It was his turn to chuckle. He patted the window seat beside him.

"Come sit by me, *m'anam*. I've something to tell before you go.”

* * *

"I was human once," he began, holding up a hand at my immediate shock. "We all are, my kind. It's a long, long, time ago now, by your world, and perhaps longer by this one."

"But how?" I asked, incredulous.

"Oh, the details aren't important. They're not a thing upon which to dwell — what's done is done and best forgotten. Suffice it to say that as a boy - a human boy - I was headstrong and foolish. I was arrogant when I ought to have been humble and rash when I ought to have been patient and wise. I let my pride guide me and it led to terrible, terrible, things."

I sat curled up on the window seat next to him, tucking the cardigan around my legs. I linked my arm in his and lay my head against his shoulder.

"Tell me what happened to you," I said, closing my eyes. I didn't want him to stop talking. I didn't even care what he might tell me, I just didn't want it to end. Because when it did, he'd take me back.

"It doesn't matter what happened, only what became of it all. I defied an ancient law and paid the price. The price was my life, in exchange for the lives of my friends. I became a half-caste faery; just another among the rest of their human victims. The only difference being that I came voluntarily, to spare my friends a similar fate. They left me with my memories, which was a cruel enough punishment itself. Sometimes I wonder if it might have been better if...."

He stopped himself and shrugged, as if shaking off the thought.

"But you're still here - you're alive," I said. "It can't be so terrible as that."

"We half-castes are not of this world, not truly," he said. "We're tolerated, for the remains of our humanity and what it means to them - to the full-blood faeries. But we're not really welcome among them. And because we hold onto the shreds of what it meant to be human, the things we have to do...."

His voice faltered and he stopped. He cleared his throat.

"It's difficult," he said, finally. "There are things which are necessary for survival. Unpleasant things. I would not burden you with my crimes."

"The water horses, you mean?" I asked. It had been a long time since I thought of him as the midnight black creature that had risen from the sea.

He nodded.

"The water horse is very much a part of me, Aibhlinn. It's more of me than I think you imagine. It was made very clear to me at the time of my.... sentencing...that I would be serving a punishment fitting to my crime. And so I've been bound to live as a water horse. And then for these nine of your days I am myself again - I can laugh, dance, love...."

His voice trailed off, choked with emotion.

"All the while knowing that, at the end of it, I become a savage, unthinking, monster."

"Those are nine days of my world, not yours — can we not stay, Fingal? Surely, if we've had these last months, it can be more? Do you not have the power to make it so?"

I was desperate, pleading. The level of torment in his own voice was too much to bear. I don't know what I'd imagined he would do when I was gone. I hadn't even considered what might become of him – supposing he'd just carry on here, in this tiny cottage, in the beautiful forest glade, so sure was I of my own grief at our parting. But I could never again think of my gentle, loving, Fingal as one of those dreadful creatures.

"No, Aibhlinn. That is a power I do not have. But not for lack of wanting." He smiled down at me. "So now do you see why it's best that you not keep the memories? What purpose would it serve to know me as such a disappointment?"

His smile widened but his eyes were impossibly sad.

There was something else, something I needed to ask but was afraid of the answer. But I knew that if I didn't seize the moment, it would be lost to me forever.

"Fingal?"

"Yes, *m'anam?*"

"Am I.... were there...are you always the bridegroom?"

I blushed furiously, partly in shame and partly in embarrassment. Would he think me a jealous harridan?

He closed his eyes and swallowed hard, as if gathering himself to answer.

"No, Aibhlinn. We are chosen only once. I am for you, and only you."

He stood up, holding out his hand.

"Let us have one last cup of tea together, shall we? Then we must be on our way."

* * *

I didn't want to go by sea. The thought of making him take his water horse form filled me with such sadness. He was as much a prisoner as I, in the end. More so, really. Neither of us with the freedom to live as we'd choose, although I, at least, had hope for my own future. Strange as it was, though, I do not think he thought his punishment undeserving. No matter how many times I'd asked, he wouldn't tell me what had happened when he was still human. It must have been a terrible thing for him to be sentenced so. It was a cruelty so immense that such a gentle soul be forced to live the life of an unfeeling beast.

* * *

He led me to the tunnel of trees.

It was a stand of ash and willow, the branches reaching across and weaving amongst one another to form a roof. It was cool and dark inside, the wind whispered through the leaves, sending them into a muffled, rustling, conversation with one another. All else was quiet but for the distant sound of the sea.

I clung to his hand, squeezing it so tightly that I'm sure it was painful for him, but if it was, he didn't say so. He hadn't spoken at all since we left the cottage, other than to direct me to the path or warn me of a rock or puddle.

The gnawing emptiness in my stomach grew into a giant ache. Something burned terribly in my chest, and I felt as though I'd run for miles. I was light-headed and panicky. I wanted to run back to the cottage, to hide in one of the hedges and refuse to come out.

But I couldn't. That much was clear. To stay was a threat to both of us. He told me that if he defied the terms of his sentence, he would be punished further and that I would no longer be protected by the terms of the covenant between our people. My nine days were his nine days. That was all we had. I couldn't bear to think of him hurt any further, so, for him, I forced myself to be brave and kept walking.

We came to a stop in the middle of the tunnel. The sound of the ocean was louder, and I could almost smell the familiar tang of seaweed and salt. I imagined I could hear the sound of a drum.

"Will I see you again?" I asked, fully aware of the answer, but needing to ask it anyway.

He shook his head.

"I do not think so, *m'anam*. Besides, even if you did, you wouldn't know me. Once you step through, back into your own world, your memories will begin to fade."

"I won't let them," I said, biting back the tears. "I've gone over and over everything we've done. I've told myself the stories over and over again. Every detail. Every colour. Every sound. Your face," I choked back a sob. "Everything about you is in here." I touched my chest - my fingers brushing my mother's pendant as I did so. "I won't ever, ever, forget."

He smiled, his barely-blue eyes brimmed with unshed tears.

"You would be fortunate, *mo chroì*, to not remember me. There is only heartache and danger in that."

"I don't believe that's true, Fingal! I can't. It's better to remember, to know what we're missing, that we might find our way back to it!"

He took my arms and held them tightly to my sides. His gaze

in mine was fierce.

"No, Aibhlinn! You must never come back. You must never try to find me. The danger.... just promise me that?"

"Why would you ask such a thing? I can't promise..."

"You must..."

The sound of drumming grew louder. They echoed down the leafy tunnel with an insistent, driving, beat.

Fingal dropped my arms and put his hands to his head, doubling over.

I reached out to him, but he stumbled back and pushed me away.

"Go!" he said. "Quickly!"

"I can't leave you like this," I cried. "What's wrong with you?"

His face was contorted in pain.

"The drums," he said. "They're intended to drive me away. Aibhlinn, I can't stay here, and you must go home to your people. They're there, waiting for you. Our time is finished. Please, do not make this a greater impossibility...."

The air around him began to shimmer. He flickered in and out of view. The sudden stench of the sea became overwhelming. He was becoming a water horse again.

"I'll see you again, Fingal. The only promise I'll give you is that one. I won't forget you. I won't."

My face was streaming with tears, the combined sorrows of my entire life so far.

"You must," he whispered, inside my head, now. A massive, black, water horse stood in his place. "You must forget me, my lady."

I took a step towards him. "Why?"

He lowered his head in a formal bow.

"Because *I* won't remember *you*."

II

Part Two

Chapter 25

Autumn Equinox

I took the cliff path down to the shore. My swollen belly made the descent more difficult; it required me to walk more cautiously and with more mind paid to where I placed my feet.

***

"Ye may come faster to yer time than with a normal child,"

Hetty had said, when she noticed the swell of my breasts and the rounding of my belly. "'Tis nary nine months to birth a faery child."

I hadn't told anyone at first, wanting to keep the knowledge to myself like a treasured secret. It was too precious to share with those who would warp it into something to gain. It felt like a connection to Fingal that no-one could deny me. Unfortunately, Hetty was right, and I began to show my state far sooner than would have been expected. Which didn't leave me much time.

I had decided from the first that I would be keeping the child. Hetty had been horrified.

"Ye cannae keep the bairn, lassie!" she'd exclaimed, her hand flying up to her mouth in shock. "Blessed Danu, have ye any notion the awful things ye'd unleash if ye tried to cheat them from their rightful..."

"Rightful what, Hetty? Property? Is that what you were going to say?"

My fuse was short in those early days. Fear mingled with extreme joy had left me in a state of emotional turmoil.

Hetty had shaken her head, reaching out to take my hand in hers.

"There now, pet. Dinna take on so. I'm sorry, so sorry. It wasnae my intention to sound so harsh. Shall I make ye a cuppa? Sit down now, take a weight off yer pins. We cannae have ye tiring out, not in yer condition."

I managed a weak smile and allowed myself to be led to a chair by the fire. I knew that she was purposely changing the subject and I wasn't in any frame of mind to fight her. All I knew was that I couldn't possibly give up the child. No matter what I had to do, I wasn't going to let that happen.

* * *

I had come down to the shore every day since I discovered I was carrying. Because there was one other thing I hadn't told anyone: I could remember everything.

I had waited, anxiously, for days after my return. I played my memories over and over again in my head, determined to hold on, but all the while fearful that the day would come when I wouldn't be able to retrieve them.

That day never came.

I kept it to myself because I was sure it meant something. I believed that it must mean that things were different somehow, that because of this failure of the faery charm, maybe things could change, after all.

I had no idea how I was going to manage it on my own, but that one difference —so small and so incredibly huge — gave me the strength to know that I could find a way to keep my baby.

* * *

I walked out to the rocky outcropping that so very much resembled the underwater cavern where Fingal and I first began to know one another. He had said it wasn't an accident that the places were so familiar so I reasoned it would be a good place to come and try to find him.

I didn't find him, of course. It was foolish of me to think a water horse would simply wander up out of the ocean simply because I willed it so. But it made me feel closer to him somehow, like being on the other side of a wall - not being able to see or touch the other person, but knowing they were there. It was a great comfort, if nothing else.

I settled myself on one of the lower boulders and began my ritual of calling out to the sea in conversation. I imagined I was chatting with Fingal, telling him of my day, asking after his.

While I spoke, I ran my hands over my burgeoning belly, feeling the ripples of movement underneath my touch. So much like the sea, I thought, the wee one bobbing about in the brine of my womb.

"'Tis that," came a soft voice from behind me. "Yon wee bairn is blessed to be floating about in an ocean of her very own."

The voice belonged to a tall, middle-aged woman. She had long, golden, hair, fading to grey at the temples, that was bound, untidily in a kerchief. Some tendrils had escaped from the binding, to which clung dried blossoms and bits of faded ribbon. She looked like the maypole in midsummer — faded by the sun and tattered by the wind and rain. Her eyes were the deep, brown of loamy soil and her skin crinkled when she smiled.

"Is the baby a girl, then?" I asked, no longer surprised to receive strange visitors in that place. "I had fancied it might be, but then supposed it was only wishful thinking."

The woman nodded. She was carrying two large wicker

baskets filled with kelp and draped over with cloth. She set them down on the sand and leaned against the rock upon which I was sitting. Rummaging about in the pocket of her apron, she produced a familiar clay pipe and set about tapping the old tobacco into her hand.

"You're different this time," I said, "Younger."

The woman nodded again.

"Not as young as once I was and younger than I'll yet be," she replied, stuffing fresh leaves into her pipe with a dirt-grimed finger.

"I suppose we can all say that, can't we?" I said.

The woman chuckled.

"I see ye're still as full of questions as ever."

I laughed a mirthless laugh. "I've far more questions than I'll ever have answered, of that I'm quite certain."

I placed my hands on my belly once more.

"Especially now," I added, softly.

The woman grunted, puffing furiously on her pipe until it caught, and smoke wreathed upwards.

"What'll ye have answered, then, child? If I were of a mind to answer, that is."

She cocked her head sideways, watching me like a curious bird, a small smile playing on her lips.

I tried to pull my knees up, like I used to do, only to have my belly get in the way. I smiled to myself and stretched my legs back down again and leaned back on the rock, my head tilted back to the sky.

"Well," I said, "If you were to promise me, say, the truthful answer to one question, I would ask how to stop my folk from giving my baby up to the sea."

"What makes ye think that's any great riddle?" she asked,

staring in an uncomfortably direct way into my eyes.

"Isn't it?" I said, surprised to hear her say it.

She shrugged, turning to spit over her shoulder.

"Not if ye remember what y'are," she said, getting to her feet and picking up her baskets.

I groaned.

"Not that again," I said, thoroughly exasperated. "Is that all you ever have to offer?"

I had to shout the last bit because she was already wandering off over the sand.

"'Tis all and 'tis everything, child."

Sighing, I slid down off the rock. The sun was starting its journey down the horizon, and I still had mushrooms to gather for tea. As I stood, dusting sand from the back of my skirt, I noticed a large square of cloth lying on the sand. It must have fallen from the woman's basket. I looked up, not really expecting to see her, then bent down to pick it up. It was finely woven and soft, not unlike the fabric of my sea bride's dress, I thought.

"It'll do for the bairn," said her voice, from inside my head. "Keep it safe, aye?"

* * *

"Where's the blessed tea, then?" shouted my father, banging through the front door of our cottage with a bad-tempered crash.

I'd stayed down at the water's edge far longer than I ought and, forgetting my inability to run as once I did, hadn't left myself sufficient time to get home and begin preparing the evening meal. I had a pan of potatoes on the boil and a mushroom and onion tart baking in the fire box.

"Sorry, Da," I said, not entirely convincingly. "I got waylaid picking mushrooms for the tart."

"Leave her alone, Da," muttered Duncan, who was sitting at the table going over the latest figures from Lord Pennorth. "Can ye not see she's getting along 'er time? She should be sitting down, not rushing about after ye,"

My father banged a fist on the table. He smelled strongly of fish and whiskey.

"Well, I dinna see ye leapin' up to help, do I now? Besides, nowt wrong wi' the lass. She's no' the first woman to have a bairn, is she? Nowt wrong wi' just gettin' on w' things. Anyroad, I'm sure the sea devils tek care o' their own, aye?"

He broke off into a wheezing chuckle before thumping across the room to the sink where he proceeded to splash water all over the bread I'd just baked while he washed his hands and neck.

Stifling my irritation, I whisked the bread out of range and handed him a towel.

"Sit down, Da," I said. "I'll bring you a mug of tea, shall I?"

"Aye, go on, lass. That'd be grand. I've a desperate thirst just now."

He sank down into his chair by the fire and stretched his stocking feet towards the flames. He'd be snoring in less than ten minutes, and I was counting on that.

I busied myself with checking on the tart until I heard the grunting snuffles that signaled he'd fallen asleep and turned to Duncan.

"Are you expecting Callum home tonight?" I asked, hoping to hear that he was.

Duncan shook his head.

"No, pet. He said he were staying up on the moor again."

Duncan put the report down and looked up at me. I think the worry must have shown on my face because he reached over and squeezed my hand.

"Aw lass," he said with a sigh. "It were terrible hard on him, ye being gone. He blames himself for picking yer name. And then to have ye come back in that way," he gestured towards my belly. "Well, he's taking it to heart. And when he cannae cope, he hides off up the hill with his ruddy sheep. I wouldnae give him a second thought, lass. He doesnae deserve yer worry, buggering off and leaving ye here wi' him."

He jabbed a thumb at Da.

I smiled at him.

"So did you!" I said, "Bugger off, that is. You and Alexander both, all over chummy with Frederick Dunn. Lord Pennorth's lackeys now, are you?"

I grinned at the indignant look on his face.

"Somebody's got to do some work around here!" he retorted. "Besides, what good is it that ye had to go off and..." He faltered then. Like most other people since my return, he seemed unable to articulate where exactly I'd been or what I'd been doing. Despite the obvious evidence of the latter.

He rubbed a hand across his face and tried again.

"Aibhlinn, pet. He'll never understand, our da, what he did when he put yer name in that sodding book. He thought he was acting the big man, like, that it would somehow make up for everything he'd done to drag this family into the muck since Mam died. He was counting on all sorts of things, y'see? But nothing comes without an effort. It weren't for a lot o' thinking on it, ye understand? Alexander wasn't ower keen on taking on with Frederick, but it means we get first sale o' the catch and Callum's wool gets first look-over. It means we dinna have to worry about yon useless lump holding us back, aye?"

This was the longest speech I'd ever heard from Duncan. He's always been the quiet one, deferring to Alexander and never quite understanding Callum.

"I know, Duncan. And I would never begrudge you any of the good things that come with me having been the sea bride. What's it all for if I can't see my favourite brothers do well by it all, right?"

I busied myself straightening the chairs and putting out the butter dish.

"And if you've the stomach to stand the face of horrid Frederick Dunn and his smarmy ways, then I'd say that's fair punishment for benefiting from the spoils of my exploitation."

I laughed out loud at the look of dismay on his face, then threw the tea towel at his head.

"Go on, you daft git," I said. "I'm just having you on. Now go and wash up, I'll be dishing up the taties in just a minute."

I left him sluicing his face at the sink and stepped out the back door of the cottage. Leaning against the rough stone, I closed my eyes and took a deep, shuddering, breath.

"Oh, Fingal," I whispered to the breeze. "Whatever am I going to do?"

Chapter 26

The women came for me at noon, one Saturday in early autumn.

I was hanging out the washing, humming a tune from the Revels, when I heard the collective cough. Turning around with a clothespin in my mouth I was surprised to see Hetty standing there, with Isabelle Dunn and Morag and five other women from round about.

"We've come to speak with ye about the bairn," said Hetty. Her face was pale, and her expression pinched. I knew that seeing me in my heavily pregnant state was probably very difficult. She'd been so strange with me in the last weeks, very vague and dismissive and I imagined it was because she and John had never been blessed with children. She'd told me that after her faery-child had been taken from her, it was as if her body refused to hold another bairn. "It wouldnae bear the sorrow of losing another one," she'd said, tears in her eyes.

"So it never let one quicken."

My heart thudded in my chest and my mouth was suddenly very dry. I looked at each of the women, none of whom would meet my eye. Other than Isabelle. She had her beady little eyes fixed right on my face, her mouth quirked into something that looked like anger.

Taking the clothespin out of my mouth and slowly placing it in the basket, I took a shaky breath and tried to pretend I'd no notion of what they meant.

"Oh?" I said, "Is this a good-will visit then? Come to share your wisdom of the birth-bed with me?"

I felt badly about the last bit when I saw the look on Hetty's face. And Morag's, for that matter. It had been made publicly known during my absence that Lord Pennorth wasn't going to offer for her, and she'd had to live with the whispers and implications since then. But for all of the humiliation of that, I daresay it didn't come close to the recriminations she was hearing from her own mother behind closed doors.

"You know fine well why we're here," snapped Isabelle, folding her hands primly in front of her fine silk dress. "I see your time...away...has done nothing to temper your impudence."

I grinned.

"You see correctly, Isabelle. In fact, I think it's just made me ever more incorrigible."

Despite the panic that was rising, I placed a hand on my hip and tilted my head with an air of innocence.

"Forgive me if I don't quite understand the nature of your visit. If not to wish me well, what other purpose? I'm quite well provided for, as you must know, Isabelle. The good nature of Lord Pennorth has my menfolk in fine standing these days. Indeed, I want for very little."

Isabelle smirked, clearly enjoying her mission of terror, as that is truly what it was. Although I wasn't about to let them know I saw it as such.

"I believe Hetty has told you of the terms involving the faery child."

She said 'child' as if it had an unpleasant taste.

"Having been blessed with such a gift herself," she continued with sickly sweetness, "she's well versed in what's expected. Isn't that right, Hetty?"

Hetty nodded, mutely.

"Hetty was the last woman of Glencarragh to be so fortunate. What a wonderful thing to perform such a duty for the well-being of her kinsmen."

Isabelle smiled beatifically around at the women of the group, many of whom, according to Hetty, were former sea brides themselves. There was a general shuffling of feet and avoidance of gazes as they were reminded of their implied failures.

To see them made so uncomfortable made my temper rise.

"Did you ever fancy yourself a sea bride, Isabelle? Is that why you wanted it for your Morag? After all, 'tis a grand thing to take a handsome faery to your bed. Still, it would've been difficult to settle for the likes of your Frederick after having such a skilled lover as that, eh?"

There was a collective intake of scandalized breath. I willed my heart to stop racing. I folded my hands into fists inside the pockets of my apron to stop them from shaking.

"Aibhlinn!" hissed Hetty, casting a nervous glance at Isabelle. "That's far enough with the likes of that filth, now."

"Filth?" I said, my voice rising. "Is that what you call it? Why would you all be so happy to send me off to it, then, if it were such a terrible thing? And why would the men want them to steal your memories from you, if not to deprive you of the joy of remembering how it was?"

The women began whispering among themselves, but Isabelle shushed them.

"That's enough, child!" she spat. "You're speaking utter nonsense. The sea bride is an honoured act of duty, an innocent ceremony, nothing more, nothing less. We are merely playing out our part of an ancient bargain, for the greater good of life here on the island."

The wind gusted suddenly, whipping and snapping the clothes I had just hung on the line. Shirts and trousers belonging to Da and my brothers and some swaddling cloths that I'd found in a chest in the attic. I'd taken them out and given them a freshening up.

Isabelle's gaze went to the line of washing, spotting the swaddling immediately. Her eyes narrowed before her face shifted into a smile of extreme benevolence.

"You are to come with us at once," she said, stepping forwards to pick up my washing basket. "You're in no condition to be slaving about after your father and brothers. They can manage on their own until your confinement, I'm quite sure. In the tradition of the sea brides, I imagine these ladies will be happy to furnish basic meals and housekeeping in the meantime?"

She glanced around the cluster of women who immediately nodded and began murmuring about what would be the best options for prepared meals and who would manage a weekly washing.

I folded my arms, reaching up to hold my mother's pendant as I did so.

Wherever you are, Mam, give me the strength to get through this…

"I'm not going anywhere," I said, planting my feet firmly. "I'm fine where I am. I'll have this bairn right here in this cottage - it was a good enough place for my own mam to birth the six of us, and it's a good enough place for me to have mine."

I should've understood the expression on Hetty's face. It was surprise and fear all at once, and then something like regret.

I felt a pair of strong arms encircle mine and a cloth smelling of something foul was placed over my mouth and nose. I tried to scream and wrench my arms away but then my vision swam and my knees buckled.

The last thing I heard was Isabelle Dunn's voice.

"See? I told you we needed the men for this. She was never going to come easily."

Chapter 27

Fingal stood before me.

He was in his water horse form, the sea streaming from the black of his coat and when he shook his head, the water sprayed like the ocean crashing against the shore. He was trying to tell me something, but the sound of the waves and the roar of the wind made it hard for me to hear him. Then I remembered he would speak to my thoughts, and I tried to listen, but the sound of a baby crying was drowning out his voice.

Then he was in his human aspect. He *was* human. The angular features and slanted eyes of his faery's face had softened into that of a pale-skinned man with bright blue eyes. His hair was as black as coal and tumbled in a snarled tangle around his face. He wore the clothes of a moor-man from long ago, one of the original pony-men; the pony-men of Glencarragh who, it was rumoured, captured faery horses and bred them to their own stock, creating herds of the finest ponies that ever ran the heather. He had something in his hand and was holding it out to me, his lips were moving but there was no sound. I tried to reach for the object - a loop of finely wrought chain with a charm attached - but he kept slipping further away from me, the closer I walked.

"Aibhlinn, pet. Wake up, lassie. It's time ye were awake."

I heard a voice, but it wasn't his. I didn't want to hear any voice that didn't belong to him. He was trying to reach me, but I couldn't hear him. I closed my mind to anything but him and what he was trying to tell me.

I was back on the shore, down at the water's edge, the sea foaming over my bare feet. My belly was large, larger than it is now, and I could feel an ache low in my back. I was screaming, calling his name into the wind, my hair blowing wild around my face. Then he was there, out over the waves, his black head cresting above the surf.

I sobbed and ran further into the water, mindless of the cold sting of rain that had begun to fall.

"Fingal!" I screamed. "Help me! They're going to take her..."

Suddenly, there he was, rising from the tide in his terrifying glory. The iron-stink of blood and sea stung my nose and eyes and I staggered backwards.

A voice in my head was roaring.

"Leave, now *m'anam*. Be gone from here and from me,"

"Fingal!" I said, weeping with relief. "I knew you'd come." I dropped to my knees in the water, my shoulders shaking with fear and exhaustion. I felt a clenching in my belly and the sudden pain left me gasping.

"Aibhlinn!"

That voice again, urgent now.

"Wake her up, she's having another terror!"

I pushed that voice away, wanting to hear the sound of my beloved.

But the sound I heard wasn't the voice of Fingal, it was deep and guttural. It hissed and spat.

"Pretty thing, poppetsssss..."

Then I remembered what he'd said.

"I won't remember you..."

The dark shape of the water horse reared above me. I screamed as it came down, pounding hooves; teeth and eyes flashing.

* * *

I woke in a trembling sweat.

The stark white faces of Hetty and Morag stared at me, horror-struck.

"Oh, blessed Danu be praised," said Hetty, breathing a shaky breath. "I thought ye were going into the fits."

She placed a cold hand on my feverish brow.

"Morag, love, get me one of the lavender cloths, there's a good lass. And pour us all a cup of ale. I warrant we all need one."

Hetty got up from the edge of the bed and pulled the curtains back slightly, letting in a shaft of sunlight.

"What time is it?" I croaked, still feeling disoriented.

"Just going on two, pet. Are ye alright then? Ye gave us a terrible scare. It's been me and Morag sitting with ye over the night and into this day. Though I don't think ye knew we were even here."

"Over the night? How long was I asleep?"

"Since they carried ye in. 'Twasn't meant to be like this, lass. I cannae tell ye how sorry I am but when ye started in about keeping the bairn, well, everyone went into a panic, like."

Hetty was babbling. She folded the edge of her apron, over and over, her fingers trembling. I thought I would be angry with her, but it all slipped away from me to see her in such distress. It's so unlike Hetty to be like this; it did nothing to ease my own mind.

"Why am I here, Hetty?" I asked, quietly, reaching out to still the fumbling fingers. She closed her hands over mine, her skin was cold on her thin, strong, work-roughened fingers. Hers were the hands of a true island woman.

She hung her head. A tear dripped slowly from her chin, and she shook her head.

"Tell me, Hetty. I've a right to know."

"You're here so everyone can keep an eye on you until the babe is born," said Morag, bustling into the room with a tray of cups and a jug of ale. She set it down on the dresser next to the bed.

"And then?"

Morag shrugged.

"Then they take the bairn and you can go."

"You can't keep me here, I'm not a prisoner!"

My voice was shrill and shaking with barely suppressed fear. I hadn't expected this sort of treatment and the implications for my baby were too terrible to fathom.

I made to throw the quilt from my legs and stand up, but Morag marched over and tucked me firmly back in. She leaned over me, her round face pale and furious.

"You will stay and do as you're told," she said from between gritted teeth. "For once in your selfish life, Aibhlinn MacFinlay, think of someone other than yourself."

I was shocked.

"How can you say that you horrible beast? I'm not thinking of me; I'm thinking of my baby! Now, let me up!"

I roared the last part, startling Morag into stepping back. I tore off the blankets and lunged for the floor. But when I tried to stand, my legs gave out under me, and I fell in a heap. Sobbing with rage, I tried to stand but my head swam, and I felt as if I were going to be sick.

"Help me, you sodding cow!" I sputtered, hating myself for my helplessness.

Morag's strong arms encircled mine and she sank down beside me, folding me in a tight embrace. I slumped against her and wept.

"I can't let them take her, Morag. Please don't let them take my baby."

I no longer cared that she might think me weak. All the pretense of courage and bluster had seeped away.

"Hush now, Aibhlinn," she murmured into my hair. "It's going to be alright. We'll think of something."

I wasn't sure I'd heard her correctly. I sniffled loudly and wiped my face on the edge of the sheet that I'd pulled to the floor with me.

"What did you just say?" I whispered, not daring to believe I may have an ally. And such an unlikely one at that.

"Shh," she said, her voice low. "Don't let on to Hetty. She's in a terrible state over this and is too afraid of my mother to raise any objections. You and the bairn have brought it all back to her, you know, the terrible upset of her own time, and she hasn't been herself these last few days. She must be remembering how she lost her own to the sea and she's terribly fragile. If you'd just behave yourself, you'll make life easier for her."

I nodded, miserable and ashamed. Of course this would be terrible for Hetty.

"Right!" she said, brightly. "Up you get and back to bed, you're in no state to be going anywhere, eh, Hetty?"

Hetty stood, ashen-faced and staring as Morag hoisted me to my feet. I wobbled back to the bed and allowed her to tuck the quilt around me again.

"I think maybe our Aibhlinn would be better off with a hot cup of broth, don't you Hetty?"

Hetty started, jolted from her stupor by Morag's brisk tone. She took a deep breath and smoothed her hands over her hair.

"Aye, pet. Ye're right, y'are. I'll just pop to the kitchen and warm some through, shall I?

"Thank you, Hetty," I said, with a faint smile. "I'm sorry for being such a nuisance."

Hetty patted my arm on her way past, returning to her usual state of bustling efficiency.

"Never ye mind, lass. 'Tis no trouble at all. Womenfolk are entitled to be a bit mad when they're expecting, aye? Just rest yer wee self there and I'll be back in a quick mo'".

I sighed shakily as she closed the door behind her, sinking back onto the pillows. Morag stood at the window, looking out across the stretch of moor towards the cliff path.

"Why, Morag?" I asked, genuinely curious, and quite a bit

suspicious of her sudden change of heart. We'd been on barely civil terms for years, and even less so since our last argument down at the shore. Her seemingly gormless deference to everyone had always filled me with such frustration.

"Why what?" she said, without turning around.

"Why would you help me?"

She chuckled and turned around. Her eyes were narrowed to slits and she folded her arms, like she always did when she wanted to appear firm.

"You always suppose it's about you, don't you?" she said, disappointment in her voice. "Everything is for, or in aid of, the lovely Aibhlinn. Lovely Aibhlinn who only ever considers herself."

I blushed and looked down at my hands where they rested on the quilt.

"Right you are," she said. "A bit of shame wouldn't go amiss."

"I'm sorry, Morag. You're quite right, of course. I'm just so used to doing everything for myself, it's hard to imagine anyone would have an interest in helping me."

I waved a hand. "Oh, there I go again. It's just all very muddled in my head, I'm sorry."

I peered out from under a curtain of my hair. "But I really do want to know why you'd...side with me, in this particular instance."

She grinned widely. Her smile brightened up her whole face, making her quite bonny. I told her so.

It was her turn to blush.

"Get on with you," she said, trying to stop smiling. "You're just taking the piss..."

My mouth hung open in shock. "Morag Dunn! I've never

heard such language from the likes of you. Whatever would your mother say if she could hear you talking like...."

"Like you?"

"A fish-wife!"

"What's this then?" said Hetty, smiling at the sound of our laughter.

She came through the door with a basin of broth and a tray of sandwiches. "It's nice to see you two lasses getting on. It does me heart good to think ye've mended fences."

I glanced at Morag who shrugged and looked away, shyly.

"Come here, you goose," I said, stretching my hand out to hers. She walked towards the bed and took my hand, squeezing it gently.

"If we lasses can't mend our fences at a time like this, what hope is there for us, right?"

Morag nodded, tears welling in her eyes.

"Oh, don't you start bubbling," I said, feeling my own eyes stinging. "Here's me never shed a tear since I was a tiny thing and now I've got the waterworks running all the time! I've no idea what's come over me these days! Now, Hetty, that broth smells lovely. I do believe I've got a bit of appetite coming back."

Hetty beamed and set the tray over my knees. She handed me the bowl of broth and a spoon and offered Morag the plate of sandwiches.

"Tuck in, lasses," she said, fussing happily about the room. "We're all going to need our strength in the days ahead, aye?"

Morag and I exchanged glances but said nothing.

Chapter 28

I'd been at the tavern just over a week when I was allowed, due to my good behaviour and Morag's own record of impeccable obedience, to start walking, daily, after breakfast. Morag would come and collect me, and we'd set off over the moors, usually with a flask of tea and a bundle of sandwiches that Hetty would tuck into a basket.

"Just in case ye get peckish while ye're out," she'd say. "Now mind ye don't overdo it, Aibhlinn. Morag, keep an eye on her and don't let her cheek ye into staying out longer than ye ought. The weather's turning and it wouldn't do to get caught out in the rain."

The weather had taken a noticeable turn since my incarceration at the tavern. I was allowed out only in the mornings, that being the time when the regular patrons of the tavern were still busy with their boats or their sheep. Despite it being universally acknowledged that my pregnancy was a boon to the island and a harbinger of great fortune, nobody actually wanted to admit my existence. Morag had told me that there was a great deal of unease in the people thereabouts, so rare was the occasion of a child of a sea bride, it had everyone in a state of nervous exhaustion.

Morag told me many such humorous stories of the people of Glencarragh on our various rambles. It turns out she has a keen sense of folk and a wicked wit. I told her I was surprised to discover that about her.

She chuckled and blushed slightly.

"I know, it's terribly un-Christian of me to say such things. But I can't help but see the pettiness of folk. They're so small-minded sometimes and yet pretend to such airs and graces."

"You mean like your mam and dad?" I said, elbowing her in the ribs. We were walking arm-in-arm, as was our habit.

She grunted.

"Exactly like my mam and dad," she sighed. "My mam is the worst offender, more so than Da because he's just doing his best to avoid having to answer to her. Everything he does, he does to prevent an argument or accusation. She can be extraordinarily cruel sometimes."

She paused, gazing off over the horizon. Then she flapped a hand.

"Never mind them," she said, smiling brightly. "Have you spoken with Father Ewan yet?"

I shook my head.

"I was rather hoping I wouldn't have to," I said. "I'd been hoping that Callum..."

I stopped, not trusting the wobble in my voice.

"Has he not come, then?" asked Morag, gently.

I'd sent a message to Callum through one of the shepherd's

lads but hadn't heard from him. I wanted so desperately to speak with him, to tell him that I was going to be okay and that none of it was his fault.

The dream I'd had when I was first brought to the tavern still haunted me. I'd sifted through it time and again, searching for meaning but finding none. I was beginning to think that it was just the effect of the noxious fumes and not a message from Fingal, as I'd first imagined it to be. I wanted so very much to talk to Callum about it. He always helped me sort things out and I was sure he'd help me make sense of it. If there were indeed any sense to be had.

I shook my head.

"I'm sure he's just busy," I said, in an attempt at seeming indifferent. "It doesn't matter, really. I'll just have to face Father Ewan, that's all."

"Best that you do, anyway," said Morag, her lips pressed together, just like her mother. "There's no point in trying to avoid these things."

"Avoid what things?" I asked, surprised to see her so adamant. "Isn't this whole venture a plot in avoiding things?"

She laughed quickly and patted my hand.

"Of course, it is. I just can't help but worry that we'll be found out, that's all. You know my mam is the world's worst for sniffing out a plot. I often think she could hire herself out to Lord Pennorth and save him the cost of keeping his hounds."

She grinned wickedly and tugged my arm. "Come on, let's walk up to the peak and then sit and have our picnic. We might as well enjoy these days while we can, eh?"

"You go on, Morag, and set up the blanket and things, will you? I fancy a moment just here on the cliff edge by myself."

She narrowed her eyes and pursed her lips.

"I'm not supposed to leave you...oh! Are you going to try and summon...him?" she asked, her eyes widening.

I laughed.

"If only it were that easy," I said. "I would've had him here long ago." I squeezed her hand. "No, I just sometimes fancy I can talk to my mam, that's all."

I blushed, suddenly feeling foolish. I rarely spoke of my mother with anyone other than Callum or Hetty and certainly not to Morag, given our history.

She seemed disappointed but nodded.

"Right, well, don't be long. I trust you won't try and do a runner?"

She smiled but there was a hint of worry in her voice.

"Give over, Morag. I'm not going to any such thing, no. Even if I did, do you think I'd get far carrying this great lump in front of me?" I gestured to my ballooning girth. "Even you could probably outrun me." I winked and gave her a good-natured shove.

She laughed nervously and gave me one last look before setting off to the peak. She looked back several times before disappearing out of sight. I waved at the last and she waved back.

I sighed.

As much as I enjoyed feeling as though I had a confidant, Morag's constant presence had become a bit stifling. I was so used to spending most of my time on my own, it felt confining to be constantly accompanied. Still, she meant well, and I really was enjoying the idea of having a friend, so I admonished my disagreeableness.

I walked closer to the edge of the cliff, enjoying the bracing coolness of the breeze. The few scrubby trees that managed to cling to the edges of the cliff were permanently bent under the constant assault of the wind. I frowned, noticing a scraggly hawthorn hedge that I didn't remember seeing before. It had clearly been too long since I'd been up that way. I saw a little hollow, conveniently placed between the columns of the bushes that created the hedge and tucked myself into the sheltered area near the base of two of the trees, settling down on the dried grass.

It felt good to take the weight off my feet. I leaned back against the rough bark of the tree and closed my eyes, trying to conjure the image of my mother from the photographs I'd seen. Hetty was being a great help to me, answering all of my anxious questions about childbirth, but I wished so very badly that I had my mother to stand by me. I just knew that if she'd been alive, she would've helped me with all of this. She would never let Isabelle Dunn and her cronies — frightened sheep, the lot of them — interfere or tell her what she could and couldn't do. And she knew how it was to want a child so badly that you'd do anything to bring it safely to the world.

The steady rhythm of the sea below soothed me and I found my breathing slowed to the pace of the waves.

I think I must have dozed off because when I opened my eyes the expanse of blue sky had darkened noticeably.

"Morag!" I thought, with a sudden surge of panic. "She'll think I've run off! They'll be after me with the dogs and flaming torches!" I stifled an inappropriate giggle at the idea.

I scrambled to my feet, not terribly efficiently, and caught my toe on a fallen branch that was hidden in the grass. I lurched forwards only to find myself steadied by a pair of strong arms.

"Gently now, *m'anam*. You wouldn't want to give the wee

bairn a jostling."

Fingal's hand covered my mouth to muffle the scream I was about to let loose.

"Hush, now. We've not much time and I don't want to waste it running from torch-bearing villagers."

His barely-blue eyes filled with tears as he folded me into his arms. I clung tightly to him, weeping great shuddering sobs into the front of his shoulder, letting go of everything I'd held onto in the past months.

Now, I thought, now everything will be alright.

* * *

"How are you here? What about..."

I had a thousand questions tumbling around in my head. I simply couldn't believe he was standing right there in front of me, after all the dire warnings and assurances we'd never see each other again.

"We've a mutual friend," was all he'd tell me. "She told me of the bairn and what you intended to do. And she made it possible for me to come to you - the veil is thinning only a very little at this time of year but, well, let's just say she held it open a little wider for me."

He smiled around at the little hollow. "And it seems you've a knack for finding fey places. It meant I could come right through and see you."

"So you came to help me!"

I clapped my hands together then reached for his and placed them on my belly. "Do you feel her? Do you feel your daughter tumbling around in her very own sea?"

I was delirious with joy. To have him there, standing in the flesh! That I could touch him was more than I'd hoped.

Fingal pulled his hands away, gently, but not before I saw a flicker of recognition in his eyes and the tug of a smile at the corner of his mouth.

"No, Aibhlinn. You mustn't. Now, I haven't long. Our friend won't be able to mask my absence for long and I wouldn't place her in a difficult position by abusing her kindness. Even one such as she has to obey the old laws."

"What do you mean?" I said, searching his face. "How long?"

"Mere minutes, my lady. I've come to warn you from your intended path. The babe isn't yours to claim. She belongs to the sea and you must let her go."

His words and his expression did not match.

I stood there, staring for a moment, my brain having trouble reckoning what I was hearing.

"No!" I shouted, finally understanding what he was saying. "No, no, NO! Not you as well. How could you?"

Something in me snapped and I started pummeling him with my fists. The pain I saw on his face was certainly not a result of my attack. He grasped my elbows and held them to his chest as I beat away at him, tears streaming down my face.

"How could you?" I repeated, my voice a mere whisper. I slumped in his arms and let him guide me to the ground where I sat in a heap, arms wrapped protectively around my belly.

"I've no choice, Aibhlinn," he said. "There are...things... that you cannot know; things that I cannot tell you, things you must discover for yourself. It's not permitted..."

"Well why are you even here then?" I snapped, interrupting him. "Why did you bother to come back if you're too cowardly to help me? If all you have to offer are warnings and cryptic faery riddles, then you'd might as well leave me now. I've no use for any of it."

It was cruel of me, but I was so angry. The look of raw pain on his face was almost enough to make me relent. I had been so hopeful and now all seemed lost. His outline began to blur around the edges.

"Fingal!" I screamed as he began to flicker and fade away.

"Remember, *mo chroì*. Remember what you are."

He was gone.

The sky lightened and the sound of the sea returned. I sat staring numbly at the place where my beloved had stood, cursing myself for my waspishness. If only I'd listened to what he was trying to tell me.

"Aibhlinn!"

Morag's voice in the distance jolted me from my stupor. How much time had passed? I scrambled to my feet and stepped out from my wind-sheltered hollow, smoothing down my dress and wiping my face.

I looked up the hill to see Morag standing at the top, waving.

"I've finished setting up the picnic! Come on!"

I breathed a sigh of relief. I hadn't been in the hollow for very long, after all.

"I'm just coming!" I called, resolving not to mention my encounter to Morag. Whatever it was that Fingal and the strange woman – for I'd presumed that was the mutual friend Fingal had mentioned – wanted me to remember, I still had to sort out. And I had the feeling that this, at least, was something

I needed to do for myself.

Chapter 29

Hetty deposited me in the big armchair by the fire in the main room of the tavern. I had brought a basket of mending and was pretending to be engrossed in the darning of some of Alexander's and Duncan's socks while Hetty bustled about the room taking the chairs down from the tables and tidying up in anticipation of Father Ewan's visit.

Morag had told me that Father Ewan had been wanting to see me – to counsel me, apparently – and I'd put him off longer than was deemed appropriate by Isabelle and her cronies. I'd finally agreed to see him after Morag pointed out that my refusal could be seen as further evidence of my rebellious nature and would result in my freedoms being greatly diminished. That was definitely something I couldn't afford.

It was too warm by the fire. What I really wanted was to be outdoors, to feel the wind on my skin and, strangely enough, to smell the sea. I've always been mostly ambivalent about the sea, preferring the moor and the woods, but my pregnancy was apparently having strange effects on me and being near the shore felt something like a compulsion.

I suppressed an impatient sigh and put down the mending to stretch wearily, easing a crick in my neck. At the bottom of my mending basket was the fold of cloth that the strange woman had left behind. "For the bairn" she'd said. "Keep it safe." Was I to keep the cloth safe, or the child? Or both. Yet another cryptic message. I rubbed the material between my fingers. It was delicately woven but very strong, and beautifully soft to the touch. It was the colour of a moonlit sea - grey and indigo-black with a thread of silver. Faery-crafted, there was little doubt of that. I wondered if it was large enough to make a wrap for the baby.

"That's a lovely piece of cloth, my child."

Father Ewan's voice startled me, and I dropped the material back into my basket, guiltily piling the half-mended socks on top.

I waved a hand in dismissal.

"Oh, it's nothing but a scrap I found at the bottom of my mending," I said. "Barely enough to be useful and certainly not a very practical weave at all. How are you, Father? Shall I ask Hetty to make a pot of tea?"

I wanted to distract him, there was something in his face that suggested he recognized the cloth.

"Tea would be lovely, Aibhlinn, thank you."

He moved to sit down in the chair opposite mine, leaning over to warm his hands in front of the flames. "The wind has turned," he said, conversationally. "The autumn tides will be upon us before too long."

"Yes, indeed," I replied, getting up and taking my basket with me. "I'll be back in just a bit with the tea, Father. And maybe Hetty will have a slice of something lovely to go with it."

"Faery-woven," he said, without turning. "The cloth is the same as that of the sea bride's dress."

I halted in my tracks, my mouth suddenly dry and my heart pounding. I clenched the handle of my basket until it dug painfully into my fingers.

"S-s-sorry?" I said, "I'm not sure I understand. It's naught but a spare scrap..."

"There's no need to lie to me, child. I've been here long enough to recognize the workmanship of those...creatures. More important, is where you got it and what you plan to do with it."

He turned from the fire and stared at me, blinking in that infuriatingly slow way that made him look like a reptile. He made me feel like a small animal trapped in the gaze of a predatory snake.

I cleared my throat and straightened my shoulders.

"It was in my mother's trunk," I lied. "I assume it was left over from something she made one of us when we were babes ourselves. So I'm quite sure you're mistaken in its origins."

The old priest chuckled mirthlessly.

"On the contrary, my dear. If it truly was your mother's cloth - which I doubt - the chance of it being faery-crafted is quite increased."

Narrowing my eyes, I hitched the basket higher to rest on my hip.

"I'll just fetch the tea, Father, shall I? Then you and I have some things to discuss."

***

"So, are you going to be counseling me towards not arguing my destiny?"

I'd poured us each a mug of tea and given Father Ewan a slice of Hetty's currant loaf. The main room remained deserted, Hetty having gone into the kitchen to begin preparations of the day's meals. The smell of baking bread drifted pleasantly around the room, blending with the tang of peat and the leftover spice of the beeswax polish she used on the wooden mantel.

"I suppose that depends upon what you consider your destiny to be, child," he replied, smiling wanly over the rim of his mug as he sipped his tea.

"All I know is that it's my own and no-one elses," I replied.

He nodded, thoughtfully, and set down his mug. He leaned back in his chair and folded his hands across his chest.

"Not even God's?" he asked, a smile tugging at the corner of his mouth.

I raised a questioning eyebrow.

"Since when did He have a say in anything that goes on around here?" I asked.

He chuckled.

"A fair point, lass. A fair point, indeed."

"Why did you stay here?" I said, "It must be horribly frustrating for you, dealing with all this heathen business."

He was quiet for several minutes, lips pursed as he frowned down at the mug on the table, as if expecting it to divine an answer to my questions. I sat and sipped silently, quite content to let the time pass without discussion of my baby.

Finally, he spoke. His voice was quiet, almost a whisper.

"Why did you allow yourself to be made a sea bride? I don't suppose there's anyone here on Glencarragh that would argue the fact you're quite possibly the most contrary child ever born. Why would you allow your father and brothers to determine your fate like that?"

The question shocked me. I hadn't ever thought of it in those terms. I'd become a sea bride because my name was written in the book and then drawn on the night of the winter solstice. I'd gone along with it because I loved this land and wanted to protect it and because it was going to give me some say over how I spent the rest of my life. I'd never once thought of it as someone else determining my fate. I'd only ever thought of it in the most simplistic of terms.

He smiled at the expression on my face.

"You see?" he said. "It's not always a matter of choice. And it's not always as simple as doing something or not doing something. There are a myriad of factors and influences, most of them buried so deeply in our stories that we assume them to be of our own choosing."

I inhaled deeply and let out a long, slow exhale.

He shrugged, then leaned forwards, putting his hands on the table. Turning them over, he pulled up the sleeves of his shirt to reveal his forearms; they were criss-crossed with ropy, white scars.

I leaned over to touch them. They were slightly raised, remnants of deep, cruel wounds.

"What happened?" I said, my voice barely a croak, because to my eye, they looked like the marks that would be left by rows of sharp teeth.

"Years ago, as I'm sure you've been told, Hetty bore a child by the sea-devils."

"I wish you wouldn't call them that," I interrupted. "You can't know...Never mind. Please, go on."

"As is your custom," he grimaced, wincing visibly as he said it. "The child was to be given to the sea. At eight days old - long enough for Hetty to have fed the child from her body and given her heart to its well-being, long enough to love - and then it — *he*— was taken from her."

I felt a heavy weight descending in my chest and my throat constricted. A flush of heat rushed to my face, and I felt light-headed. No, I screamed inwardly. No! That will *not* be how it happens for me.

Father Ewan's own face was a mask of misery, his voice raspy with emotion.

"It was my task to remain here with her, to pray and to attempt to guide her to peace. Folk have a wary tolerance of me, you see. But no more than that. Certainly, there's no trust. They wouldn't have me anywhere near the water's edge that day, no matter how I tried to convince them to see the error of their ways. Oh, I suppose a wiser man may have left the island, left your folk to themselves, but I felt it was my calling to stay — to try and help the ones that perhaps were not so convinced of the presiding ways."

"But you didn't help Hetty," I said. "You let them take her child — how can you call that helping?"

I hated that my voice was so shrill. I'd promised myself I'd keep a level head, so that I could convince him sensibly that he ought to help *me*. Morag had me convinced that he would be the one, despite my reservations. I tried not to think of all of the times I'd cheeked him.

"A man of God," she'd said, "is bound by his duty to help those in need. Especially the bairns."

Father Ewan shook his head.

"But I did try, Aibhlinn, my child. I did a foolish thing and I fear I may have made things worse, in the end." He paused and took a large drink of his tea, draining his mug. "I went down to the shore that day, against the tenets of my faith and against the strict instruction of the island folk."

His voice shook and he passed a trembling hand over his brow.

"I cannot speak of the horror of it," he said. "To this day, the stench..." He shivered. "I watched one of those terrible beasts rise from the sea. I thought the child was going to be slaughtered - to be fed to the creatures like some hideous sacrifice from the days of old. I was wild with grief and shock and anger. I'd seen Hetty - the expression on her face when she begged me to save her child. That she'd been used so awfully, that she'd even conceived the child was enough of a horror to my mind. I thought to drive the beast back, so I held high my crucifix and began to pray. I walked towards it. Oh, the commotion! Everyone was shouting and suddenly another creature appeared. It was.... well, it resembled a woman, I suppose. But I barely saw it, I was full of conviction, you see. I lunged for the baby - some misguided fool or other was cradling the bairn, so terribly close to the beast. Well, I'm not certain what took place next. Someone, or something, knocked me down and I'd a face full of seawater. Then something grabbed me by the arm and the pain was so intense, I'm ashamed to admit I may have fainted. When I came to myself, we were back here, at the tavern and I'd a bandage on my arm and the rage of the island folk to welcome me. I spent three weeks in and out of a violent fever and was left with these scars to remind me of my trespass."

"And Hetty's bairn?" I asked, even though I clearly knew the answer. "What happened to the baby?"

His eyes filled with tears, and he shook his head.

"It was taken by the faery-woman, Lira" he said. "Folk said I'd almost ruined everything. Even with the babe given over to the faeries, it was a bad year that followed, and I was blamed for angering the beasts with my interference. It was a near thing that I wasn't driven from the island altogether."

He pulled a large, spotted, handkerchief from the pocket of his coat and wiped his eyes and blew his nose.

"I took it as a sign from God," he said. "That to acknowledge the creatures was a terrible mistake, a grave misjudgment and a lack of faith on my own part. As far as the church is concerned, none of this exists." He waved his hands to encompass the tavern and myself. "The only intervention I'm allowed is that of forgiveness and reform. And so from that day, I vowed to follow that path."

"Bollocks. Utter, bloody, bollocks," I said in disgust.

The reaction on his face wasn't what I expected. Instead of shock at my language, there was a sense of profound sadness and defeat. He suddenly looked his age. There were deep lines etched on his narrow face and dark circles under his eyes. His thin shoulders were slumped, and he seemed to have shrunk inside his clothing. I could almost feel sorry for him. But then I thought of Hetty and the way she'd been wandering around for the past few weeks like she'd seen a ghost. Every care and kindness that she was tasked with offering me was a brutal reminder of what she'd lost; what had been taken from her.

I reached across the table and picked up the teapot. It was still half full and warm.

"More tea, Father?" I asked. He looked surprised at the question.

"Oh, no," I said, pouring him a fresh cup and stirring in a dollop of milk. "You're not getting away with any of this. You've a debt to pay and you're going to have to sort out exactly how you're going to do it."

***

"Did you know my mother?" I asked, wrapping my hands around my mug.

Father Ewan nodded.

"She was a lovely woman, Aibhlinn. To that, I can surely attest. She showed me great kindness always, even though she didn't follow the teachings of the church. I would often see her, walking up on the cliffs. I like to walk there myself, it's a marvelous place for reflection up there, on the edge of the earth. Sometimes we'd walk together and discuss the finer points of poetry and the weather."

"Poetry?" I said, surprised.

"Oh yes. Your mother loved music and poetry - her kind always do. I would recite the psalms to her - they're a form of poetry, after all. And she would sing the most haunting songs. I never understood the words, but they were simply magnificent."

He smiled at the recollection, his face transformed from tired, old, man to that of a younger one. He saw me watching him.

"Ah, we were all a little in love with Anwen, lass. Even a chaste old priest such as myself. She just had that effect on folk. Everyone loved her."

"You said, 'her kind'. What does that mean?"

His face reddened and he shifted uncomfortably in his chair.

"Well, I-I-I don't mean any disrespect, of course. But it was fairly common knowledge, and she would never confirm nor deny it."

"What? That she was a selkie, you mean? I thought that sort of thing didn't exist, Father. Were you trying to reform her existence when you were chatting about poetry and music and the like?"

"You misunderstand me, child," he said, clearly flustered.

"No, I don't think I do. I think it's quite obvious that you are both a coward and a hypocrite," I fumed, slamming my mug down on the table and making him jump.

"You'll happily mingle with the sea-devils, as you call them, when they're beautiful and singing pretty songs, but you won't face the obvious when it's sitting right in front of you." I placed my hands on my swollen belly and leaned forwards.

"This is her grand-bairn," I said, furious and desperate and seeing my only chance slipping away with his helpless surrender. "Don't you see that? Does that even make a difference to any of you? That these are children and grand-children and great-grandchildren of the women of this island, as much as they are of the sea-folk. Do any of you even consider that?"

Father Ewan sighed, a heavy, world-weary sigh.

"It doesn't matter, my child. It never has, and it never will."

I stood up from my chair, hands still encircling my belly.

"That, Father Ewan," I said, my voice steady and my head held high. "Is where you're so very wrong."

Chapter 30

I didn't cry until after he'd gone. I couldn't bear to let him see how much I'd been undone by our conversation. The hardest part was hearing how he'd known and loved my mother and yet couldn't see the connection between her and my unborn child. How none of them could see it. That had been my final hope. Of course, no-one would be predisposed to help *me* — I'd made sure of that with my contrariness and determined otherness - but surely, they could see that this concerned more than just me? How could they not see that they were overlooking the sacrifices of generations of women from the island?

The words of the strange woman, and of Fingal, crept in to niggle at the back of my mind. "Remember what you are." Not *who* I am, but what. For once, I wished I were a simpler creature - one for whom the answers would be quite clear. Instead, I'd managed to create a wretched tangle of things.

Oh, how I longed for someone to talk to that would understand! Hetty was that person once, until I went away. Now she was distant, almost afraid, and I'm sure it's my own presence that conjures the ghosts that haunt her. I can't possibly expect her to help. Callum is gone from me, too caught up in his own guilt and shame it seems – but he would at least have listened, if not understood. And while I appreciate the company of Morag – to a point – I can't help but feel that she, too, still considers me at arm's length.

I sighed and walked to the dresser to splash some cold water on my face. I had to pull myself together. Hetty had said a faery-child arrives sooner than a human one, so I hadn't time to waste. I patted my face dry and dragged a brush through the tangle of my hair. It was even thicker and more wildly curled since I fell pregnant. I closed my eyes as I brushed, imagining the time, not so long ago, when my beloved Fingal would brush it for me. An old rhyme from my childhood came to mind, one that Callum and I used to recite together as we tramped over the moors. He told me that our mother had taught it to him when he was small.

To the hollows, the hollows, the hollows I'll go,
Over the hills where the north winds blow;
Follow the raven, follow the crow,
To find my beloved in hollows below.

The memory of it made me feel weepy again. It seemed like such an eternity ago – Callum and I, out roaming the moors, for hours on end. To excuse my absence from the house, he would tell Da that I was helping him find lost sheep. As long as we came home with some blackberries or wild mushrooms for the tea, the outings went unpunished. I hadn't realized until now how much Callum had shielded me from our da's temper and cruelty. It got easier as I got older - I had a temper to match Da's and then, when he started to spend more time in the tavern than on the fishing boat, it got easier again, simply because he wasn't around as much.

I shook my head. It wasn't going to do anyone any good to wallow in the past. I decided right then that I needed to get out of my little room. With or without Morag. It suddenly chafed me to think I needed a constant chaperone. If none of these people were going to help me, then why should I submit to the pretense of co-operation?

Feeling better for having made the decision, I pulled on my thick stockings and took up my heavy, woolen jumper that had once belonged to Callum. I breathed in the smell of it - it was infused with the scent of lanolin and pipe tobacco. If Callum wouldn't come to me, then I needed to go to Callum.

I stood at the door to my little room - it had been both prison and sanctuary. I'd known great comfort and great despair, all at once, within its walls. I knew then, with a firm certainty, that I wouldn't be coming back. I crossed back over the creaky wooden floor to my work basket. Digging through it, I pulled out the length of cloth - faery-cloth, even Father Ewan had recognized it - and lay it on the quilted bedspread. I took the remains of my breakfast - half a loaf of Hetty's bread, a wedge of hard cheese and some dried blackberries - and wrapped it in one of my spare aprons. This, I put on the faery-cloth, along with another pair of stockings and the shawl that Hetty had given me on the eve of my betrothal. I rolled it all together and tied it into a bundle with a length of darning yarn from my basket. A tiny pair of scissors that had belonged to my mother, I slipped into the pocket of my overcoat - another cast-off, this time from Alexander and, on strange impulse, I grabbed one each of the socks I'd been darning from my basket; one belonging to Duncan and one belonging to my da. I hesitated at that, but then reasoned if I were to be throwing myself at the mercy of the impulse, I might as well be thorough. Besides, who else but my da could claim first responsibility for the situation in which I found myself? Now I had something from everyone; I thought of them as ingredients of a charm intended to strengthen and shelter me.

Standing there, with my pitiful bundle in my hands and nothing more than a niggling thought to guide me, I suddenly wondered if it wouldn't just be so much easier to stay. I could ignore the signs that told me differently, I could simply do what was expected of me and think no further of what had befallen me these past months. I could just surrender all of this struggle and, in time, there might even be a husband - possibly a tolerable one - and other children, surely; I could live a simple, predictable, life on my beloved island with the few people I loved best. No-one could fault me for that. I might even make more friends among the womenfolk.

But then I thought of Hetty, and her haunted eyes and of Morag, forced to live someone elses idea of her life; I thought of all of the women, generations of them, who'd borne the title of sea bride and paid the price in loss and heartbreak. I thought of how even what they'd done - what they'd given of themselves for the safety and prosperity of their kin, the memory of the wonder that it was - even that had been taken from them. Memories wiped clean lest they yearn for a return to a time and place that honoured them and their contribution. This wasn't just about me, after all.

Then I felt the ripple, the undulating movement of the life growing within me. This child, this unborn daughter of land and sea, a child of neither world and both worlds; she then, if nothing else, would be the reason for whatever came next.

Seizing a courage that wasn't mine alone, I opened the door of my little room and walked out.

Chapter 31

There was an old bothy, high up on the moors, that Callum and I used to visit on our ramblings when I was still very little. We'd often sheltered there during the sudden downpours that would sweep rapidly over the braes from the nearby sea. Eventually Callum claimed it for his own, saying it was sometimes easier to spend the night on the moor, caring for his sheep, than it was to come home. Of course, I know it was more than that - because that's what my own wee croft represents - it was escape and freedom. As the years went on, he took to spending more and more time there, leaving me to cope with da on my own. I couldn't blame him though. Wasn't I, too, plotting such an escape? I stifled a sigh, thinking of my poor, neglected cottage. Still, if all went according to plan, I'd be there sooner than not.

Anyway, it was to Callum's place that I set off from the tavern. By some miracle, no-one saw me leave. John would have been out on the boat, but I've no idea where Hetty could've been. I had a story prepared anyway, just in case, but I saw neither her nor Morag when I crept down the back stairs and left by the door leading off the kitchen. I murmured a quiet thank you to whatever unseen forces may have orchestrated their absence.

The wind was gusting and sharp. The softer, welcome, breezes of summer had been replaced by their pricklier cousins of autumn. I pulled the collar of my coat more tightly to my neck and walked as quickly as I could, up the hill towards the bothy. I wanted to put as much distance as possible between myself and the tavern, not trusting my absence to go unnoticed for too long.

It felt enormously good to be outside. The wind, biting though it was, had its usual effect of clearing my head and my heart. I took great, deep, breaths, rejoicing in the sting of it on my nose and the tips of my ears. I fancied the baby could feel the benefit of the wind through me, I patted my stomach gently, delighting at the answering ripple.

Despite my bulk, I still made good time. The sun sets quickly at this time of year and already, early in the afternoon though it was, the shadows had begun to lengthen. I spied no-one as I walked, which had been my other concern. Most of the sheep had been brought down from the high ground by now, but it wouldn't have been unusual to see a shepherd up on the hills, looking for a straying ewe or doing repairs to the walls of pens. All I could think of was reaching the bothy before dark, hopefully with enough daylight spare to build myself a small fire and settle in to wait for Callum.

At last, I reached the crest of the hill and there, in the small hollow created by the undulating landscape was the tiny, stone, building. I wasn't entirely surprised to see a thread of smoke curling from the chimney, having caught the scent of it on the wind. I had thought I'd be the one waiting, but it looked as if someone was already there. I murmured another prayer, this time that it be the person I hoped and not someone who would march me back down the hill to the tavern.

I slipped and slid down the hill, keeping my bundle tucked tightly under my arm, until I reached the door of the little dwelling. It was more sturdily built than some, with thick stone walls and small windows. The door was a crooked and weathered contraption of driftwood and oiled canvas but gave the bothy the look of a home. If only for a night or two at a time. As a child, I'd often daydreamed of running away and living up there, all by myself - well, Callum could visit whenever he wanted, and Hetty. I would've been quite content with only the company of badgers and foxes and the occasional wandering sheep. Obviously that daydream had taken root, although with the hope of something slightly more well-appointed than this little place.

The tiny slits of windows glowed with a yellow-orange light, evidence of a warm fire and lamplight. I took a steadying breath and pushed open the door.

I stood blinking in the light, at the figure seated by the fire.

"Oh," I said, stupidly. "It's you."

Chapter 32

Her golden hair was more grey than gold now, and her face more deeply lined. Funny, that she could appear, outwardly, so different and yet I knew, instinctively, that she was the same person. Although, thinking on it, she wasn't likely a person at all.

She grinned at the expression of dumb surprise on my face, her eyes, as sharp and blue as ever, crinkled into slits. Her teeth, white and straight, were clamped onto the stem of her ever-present clay pipe. The smoke from that mingled with the tangy scent of the peat fire, creating a lovely, earthy, smell that took me back to the underwater cave where Fingal had first taken me.

"Who were ye expecting, then?" she asked, gesturing towards the chair opposite hers. "Take a load off yer weary pins, lassie. Am I a great disappointment?"

"What? Er - no, not as such," I said. "I was hoping my

brother would be here, that's all. Not that I'm sorry that you are instead. Only, I'd really hoped..." my voice trailed off. I was more tired than I'd thought and even though the chair was wooden and not terribly comfortable, it may as well have been a feather bed for the welcome it was.

The woman nodded.

"Aye, 'tisn't far off yer time, I warrant." She tilted her head and studied my face. "How're ye keeping, then, lass?"

"Oh, fine," I lied, not wanting to fall into my recent pattern of self-pity. It really was a sore disappointment that Callum wasn't here. I was so sure...

"Och, lass. He's here, alright. Just off over the moor for a bit. He'll be back. I thought I'd just keep his seat warm while he was gone, aye?"

Relief washed over me like a warm draft of air. It must have showed on my face because the woman chuckled, a deep, rumbling sound like stones tumbling over hard ground.

"You helped us," I said, suddenly remembering. "You helped Fingal come to me, in the little hollow near the cliff edge."

"I did, aye," she said, puffing furiously on her pipe. It appeared to have gone out. She took it from her mouth and leaned over towards the fire. She reached her hand in and plucked out a spark, transferring it to the bowl of her pipe.

My mouth hung open in shock. Her hand remained unscathed.

"You just put your hand in the fire," I said.

She laughed again.

"Ye're ever one to be pointing out the obvious, eh?"

I blushed, realizing how very gormless I must seem.

"You must think me quite stupid," I said.

She grunted.

"No more than most of yer kind, and far less than many," she replied.

"Am I meant to take heart from that, or feel worse than I already do?"

The woman laughed, loudly this time, her laugh reverberating around the tiny cottage until I was sure that everyone on Glencarragh could hear her. Tears streamed down her lined face, and she slapped her knee with apparent delight at what I'd said.

"Oh, lass," she said, after her laughter died down. She wiped the tears from her face with the back of her thin hand. "Ye're a right tonic, that's to be sure. A right tonic."

"I'm happy to oblige," I said, primly. I didn't much enjoy bearing the brunt of her odd humor.

"Och, dinna take on so," she said, reaching over to pat my knee. "Let a body enjoy herself. It's not often I have the pleasure of sharing a laugh."

Suddenly, all laughter was gone from her yes and she drew back in her chair, appearing to become larger, darker.

"Tis a small price to pay for the life of yer bairn, is it not?"

Her tone had shifted like a winter wind.

I, too, shrank back, to make myself smaller in the face of her sudden change.

"What do you mean?" I said, my voice barely above a whisper.

"Only this," she said, her own voice strong and sure. "By the ties that bind and the bargains that seal the fates of foolish men, aid is not allowed ye. Ye willnae see me again, lass, this side of the veil, and I can leave ye with only this. The life of the child and all that follow her lies in what happens next."

She stood up from her chair, rising so tall as to surely go through the low roof of the bothy. But up she went, taller and taller until she was as high as the hill on the opposite side of the hollow. The walls of the cottage had fallen away, and we were both standing, buffeted by wind and rain. She carried her basket over one arm and held a long, wooden staff in the other. Twice, she banged the end into the heather and twice the wind surged, sharper and crueler than before. When she spoke, her voice carried out over the darkening moor,

"Let no man, mortal or faery, come between ye.
  Ask not for help from without, for the answer lies only within.
  Take what is given and give back what you possess."

The wind roared in my ears, stirring up my coat and my skirts, sending my hair in a wild dance around my head, obscuring my vision. I staggered slightly with the force of it.

Go then, lass. Do what need be done. They'll not find ye this night but as the sun rises, so does the danger. I give ye every blessing as is mine to give. Her voice echoed inside my head as the wind suddenly dropped.

I took a backward step and fell, once more, into the chair by the fire.

* * *

I was still sitting in the chair, slightly dazed by what had just happened, when the door flung open, and Callum burst in.

"Aibhlinn!"

"Callum!"

We met in the middle of the room. I flung my arms around him, and he lifted me clumsily into the air and swung me around. The embrace was slightly hindered by my protruding belly which made us both laugh like children.

"Look at ye!" he said, his face alight with joy. "Blessed Danu but ye look fit to pop!"

I grinned foolishly.

"I know, aren't I just a great bloated thing? I feel like I haven't seen my feet for months."

His face suddenly clouded, and he held me at arm's length.

"But are ye alright, lass? Hetty said ye'd taken poorly and couldn't have any visitors. I tried to come and see ye but they wouldn't let me in. I've been out of my mind wi' worry. All I could think about was our mam..."

"They said what?"

I kept my voice and my expression calm, but inside I was in a turmoil. A sickening wave of disappointment swept over me, leaving me feeling nauseous. I could've wept with rage and frustration. They'd lied to me! They said Callum hadn't bothered to come to see me. He must not have got the message I sent by the shepherd's lad. And Hetty, how could she? I realized how I must have underestimated the strain she'd been under.

"Here, sit yerself down. I'll put some water on to boil. I've a bit of a stew I was planning to heat up for tea, there's plenty for both of us."

He bustled around the tiny room, displaying a comforting degree of bumbling domesticity that made me slightly wistful for my old home.

"Callum, what did they tell you? I haven't been poorly at all. They bloody well kidnapped me, right from our own garden and I've been kept under lock and key this past month."

The spoon with which he was stirring the stew fell with a clatter into the iron pot. He whirled around, his face like thunder.

"They did what?" His face had turned an alarming shade of red.

"It was the women - Isabelle Dunn and her cronies. They set upon me while I was hanging out the washing. I imagine I was supposed to go quietly, but when I didn't, one of the men came up behind me, shoved a rag soaked in chloroform over my face and they bundled me off to Hetty's."

He sat down in the chair with a thud, leaning over and putting his face in his hands.

"Hetty?' he said, hoarsely. "Hetty was in on this?"

"Don't blame her, Callum. I can't bear any ill-feeling. She isn't herself at all. It was Isabelle who organized the whole thing. Everyone's afraid of her so poor Hetty didn't stand a chance. She's looked after me, anyway. Made me as comfortable as I could be, considering I was basically a prisoner."

He shook his head in disbelief.

"Oh, and Morag, if you can believe that! She's been keeping me company, taking me out for walks along the cliff path."

"Not Morag," he said. "Couldn't be. It were Morag as kept turning me away."

I felt the blood drain from my face. How could it be? I thought Morag was on my side. My hand flew to my mouth, and I felt the prickle of panic creeping over my scalp. What had I told her? Did I give away anything important? My fear turned to anger in a flash. I was furious - with myself for being taken in, and with Morag for pretending to be my ally.

"I trusted her," I fumed. I made a fist and smacked it down on the arm of the chair. "I can't believe I fell for it. She seemed so genuine..."

Callum sighed heavily.

"It may be that she was," he said. "That poor lass is as much a puppet to that harpy of a mother as the rest o' the women. Mebbe even more so."

"Hmmm, perhaps," I said, because it was certainly true that her mother ruled her. "Still, it's a horrible, sickening, disappointment."

I didn't want to show him how *much* of a disappointment it was to think that Morag had betrayed me. Despite her suffocating presence at times, I had become quite used to having a friend. But I couldn't allow myself to be sidetracked by such things. I had to think only of the road ahead. I was on my own again, but it wasn't as if it *that* was a new sensation.

"Never mind all that, anyway," he said, getting up and resuming his stirring of the stew. "Ye're here now and that's all that matters, aye? I'll have a word with that lot tomorrow about how they've treated ye. Why on earth would they want to keep ye locked up like that anyhow? And why'd they let ye go?"

"Oh, Callum," I smiled at the broad back of my favourite brother. "You've missed a lot since you've been hiding out here with your sheep."

He grinned back.

"I weren't hiding, as such," he protested. "Just staying out of the road of all those mad women." His face grew somber again. "And I couldn't bear to think of ye not well. I came up here because it's our place, aye? I felt like I could be closer to ye…" He flapped a hand. "Never mind, it's all a bit o' foolish nonsense, really. Just me old imagination running off wi' me. Too much in the company o' the woolly ones and not enough o' people. Makes a body a mite batty after a bit."

I chuckled, getting up to take the spoon from his hands. I lay my head on his shoulder, leaning slightly against his familiar warmth.

"I know what you mean, Callum. You don't need to explain. It's why I came here first. I had a feeling…a hope, really, that I'd find you here." I scooped up a bit of the stew and brought it to my lips to taste. It was a bit sparse and salty but would be a welcome meal. "I think it's warmed through enough. Will you make the tea and I'll dish this up? We can have a grand feast while I fill you in on what's been happening since you wandered off and left me with those lunatics."

I laughed at the look of horror on his face.

"I'm just having you on. Go on with you!"

He gave a nervous laugh.

"I've only got the one bowl," he said, sheepishly. "I can eat mine out o' the pot."

"Quite alright," I said, suddenly overcome with a sense of relief at being here, with him, safe and warm and on my way.

"I'd imagined I might be sleeping under a bush tonight, so a lovely bowl of stew and a warm fire is as close to heaven as I could ever imagine being."

Chapter 33

We sat in silence after we'd eaten. The wind had picked up again and was lashing rain against the small windows. A draught seeped in through the cracks between the door and the floor, sending the candle flame skittering and dancing.

I'd told Callum everything. I didn't think there was any point in holding any of it back. I told him about Fingal and how I loved him and how, despite the faery charm set against it, I remembered everything.

"I don't know why," I said. "Maybe it's because there's true love between us. Maybe it's because I was so determined to hold on. Anyway, it doesn't matter. All that matters is that I do remember and because of that, I'm determined to save this child."

Callum stared into the flames. He'd stretched his long legs out towards the fire, his stocking feet only inches from the hearth.

No wonder I was always having to darn his socks, I thought, fondly. The holes must start as singes from the fire. I suddenly wished that he and Fingal could meet. I felt sure they would become fast friends.

"It's the pendant," he said, suddenly breaking his silence. He looked up at me, his eyes bright. "The pendant our mam left for ye. She must've known somehow..."

I blinked in surprise, reaching up to touch the charm beneath the material of my dress. The strange, twisted shape settled perfectly into the hollow between my breasts.

"But how can that be?" I asked, although I thought perhaps, I knew the answer.

"Faery-begot," he said, softly. "That's what folk have always said of ye. And even though they'd say it like a curse or a slight, I've always taught ye that it were a thing to be proud of, haven't I?"

"Of course you have, Callum. And of course, I've always been proud of it. Haven't I always thrown it back in their faces?" I grinned, trying to pierce the sudden seriousness.

He smiled a rueful smile.

"Aye, and haven't ye always got yerself in more trouble than ye ought by being as contrary?"

I shrugged.

"I suppose there's a bit of Da in me as well,"

He nodded.

"'Tis a fearsome combination, isn't it?"

"But how could our mam ever know I'd become a sea bride?" I asked, wanting to steer him back to the matter at hand. If the pendant really did hold some selkie magic, then it might aid me in my quest.

Callum shook his head.

"I don't know, lass. She knew all sorts o' things she ought not to have knowledge of. Folk always said she had the Sight. Or the devil, depending on who ye asked."

I smiled, thinking of Isabelle Dunn.

"She was that desperate for ye. She walked the cliff path for weeks, calling out to the sea in the way that she did. I told ye, I were convinced she sang ye into being." He laughed softly. "Och, but I were just a silly wee laddie at the time. I thought she was the most beautiful creature in the whole world." He sighed and lapsed into silence again, occupied, I imagine, with thoughts of our mam.

My mind was turning over and over. If it were true, and it had been implied to me often enough even though I only dared half-believe it, that our mam really was a selkie-woman, then it was almost certain that it was faery-magic that made the pendant that hung around my neck. But how much power did it have? Was it just a gift of memory? That was gift enough, to be sure. But what if it had other power? What if it's true power was as a shield from other faery charms? The sea bride's dress, after all, held such power.

"Do you think the pendant carries a charm against faery magic?" I asked, jolting Callum from his reverie.

He shook his head vehemently.

"Now don't ye go expecting it to be something it isn't," he said. "Ye cannae predict these things and it's far too dangerous a thing to be playing about with."

He narrowed his eyes.

"Why do ye ask?" he said, suspiciously. "What're ye up to now?"

And so I told him.

* * *

The expression on Callum's face was almost enough to make me change my mind.

"But why don't ye just stay here?" he said, pleading with his eyes. He'd put down his mug of tea and reached across to grab my hands, as if by holding them, he'd keep me there.

I shook my head.

"I can't, Callum. Don't you see? This will be the first place that they look for me. The old woman said they'd not find me tonight — I imagine she's put a shield or something on the bothy. But whatever enchantment she puts on it, it'll be gone shortly after dawn."

"This is madness," he said. "Utter bloody madness. All this talk of enchantments and strange old women. How did things get into such a mess? I cannae believe the way folk are carrying on. It's like they've lost all sense of themselves."

He scrubbed a hand across his face and through his hair, making it stand on end.

"Are ye sure Hetty willnae help ye? I cannae fathom the way she's letting that poxy cow Isabelle Dunn take over things. She's always the one to stand up to the likes o' that lot."

"I told you, she's not herself just now. It's the bairn, the one she lost."

"Aye, but ye'd think that'd make her want to help, wouldn't it?"

I sat and thought about that for a moment, letting the dancing flames of the fire mesmerize me. Oh, how simple it would be to just wait here and let them find me. I felt suddenly very weary. All of the planning and intrigue and all I really wanted to do was lie down and sleep for days.

But that wasn't the path before me. I'd made my choice and now I had to follow through.

I sighed heavily.

"Maybe so, but I can't depend upon it. I know where I need to go — I remember how to get there, but I'll need someone when my time comes."

"What?" He paled visibly and his mouth hung open. "Oh no, dinna ask me that, lass. Birthing bairns is women's work. Ye cannae expect me to take part in any o' that business. Absolutely not, I'm sorry to say." He shook his head firmly back and forth.

I'd expected as much, but I had to ask. At the very least, I had to tell him where I was going. The old woman said I wasn't allowed aid, but I couldn't believe that meant I had to be alone during childbirth. Surely, I'd be given some help then.

"Can I at least tell you where I'm going?" I asked. "Maybe you can convince Hetty to come at some point, but I'd feel better knowing someone knew where I was."

"Aye, go on."

I explained, as best I could, about the cluster of boulders down at the beach. I wasn't even sure where to go once I got there, but I was relying on faith and the rightness of what I was doing to guide me. As long as Callum knew the starting point, I imagined I could do the rest myself.

"But it's nowt but a pile of crag, lass. Surely that's not enough of a shelter for ye when ye're on your time. Think of the wee bairn," he objected. "Please let me try an' talk to the folk. Ye can stay here while I go down into the village, they willnae bother ye, I'm sure of it."

I shook my head.

"No, Callum. I have to insist you don't try that. If they find out where I am they'll just come and get me, and I won't let them anywhere near this child. Don't you see? They've got it all wrong. They think that the sea-folk have some sort of sway over what happens here on the land — that they can control how well our sheep fare or even how well the fishing goes."

"Well, they do have a bit o' say, if you think on it, lass. Aren't we saved the awful times when the water horses would come ashore and hunt? Would ye want to go back to those days?"

"What's worse, Callum?" My voice had become shrill again. I forced myself to take a deep breath. Long hours on my own in the little room had afforded me plenty of time to consider the whole premise of this so-called bargain.

"The custom of the sea-bride is one thing, the giving over of children is entirely another," I said, trying to stop the note of hysteria creeping in whenever I mentioned the children. Those nameless, faceless infants of years gone by had suddenly, with the presence of my own unborn baby, become just as important to me.

"If anything, the children of the sea-bride should be cherished and celebrated, here, on land. They represent the best of all the worlds, do you see? That awful Lira with her hateful vendetta, stealing what we should think of as our most precious commodity, under the pretense of protecting something that's none of their domain anyway. Surely our children are worth a few sheep?"

"Bloody hell, Aibhlinn. That's a right terrible way to put things. Surely ye cannae think it's a choice between the bairns and some sheep?" Callum was incredulous.

"Isn't it, though?" I asked, determined to make him see what was right in front of him. Too much, I thought, folk had just carried on with this without ever questioning it. Father Ewan had said as much — folk just accept things assuming that it's the way it has to be. If I could convince them there was another way, perhaps this would end for good.

"How do you suppose the sea-folk, the water horses, have any influence over how many lambs our ewes have, or how much cod there is in the sea?"

"'Tisn't that, Aibhlinn, and you know it. It's about the hunting grounds and protecting ourselves from them, protecting the children. How d'ye fancy it if there were bloody water horses coming ashore and rampaging about, snatching anything warm-blooded..."

"Did you just say 'protecting the children'?" I asked, smelling victory.

Callum's mouth snapped shut. He frowned then leaned over to prod the fire. Sparks flew up the small, stone chimney and the wind whistled down from above.

"I suppose there's a point there, lass. But still, there's more to it, I'm sure. It's not so simple, it cannae be."

"Oh? And why not? Could you not entertain the idea that this has all been an elaborate bit of trickery on the sea-folk's part? And maybe there's some ill-doing among us mortals as well. We can't know what happened all those years ago, we've just been going along with the old stories. Think about it, Callum. No-one has ever questioned or challenged them, not ever. We've just carried on. Whatever the original bargain was, it's been twisted into something else entirely and we've just gone along with it all these years."

My brother remained silent. He was the thinking one, the

one who questioned things. If anyone was to reconsider what had been held as truth, it was him.

"How can ye be sure o' this, Aibhlinn, pet?" he said, finally. "What if ye're wrong?"

"I'm not wrong, Callum. And I'm sure enough to pledge the life of my child on it."

He sighed again.

"What d'ye need me to do? Besides catching the bairn," he added, hastily. "I cannae help ye wi' that business."

I grinned, my eyes filling with happy tears.

"You don't have to do anything, Callum. All I needed you to do was believe me."

* * *

Callum woke me just before dawn. It was so quiet up there, the hollow in which the bothy stood muffled much of the sound of the nearby sea. Only the lone cry of a curlew and the distant bleating of a sheep could be heard. A weak light was just creeping in around the edges of the curtains and Callum handed me a steaming mug of tea.

"Ye'll have some provisions then?" he asked, fussing about, prodding the fire and tidying away the previous evening's dishes.

"A few," I said. "I won't need much, I don't think. I just have a feeling — or maybe it's a blind hope, that everything I'll need will turn up when I need it."

"That's a helluva leap o'faith, lass," he said, his face creased in a worried frown. "Are ye quite sure? I don't mind telling ye that I think this is madness, utter madness."

I smile, a rueful smile, because part of me agreed with him.

"No more so than what I'm trying to change by doing it."

He nodded, his lips pressed tightly together.

"Right then," he cleared his throat and looked out of the window. "The sun's almost up," he said. "Yer one said the enchantment would lift at dawn, didn't she? I dinna expect folk to have been out looking for ye in the night anyway, but it willnae take them long to get up here once there's daylight. Hetty knows I'm up here, along wi' a few o' the other men."

I nodded, swallowing down the last of my tea. I didn't have anything to pack, my bundle had remained where I'd left it when I arrived the previous night. I stood and picked up my overcoat from where it was draped over the chair.

"Here," said Callum. "I know ye didn't want to take anything more, but I've a bit o' Hetty's bannock left and a packet of tea. I don't know about ye, but if I've a cup o' hot tea at the end of a long day, I'm all the better for it."

I smiled, willing the tears not to fall. I couldn't let him see that I was frightened out of my wits. I wanted his mind to be easy when I left him.

"Right you are," I said. "I'll raise a mug to you once I'm settled in, shall I?"

"Come here, lass." Callum enveloped me in his strong arms, and I breathed in his familiar warmth and strength, taking a deep breath of him to sustain me for the journey ahead. I held him as closely as my bump would allow and promised myself that I'd be strong enough to be worthy of his faith in me.

"Thank you," I said, my voice muffled in the scratchy wool

of his jumper. "For believing me and for not trying to talk me out of it."

He nodded, allowing me to step back.

"Go on wi' ye," he said, his voice hoarse with emotion. "Get yerself away. I'll hold them here as long as I can."

I took one last look around the tiny cottage, arming myself with the vision of its simple comfort and what it represented - home and family. This is what I was fighting for; this and my right to define it and live it the way I saw fit.

"I'll see you, then," I said, giving Callum my best and most cheerful smile. "Don't worry about us," I added. "We've got love on our side, after all."

I walked out the door and didn't look back.

Chapter 34

The only drawback of having climbed the hills to the bothy, was that they now stood between me and the path that would take me down to the sea. Not to mention the fact I'd be likely to meet anyone who was coming to look for me on the way. That meant I had to travel over the moor, rather than by the well-trodden footpaths that criss-crossed the hills.

The footing was uneven and tricky - hummocks of grass and heather tripped me up and snarls of low-growing thorns snatched at my skirts as I blundered along, trying to walk quickly and carefully at the same time. An underlying feeling of panic pushed at me, hurrying me along. I clutched tightly at my bundle of supplies, fighting back tears as I stumbled over the hostile ground. I had felt so sure of myself as I left the tiny cottage, but the further away I traveled, the more exposed I felt; the chasm between safe points widened with every step I took, and I had to fight the urge to turn around and run back to my brother.

The sun was fully risen and shone in a cloudless sky. The wind bit and snapped and I wished I'd thought to wear a hat. My back ached and my feet were sore and all I could think about was how much I was up against by doing this. How could I ever have thought I could undo generations of needless sacrifice all on my own? Wasn't this just another example of the impertinence everyone saw in me?

I shook my head, trying to silence the nagging voice of doubt and instead concentrated on not getting lost. Going across the moors instead of using the footpaths was harder than I'd thought, the familiar landmarks were in unfamiliar places and so I navigated by the sound of the ocean. I forced myself to take deep, steadying breaths and started to call out to the wild things, reciting their names in my head - deer, badger, fox, crow, hare. Saying their names and remembering their shapes, settled me into a comfortable rhythm. Soon, the terrain felt less hostile, and I found myself stumbling less as I relaxed into my stride.

I was almost to the last incline - I had one more hill to crest before the land sloped down towards the cliff path. I was lightheaded with relief and beginning to think I'd make it all the way down to the water's edge without anyone seeing me. And that's when I heard it. The bark of a distant dog and an answering shout. I tried to convince myself it was just a shepherd out looking for a lost sheep but quickened my pace as best I could.

Suddenly, the enormous black outline of a raven burst from the undergrowth on my inland side, cronking loudly as it veered upwards towards the top of the hill I was climbing. I'm coming, I muttered, imagining that the raven was leading the way. The old well of panic began to rise as I heard more voices echoing across the heather. I daren't look back; if I was to see any sign of pursuit, I'm sure I would have given up there and then.

At last, I staggered to the crest of the hill. The raven circled in the sky above me and the wind, rising over the top of the brae blew my hair into streams away from my face. It was wonderfully refreshing and now that I could see the ocean on the horizon, I felt re-energized. The familiar worn track of the cliff path was visible at the end of the rolling descent. I imagined myself there and after a few more replenishing breaths, I struck off down the hill, determined not to look back, despite the frequent shouts I could hear in the distance. I prayed to whomever would listen, that Callum had managed to delay any searchers that had made their way to the bothy long enough for me to outpace them.

It was in my haste to get to the bottom of the hill that I made my first mistake. I let the promise of my destination carry me too quickly, and I snagged my toe on a particularly rough patch of sod, which sent me flying forwards. I dropped my bundle in an effort to prevent myself from falling, sticking out my hands to cushion the impact and twisting sideways to avoid falling onto my belly. Thankfully, the heather was soft from the previous night's rain, but I still landed with a thump, knocking the wind right out of myself. I lay there for a moment, mentally checking for pain or possibly injury. The raven was still soaring overhead, it banked and dived, crying out in its strange, raucous voice. Feeling myself to be unhurt, I slowly rolled onto my knees and attempted to stand. There was a stabbing pain in my right foot, the one which had caught on the hummock of grass, and I staggered slightly. A hand reached out and caught my elbow, bracing me from falling again. I shrieked and pulled back, immediately sorry as pain shot through my foot.

"You ought to be more careful," said Morag, smiling sadly. "It isn't very clever of you to be running down hills in your state."

Chapter 35

"**M**orag!" I said, my mouth suddenly very dry. I ignored the pain of my foot and allowed her to help me to stand. "What are you doing here?"

"Looking for you," she answered. "Just like the rest of them. The only difference is that I knew where you'd be going."

Her face was stark white, and her lips were trembling. Her almost colourless hair washed out her already-wan features, making the dark circles of her eyes stand out even more dramatically in her round face.

I swallowed hard.

"Please, Morag," I said, pleading, "Don't try to stop me, you have to let me keep going. I don't know why you pretended to be my friend, I don't know why you lied to Callum, but I won't hold any of it against you. None of it needs to matter, if you just let me go."

It was a strange position to be in, me pleading mercy from

Morag, who had so often been on the receiving end of my sharp tongue and ruthless humour. I regretted every single thing I'd ever said to her, knowing that if she did grant me such mercy, I hadn't earned it.

She seemed to be thinking the same thing, although there was more than that in her eyes. Regret, was it? A look of loss or despair? I couldn't place it, but knew somehow that whatever it was, it would decide my fate.

She bent down and picked up my bundle. I moved to take it from her, but she took a step back.

"You'll never get away with it," she said. "The men are already down at the beach, waiting for you. I told them that's where you'd be going," she added, tilting her head and looking at me, slyly, wondering, I suppose, how I'd react. "They plan on taking the bairn from you, as soon as it's born. They know they can't trust you to care for it for the first eight days. They said a ewe's milk is good enough for the faery-begot."

My shoulders slumped and I took a deep breath. The sound of voices carried up and over the hill.

"I suppose they're following me, too?" I asked, my mind racing. I had come so far and was so very close. No matter what happened next, I decided I wouldn't be taken easily. In a sudden, despairing and dramatic thought, I resolved to die rather than let them take me back to the tavern. I don't know that I'd've acted on it, but it was enough to fuel my rebellion once more.

She nodded.

"They went to the bothy first. I imagine you had Callum ready to put them off with some story or other?"

I narrowed my eyes.

"Why, Morag? Answer me that at least. Why befriend and

then betray me? Was it revenge? I've not been kind to you over the years, I know that. I don't suppose it matters now, but I truly regret the way I treated you. I've been vain and selfish and quite stupid, really. I don't blame you at all for turning on me."

I was stalling for time. A new plan was bound to come to me. At least, that's what I hoped. I briefly entertained the idea of trying to overpower her - to push her down and just run for it. I abandoned that idea almost immediately. She was far bigger than I, even in my heavily pregnant state, and that state considered, I wasn't really in the best shape for a downhill sprint.

Her face registered surprise, then clouded over.

"I didn't plan it like this, I really didn't," she said, defiance in her tone. She crossed her arms over her ample chest, tucking my bundle under her own arm. "I didn't want..." Her voice trailed off and she shifted her gaze from mine, avoiding my eyes.

Suddenly, I understood.

"It was your mother all along, wasn't it?" I said, everything suddenly making sense. "She put you up to it, didn't she? Everything - the pretending to be my friend, pretending to be on my side, all the while you were just her puppet. Just like always, eh, Morag? Doesn't that ever get tiring? Not being allowed to have any thoughts or opinions of your own?"

I was gambling heavily. I had an inkling that somewhere in the midst of all her troubled emotions and torn loyalties - because I really believed that she felt some pity for me - that what Morag really wanted was to defy her mother.

She scowled, her face flushing, reddening her pasty skin to the roots of her colourless hair.

"I have my own opinions," she spat. "Plenty of them."

"I know," I replied, inching towards her, wincing at the pain in my foot. "We had some good conversations, you and I, didn't we? I really thought you were quite clever, cleverer than I'd ever imagined. You always seemed such a dunce, but then I realized that was just a show you put on for your mother. So that she wouldn't know what you were really thinking."

I shrugged.

"I suppose I was mistaken. It was all just an elaborate hoax to fool me into trusting you."

"It wasn't!" Her voice rose to a shout, her eyes suddenly wild. "It wasn't a show. That's really who I am!"

She was breathing heavily. I could see that she was struggling. If I could just tip her over the edge of herself, back to the person I thought I'd come to know.

"Then why do you let her do it?" I asked, softly. I looked up and saw my raven perched on the tangled branches of a stand of hawthorn. It cocked its head to one side, then hopped to a higher branch. *I'm working on it*, I said to it, silently.

Work faster, said a voice inside my head.

My eyes widened and I stifled a gasp. Even so, Morag eyed me curiously. I shook my head, glancing quickly in the direction of the bird who began to studiously preen its wing feathers. Acting for all the world like any other raven.

I turned back to Morag.

"Why do you let her control you?" I asked again. "Surely you don't want to live like this forever. Constantly under her thumb, at her beck and call?"

"What choice do I have?" she retorted. Her eyes filled with tears, and she bit her lower lip. "It's not as if I've some handsome faery-man come to spirit me away," she said, attempting a smile. "No man is ever going to offer for me. I've no choice but to do as my mother says. It's just the way it is in our house. If you want a bit of peace, anyway."

My heart broke for her. Here was a girl with a good heart and a quick mind. Her only fault was having a mother with a stronger will than her own and who'd taught her to believe that she wasn't worthy of love and attention on her own merit.

"Oh, Morag!" I cried. "Surely you can't believe that's the only way!"

The voices over the heather were getting louder.

Impulsively, I reached out and grabbed her hand.

"Come with me!" I said, my eyes shining. This could be the perfect answer! "You don't have to stay here, there's no reason to."

She shook her head, withdrawing her hand from mine.

"I can't, Aibhlinn. I'm not like you, don't you see? I'm just good old, wishy-washy, weakling Morag."

I winced, recognizing some of the awful things I'd said to her over the years.

"That's not true, Morag. Please don't believe that. There's always another choice, you just have to do the choosing."

"That's not for me," she whispered.

"Of course it is," I said, losing patience. I was running out of time and her inclination for feebleness was as exasperating as ever.

"Do you know why I've been so horrible to you over the years?" I asked.

Her eyes widened. "Because you're horrible?" she answered, with a trace of the quick-witted girl I'd come to know over my weeks of imprisonment in the tavern.

I laughed, encouraged to see her spark.

"Well, yes. I am, that's true. But mostly because you frustrated me. I just knew there was more behind that cringing demeanour. The fact that you allowed your mother to run rough-shod over you and squash your spirit was beyond my understanding. You exasperated me and so I wanted to bully you out of it!"

"Didn't work, though, did it?" she replied, a thin smile creasing her plump and waxen face. She waved behind me. I turned to see Isabelle Dunn leading a group of men and women over the crest of the hill.

My heart thudded in my chest. A prickle of fear crept up my scalp. I placed my hands on my belly, trying to draw strength from the child within.

You'd best get a move on.

That voice again! I looked around to see the raven staring at me from the hawthorn. *No time left for bargaining lass, the pasty one's made her choice already.*

"I'm sorry, Morag," I said, drawing myself up as tall as my throbbing foot would allow me.

"For what?" she looked surprised, then wary.

"For not treating you more kindly, for not realizing how much you were suffering."

"Are you trying to sweet-talk me out of keeping you here?" she asked. "Because my mother...."

I placed my hand on hers again and squeezed it gently.

"I've no right to ask you anything," I said. "I only wish you could see how strong and lovely you really are."

I took a deep breath and started to walk towards her, intending, not to force myself past, but to give her the option to stand aside. My plan to get to the rocky outcrop at the beach was obviously in ruins. There was only one other option left open to me.

"Oh, bollocks!" she said, thrusting my bundle into my hands, and stepping aside.

I tried, unsuccessfully, to suppress a grin.

"I can't expect to slow them down for long," she said. "Although my mother's going to have a grand time tearing into me in front of her pet cronies, so that'll delay them a bit. You'd better bloody well get a move on."

She grasped my arm and looked fiercely into my eyes.

"Don't make me sorry I've done this," she said. "I expect to see you emerge from wherever you're disappearing to with a ten-day old baby in your arms."

I couldn't stop the grin this time, nor the tears.

"I will, Morag. I promise you that."

Chapter 36

With the water's edge and the rocky outcropping lost to me, my only other thought was to make for the little hollow in the hedge in which I'd found myself when Fingal appeared. The fact that the raven seemed to be flying in that direction rather made me hope it was the right decision.

My foot was on fire. I must have sprained my toe, but I offered up another thank you that it was at least just my toe and not something more hindering like an ankle. I ignored the pain, promising myself I'd take care of it once I had myself and my baby to a place of safety. I reasoned that I'd be able to hide within the protection of the hollow until my pursuers had given up looking for me. The realization that I may have to make my way down to the sea under the cover of dark filled me with dread, but I pushed that aside and concentrated, instead, on getting to the hollow. Tending to the immediate threat was my only concern.

The sound of voices behind me had diminished so I assumed that Morag had made good on her promise and not revealed my direction to them. With any luck, they'd carry on towards the shore and I would be left alone. I still wasn't sure where her loyalties lay – or perhaps I was – rather it was her strength in resisting Isabelle that I questioned. I knew from experience the level of cruelty that Isabelle was willing to leverage at her own daughter. While I'd always keenly felt the absence of my own mother, I simply couldn't imagine being burdened by one such as Isabelle Dunn. As wretched as my father may have been, there seemed to me a much greater potential for infinitely deeper, and more lasting, wounds, between mothers and daughters.

Huffing and puffing, I finally limped down off the hill and onto the cliff path. My heart was in my mouth, fearing that someone had been left to watch this stretch of the path. It would probably have been faster and easier to simply walk along the crest of the hill and then down towards the hollow, but I was afraid I would be far too visible a silhouette on the horizon. By going down the hill and then having to travel halfway up again, at least I was tucked into the sheltering side of the land itself. I also imagined that it was close enough to the tavern to make it seem unlikely to my pursuers that I'd be back this way. I could see the chimney smoke from the tavern, curling in the distance, and its closeness – now frighteningly obvious – was enough to trigger the barely quelled panic in my breast. Breathing deeply, I turned away from it and moved as quickly as I could off in the direction of the hedge.

Easy on, lass, said the voice in my head. *'Tis within reach now.*

I looked wildly around me, searching for the raven, but all I saw was the red brush of a fox disappearing over a clump of gorse.

I was too tired and too panicked to question it. Perhaps it was just fatigue and terror causing me to imagine I was hearing things. At least they were encouraging things, I thought to myself.

Finally, I could see the outline of the stand of hawthorn. I laughed out loud and hoisted my bundle more firmly under my arm. Even the pain of my foot seemed to ease, knowing that my destination was so close.

Suddenly, I heard a high-pitched keening off to the side of the path. I recognized the sound immediately.

Oh no, I thought, *not now. I don't have time...*

The sound came again, higher in pitch, with a panicked urgency.

Swearing softly, I dropped my bundle on the path and started parting the fronds of bracken and tangles of scrub.

Is that wise? Ought you not be more concerned with getting to your destination?

I ignored the voice, unwilling to acknowledge it was asking the very same questions I was asking myself. I followed the sound which had softened into a whimpering cry.

Just then I heard a shout.

No, I wailed internally, *it can't be!*

I spared a moment to turn around and look up. Sure enough, at the place where the hill met the cliff path, where I'd been only moments before, stood a group of people, all pointing and waving towards where I stood.

I groaned quietly, not believing it possible, as I continued casting about in the undergrowth, my movements panicked and hurried.

My hand closed over a fine wire, which I followed to the

source of the crying. A small hare trembled; her hind leg caught in the snare. On seeing me, she panicked and started thrashing.

"Hush little lady," I murmured in a sing-song voice. "I'm here to help but you have to lie still as I've not much time. I've my own wee bairn to think of."

I slipped trembling fingers between the wire and the hare's leg, willing her to be still. She flattened herself against the heather, quivering violently. Sweat beaded my upper lip as I worked the noose free, trying to ignore my inner voice that was screaming at me to run. With one swift tug, the binding came free, and the hare dashed away, none the worse for wear. I took the offending snare and unraveled it, determined that it wouldn't catch any other innocent creature unawares.

The sound of voices seemed suddenly closer, and I stood up and looked back down the path. They were halfway up the hill and gaining steadily. There was no way I could make it now.

A sharp bark sounded from further up the hill. The fox, again. It was standing on the path, watching me, its tail held low and its head high, ears pricked.

Never mind them, lassie. Look where you're going, not where you've been.

The fox turned and bounded up the hill towards the hawthorn.

That was no coincidence, surely. I couldn't have imagined it. It must be a sign!

Real or imagined, I took strength from it. Summoning the last of my reserves, I took another deep breath, bent down to retrieve my bundle and kept going - somewhere between a walk and a run, anything to put some distance between myself and the villagers.

"Aibhlinn MacFinlay!"

My father's voice was unmistakable, booming up the hillside the same way it had boomed through my entire childhood, constantly reminding me of my wrongness. "Stop where ye are, ye feckless wretch. There's nowhere for ye to run to. Ye've no choice in this. 'Tis not to be meddled wi' by the likes o' ye!"

Oh, how very wrong you are, I muttered, gritting my teeth and pushing myself to go faster. My legs were aching, and the sheer size of my belly made it difficult to get a proper lung full of air. I stumbled, pitching forwards onto my knees. My bundle fell and for a moment I truly considered giving in.

Just then, a pair of hands seized me under the arms and hauled me to my feet.

"Get off me!" I shrieked, imagining it to be one of my captors. I twisted in the strong grip, trying to turn and see who it was had managed to catch up with me. "Let me go! I won't come with you!"

"Shhhh, lass. No, don't look back," added the voice. It was a deep, sonorous voice, vaguely familiar. "Pick up your bundle and keep going. You're almost there and have every blessing to carry you. Face forwards, young one. Always forwards. I can't help you if you're looking back."

Trembling with fright and fatigue, I leaned down to pick up my bundle where it had fallen. Glancing to the side I saw a strange shadow behind me – the figure of a tall man wearing what looked like a head-dress made of deer's antlers.

"There she is!" came a shout.

I almost turned, then remembered what the voice had said.

I kept going.

Chapter 37

I really don't know how I managed to get to the little patch of hedge ahead of the village-folk. I could almost smell the whiskey on my father's breath as the group of them came closer. I honestly didn't think I was going to get there – and even when I did – they'd have seen where I went and would only follow me. The whole idea suddenly became madness.

But with one last surge of strength, and a heartfelt prayer of gratitude, I stumbled down the slight incline towards the cluster of scrubby trees. Slipping and sliding on some loose rock, I ducked under the low branch of the one closest to me and scrabbled my way into the little opening that was made by the overhanging branches of its neighbours.

But instead of finding a small, person-sized space in which to tuck myself, I was met with an impossibly large glade. The trees surrounding it weren't hawthorn at all, but a collection of oak and ash and, just off to the left, a giant willow that trailed its branches into a merry stream. I looked behind me, not quite believing what I was seeing, expecting to see the angry red face of my father, bursting into the hawthorn. But the trees had closed in behind me and there was no sign of the cliff path or my pursuers.

"Now, what have I told you about looking back?" said a voice. "You're never going to find your way by always dwelling on what lies behind."

I wheeled around, but saw no-one, only a curious-faced fox sitting across the glade, its bushy tail folded neatly around its black feet.

"Who's there?" I called, fully aware it was very likely the fox who'd been speaking. Furthering the impossibilities, it was probably the one I'd seen when I was climbing the hill.

I took a shaky breath and sat down. The grass of the glade was spotted with violets and snowdrops — spring flowers. I inhaled the sweet scent of them and tried to sort out what had happened.

I'd clearly found my way back into Fingal's world, a fact which filled me with equal measures of relief and worry. I was no less alone here than I was in my own world, but at least here, I was safe from the island folk.

"Ah, but you'd much rather be here, wouldn't you? I can't imagine you'd prefer the surety of imprisonment over the unknowns of freedom."

A pair of long, trouser-wearing, legs appeared in front of me. I looked up but was temporarily blinded by the dappling of sun through the canopy of trees. Blinking, I put my hand up to shade my eyes. The owner of the legs crossed them and folded himself onto the grass in front of me.

"But perhaps I'm mistaken about you, daughter of the sea. I

often am, when it comes to those not born of the earth. Then again, that's not quite true. I see that you are also a child of the land. How curious. Incidentally, that was rather foolish of you to stop and help that little animal."

It was when he tilted his head in a questioning gesture that I gasped.

He was painfully handsome, with deep brown, almost black, eyes and skin the colour of rich, loamy, soil. His black hair came to a point on his high forehead, and it was suddenly quite clear that he wasn't wearing a head-dress at all. A pair of many-tined antlers was actually sprouting from his forehead.

He smiled at my less-than-surreptitious glance at the unexpected appendages.

"Cernach," he said, bowing his head slightly. The antlers tipped dangerously in my direction, and I resisted the urge to draw back, imagining it might be taken as offense. "That is the name by which I call myself, although sometimes I'm known by others, but never by the name that's mine and mine alone."

I frowned, trying to untangle what he'd said.

He laughed, a deep, reverberating laugh.

"So," he said, "Am I wrong?"

I gathered my wits and straightened my shoulders, flicking my hair back from my face. I dared not think what a sight I must be. His extraordinary beauty made me feel quite grubby.

"No, sir," I replied. "You are not. As to the other, I couldn't very well leave her to get torn to pieces by the dogs, could I?"

I paused, noting the satisfaction flicker across his face.

"Am I correct in assuming it was you who helped me when I fell? And who spoke the words of encouragement in...in my head?"

He shrugged. I noticed that he wasn't wearing anything above his trousers. His rather wide and muscular chest was bare. I flushed and looked away, a point which he noticed and at which he smirked.

"I intervened only to remind you of what you already have," he said, quite huffily. "None of us are permitted to help you, but there are no rules about reminders."

"Who decided these so-called rules?" I asked, having become quite tired of being reminded how very much alone I was.

He shrugged again, making sure to flex his shoulders to their best advantage. It was my turn to smirk, aware as I now was of his obvious vanity.

"It matters little," he said, waving a hand, curling his muscular arm as he did so. I suppressed a grin. "It was long ago and forged by the whims of greed and foolishness. Neither party entered the agreement without malice or deceit, and so neither party can claim superiority of virtue over the other."

"Meaning?"

"Meaning, my lovely creature," he leaned towards me, his eyes like endless night. "That the way is now clear for you to break the seal of this unsavoury bargain, and end this particularly ridiculous battle in the war between our worlds."

I raised an eyebrow, remembering what Fingal had taught me of the faery kind.

"Why would you even care?" I asked, blithely. I stretched out my legs to ease the ache of my back and smoothed down the folds of my skirt, placing my bundle neatly across my knees. Doing so forced him to lean back. "Surely the trifling grievances of us mortals are of no interest to one such as yourself."

I had an inkling of who he might be, but I dared not believe it to be true. If it were true, I was treading on treacherous ground by challenging him. Once again, I cursed my incurable impertinence.

He grinned, showing his impeccably white teeth.

"You are indeed everything I'd hoped," he said. "Brave, clever and just the right amount of incorrigible." He pulled his knees up and crossed his hands in front of them. "I care, my lovely creature, because there are bigger battles than yours to fight. But until this particular unpleasantness is tidied away, I feel that I cannot move on with the task at hand."

"So, I am an unpleasant mess that needs tidying, am I?" I could feel my temper rising. Whatever awe I should have rightly felt to be in conversation with this creature was quickly disappearing in the face of his unabashed arrogance.

He, at least, had the decency to look mildly apologetic.

"That isn't what I meant," he said. "Of course, you cannot be familiar with the way things work in my world. There are greater forces at play, more lives which hang in the balance. Until my wayward, sea-dwelling cousins are brought in hand, then energies cannot be directed in the way they ought."

"You're a...being...of the land, aren't you?" I asked, trying a different tactic. "So, you have no domain over the sea?"

I took his lack of response as an admission of my having spoken the truth.

"Then your people have no concern in this at all, it's between humans and sea-folk," I narrowed my eyes. "So why don't you tell me - really - why you're bothering to help me?"

He cleared his throat, regarding me steadily for a minute or more. I willed myself to lock his gaze and not look away. I somehow believed it meant something that I wouldn't let his explanation slide.

"Once, a long time ago, even by our measuring, I loved a daughter of the sea," he paused, closing his midnight eyes for a moment. "What happened is a story for another time but suffice it to say I owe a great debt and have pledged my days to honouring it. That I might put to rights a great wrong that was wrought by such greed and deceit and has been replaying itself in this foolishness," he waved a hand at my swollen belly.

I swallowed hard, wishing that, just for once, I could let things stand instead of feeling the need to exert my opinions.

"I thank you for your honesty, my lord."

He glanced sharply at my use of the title but said nothing, only inclining his antlered head.

"I know now that your aid comes at a great price, which honours me, but I feel I ought to tell you that what you call foolishness, is not entirely so."

I placed my hands on my belly, marveling again at the ripple of life that I felt there.

He sighed, holding up his own, long-fingered, hand to halt my speech.

"I know, my child, I know. You love him. The one who fathered your babe?"

I nodded, not trusting myself to speak.

"But surely you know what he is?" he asked, gently now. "You know the nature of such a creature?"

I nodded again, summoning my courage for one last effort.

"But he was human once, my lord. A human who, I believe, played a part in this bargain of which you speak." I saw the recognition flash through his eyes. It was a wild guess, but it emboldened me.

"If I am to play a part in the dissolving of this bargain - this untidiness that you need to clear up," I glanced towards him, seeing the corners of his mouth twitching into a crooked smile. "I would ask a favour,"

There! I said it!

He threw back his antlered head and laughed, the sound echoed through the glade, startling a blackbird which had come to perch in a nearby tree.

"I would have been disappointed had you not, my little pet."

He unfolded himself into a standing position, towering above me. Leaning down, he offered his hand. I took it and allowed him to assist me to my feet.

"Now, if you've rested sufficiently, shall I escort you to your accommodations for the duration of your stay here?"

Mustering all of the composure I had left, I nodded primly and tucked my hand in the crook of the elbow which he offered.

In that way, I was escorted, by an old, old, god, back to the cottage where I'd been so happy.

Chapter 38

It was just as we'd left it. Even the bed remained unmade, still in a state of contented rumple from the last night, the only night, when my beloved Fingal slept by my side. I tried, unsuccessfully, to quell the rush of emotion that flooded over me when I saw it.

Cernach made a tactful exit at that point, promising to return at sundown. I nodded, without speaking or turning around, and heard the door close quietly behind him.

Sinking onto the bed, I buried my face in the bedclothes, inhaling the scent which still lingered there - Fingal's scent - and cried.

Eventually, I fell asleep. Fear, exhaustion and the blessed relief of sorrow had drained me. When I awoke, the light of the day had waned, and the cooling breeze of night wafted through the open window. I sat up, scrubbing a hand across my face. I was still dressed in my thick jumper and overcoat, still with my boots on my feet. If Cernach was coming back, I supposed I ought to make myself slightly more presentable.

I unlaced my boots, letting them drop with a thud onto the rug at the side of the bed, and padded my way into the sitting room area. The makings of a fire were stacked in the hearth, so I struck a match and set to lighting the crumpled wads of dried grass that served as kindling. As soon as it was flickering steadily, I rose from the hearth and went to the corner that was the little kitchen.

Cernach had left my bundle on the table, so I undid the strand of yarn which bound it together and emptied the contents onto the table. A stab of wistfulness struck me when I saw the packet of tea which Callum had given me, and the wedge of Hetty's bannock. It seemed like a lifetime ago that I'd seen either one of them. Another life and another world, which wasn't quite so far from the truth, I suppose.

Between that and the bread and cheese I'd hurriedly thrown into my bundle at the tavern, I thought I might be able to rustle up a small meal worth sharing with the lord of the forest. I grinned to myself, as I filled the kettle from the water barrel by the sink, not quite believing my nerve in asking him for a favour. I hadn't expected him to entertain the notion at all, but I was encouraged that he hadn't exactly said no.

The fire soon filled the cottage with a merry light and a warmth against the chill of spring air. I was still trying to adapt to it being spring, and not autumn, as it was in my own world. If it had been approaching the end of summer when I'd left here, only a month or so ago in my own world, then an entire turn of the seasons must have passed here. I suppose it could've been even more than that. I shook my head, getting muddled and overwhelmed with the possibility.

I poured the boiling water from the kettle into the teapot, letting the fragrant steam waft upwards before tucking the pot under its cozy. I'd always thought it a strange thing to find in a cottage of the faery realms – a knitted tea cozy. Fingal had laughed when I'd pointed it out, telling me it must've been left as a token by some other soul who'd wandered through the forest at some point. I remembered wondering where they'd ended up, that particular traveler who had a tea cozy on their person. It didn't bear thinking about, really. So frightening and dire were the warnings about those hapless victims of the Otherworld – returning to their own world after a week only to find that decades, or even centuries, had passed. I shuddered, thankful to have had Fingal's protection.

Oh, Fingal, I thought, perilously close to another bout of weeping. *Where are you and why can't you come?*

Sighing, I lit the oil lamps and settled myself in the chair by the fire to wait.

I didn't have to wait long before there was a knock at the door.

"Come in," I called, rising from the chair and heading back to the kitchen to get the teapot and a pair of cups.

"You'd best not be so free with your welcome here, my lady. You never know what sort of undesirables might wander past of an evening."

I almost dropped the teapot. Indeed, I sloshed the hot liquid over the tablecloth in my haste to set it down before spinning around.

"Fingal!" I shrieked.

In two strides he was across the room and in my arms, happy tears coursing down both our cheeks.

"Now, now," said Cernach, his deep voice held a note of

laughter. "Let's not get carried away. As much as the reunion of young love delights me, there are serious matters at hand."

Fingal and I tore ourselves apart but stood, arm in arm, grinning like a pair of simpletons. I couldn't believe my eyes. I'd been convinced we'd never see each other again!

"I'll get another cup. Sit down, both of you," I said, trembling with happiness.

I came back to the table and poured us each a mug of tea then sat down beside Fingal, opposite Cernach. It was then I noticed something odd about the forest lord.

"Your antlers!" I blurted. "They're gone."

Cernach just smiled. "Not gone, just not there," he replied, in his fanciful cryptic fashion. "Some matters are best served in a different guise." He tilted his head and grinned lasciviously. "Although I suppose you have some knowledge of that, Fingal my lad."

Fingal blushed a bright red to the roots of his black hair.

"There has been nothing between us that was anything other than consensual, my lord."

Cernach laughed, a throaty chuckle.

"Aye, and you know something of how that works too, I don't doubt."

This time Fingal's flush was one of anger. I saw him tighten his lips and clench his fingers around his mug. His other hand held mine, resting in my own lap. I closed my other hand around it and gave it a squeeze. He acknowledged the gesture by lowering his gaze from Cernach's.

"Indeed, my lord. I have been well-schooled in the various forms of trickery available to my kind. But I'm truthful when I say that no such tactics have been employed between Aibhlinn and I."

"Perhaps not on your side," mused Cernach, steepling his fingers together in front of him. He regarded Fingal's quiet defiance for a moment and then turned to me. "But what of you, lovely creature? Have you not used faery wiles against your beloved?"

"Me?" I couldn't have been more surprised. "How could I do that?" I asked, genuinely curious as to his line of questioning. "I haven't got any faery wiles." I looked at Fingal who just shrugged.

"Oh, I wouldn't be so sure of that," said Cernach. He waved a hand in front of us. "Never mind that, it's not important just now. You're probably wondering how I managed to get your Fingal here and why."

"Well, actually, I hadn't thought of that at all. I was too busy being happy to see him," I admitted, truthfully.

Fingal smiled down at me and reached out to place his hand on my belly.

Cernach cleared his throat loudly.

"Can we forgo the besotted lover performance for the time being?" he asked, drily. "Time is short and there's much to be discussed."

I straightened in my chair, squaring my shoulders and tilting my chin upwards.

"It's not a performance and I'd thank you to show a little patience, my lord. It's been quite some time since I last saw Fingal and our parting was on less-than-agreeable terms. Surely, you can forgive the joy of our reunion?"

Cernach smirked.

"You can have all the joy you want once I'm gone," he said. "Right now, I need you to listen to what I have to say."

"Fair enough," I said, blushing at his insinuations, convinced he could see the thoughts written plainly on my face. Fingal, I noticed, was doing his best to avoid my gaze entirely. "Before you carry on, I just want to express my gratitude to you for bringing Fingal back to me."

Cernach held up a hand.

"Mind how you throw around the gratitude and don't get too comfortable with his presence, lovely creature. You can have him for a few hours then he's mine once more. He's here on sufferance and to ensure you uphold your end of our bargain."

I tried not to show my disappointment. I felt Fingal's hand tighten in mine.

Cernach raised a perfectly arched eyebrow. "Oh, surely you didn't think it would be that simple?" he said. "No, no, no, my poppet. One does not enter lightly into dealings with one such as myself. If I'm to guess correctly – and I usually do – the terms of your favour, then what you're asking requires me to defy and intervene in some very old laws and customs. Not to mention incurring the inevitable wrath of one who already has more than enough to go around."

He glanced over at Fingal who stiffened slightly.

"I suppose he hasn't told you what he did to deserve his punishment? And what happened afterwards?"

I shook my head.

"Nor will I ask him to, unless he wishes," I added. "You say yourself, my lord Cernach, that we must look ahead and not behind us."

The deep, rumbling laugh filled the small cottage.

"Well said, little minx, well said! You are a worthy challenge, I think."

I smiled, in what I hoped was an expression of calm confidence. Inside, my heart hammered loudly in my chest. Always, it seemed, I was placed in a position of having a frighteningly tenuous hold on what I loved best. Trying to stay one step ahead of the next crisis was an exhausting exercise. I braced myself for what Cernach had to say.

"Right then, we shall not dwell on the sordid details, although you," he gestured towards Fingal, "you may wish to reconsider the depths of your shame and ask yourself how great your pride."

"It is not a matter of pride, my lord," said Fingal, stiffly. "But one of duty."

Cernach snorted dismissively. "I find the two become wearyingly interchangeable in the hands of those who seek to justify their own suffering in lieu of necessary transformation and growth. But that's not the issue at hand."

He leaned back in his chair and stretched out his long legs. The absence of his antlers was balanced by the inclusion of proper dress — a pristine white shirt after the old fashion, a froth of lace at its throat. He also wore a well-tailored frock coat that he'd unbuttoned when he sat down. He looked every bit a lord, albeit one whose domain covered more than just wool and fishing interests. Looking at each of us in turn, he sat forwards again and placed his hands on the table, palms down, and spread his fingers.

"Even if your beloved refuses to share his part in it, this much you should know: the taking of the sea bride children was not, and never has been, a part of the original bargain forged between mortals and faery."

I gasped and opened my mouth to speak but Fingal's hand tightened in mine, so I closed it again.

"This particular addendum was created between Lira and certain factions amongst the mortals who believed her to have a power over them which she categorically does not. Her domain remains that of the sea, nothing more."

"So that means she can't send the water horses?" I glance quickly at Fingal, but his eyes are lowered. "What about the storms?"

Cernach nodded.

"The storms and how they affect the ocean are indeed within her realm, that much will not change. However, what I propose to set in motion has the potential to aid the mortal world even from that aspect of her tiresomely vengeful nature."

"What I have to offer you is this: I will endeavour to have the crimes of your lover here, absolved, that he may be granted a modicum of flexibility in his appearance and geography," He held up a hand as I attempted to speak. "Do not get ahead of yourself, lovely creature. Absolution does not guarantee a full reversal to humanity. Some things are well beyond even my reach, but I do believe the result will satisfy. In return, you will bear his child and keep it, to be raised by you, as a half-breed, but among humankind. You will promise to protect this child from the sea-folk — and your own folk, for that matter — until she is able to do so herself. Agreed?"

I sat with my mouth open, incapable of speech.

Of course, I would agree — is that not everything I wanted? I turned to look at Fingal, expecting to see my joy mirrored in his face, but he remained impassive. His translucent eyes were troubled and questioning.

"What else?" he asked, softly, regarding Cernach with that questioning glance. "It's never that simple. What have you left out?"

A flash of irritation flitted across Cernach's handsome features, which he quickly schooled into a mask of blithe unconcern.

He shrugged nonchalantly.

"Do you accept, lovely creature?" he asked, ignoring Fingal completely.

I leaned over, eager to do just that. Fingal placed a warning hand on mine.

"Ask him, *mo chroì*," he said. "If you ask him, he's bound to answer truthfully."

I frowned. Cernach made a noise that sounded like an animal growling.

"Alright," I said. "Is there anything else to this bargain that you propose, that I need be aware of before I accept?"

Cernach sighed and shook his head.

"Fair enough," he replied. "Only this – you may stay here, in our world, until the time of the child's birth. However, you must return to your own world when your birth time is upon you."

My stomach dropped. I looked wildly between Fingal and Cernach.

"But it's not safe there! They'll take the baby from me as soon as she's born. That's what they plan to do!"

"That is not my concern," said Cernach, coldly.

"But..."

He held up his hand again, halting my protest and then stood; his shadow, cast by the light of the fire, showed the missing antlers. He was tall and imposing and irrefutably powerful. When he spoke, it was the voice of an ancient being, older than anything in human memory.

"The child must be born in the mortal world. Otherwise, the bargain is forfeit and your beloved will be lost to you forever. You decide. The choice is yours to make."

He turned to Fingal.

"You have until the moon turns in the sky, then you must return to the sea."

He paused in the doorway then turned back.

"Do not test the time I'm giving you," he warned. "She has no bride's dress to shield her this time."

* * *

"Will you tell me?" I asked, as we lay entwined.

We had drunk of each other like thirsty travelers deprived of fresh water. Despite the slight inconvenience of my belly, our love had left us both bright-eyed and breathless.

He stroked the length of my arm. His long fingers lingered over my hands, and then traveled to trace the circle of my rounded belly.

"I cannot, *m'anam*," he said, at last. "Telling of it will not lessen the effect, and that is all that matters to us now."

"Was it so horrible?"

He didn't answer.

"I'm going to go back to have the baby," I said.

His fingers stopped their travels, briefly, and then resumed.

"You mustn't do it. Not for me," he said, his voice soft in my hair. "I have had the gift of you. More than I ought to have had."

I smiled, although he could not have seen it.

"I told you I wouldn't forget."

I felt him smile into my hair.

"Aye, *mo chroì*. That you did. Still, the danger is too great, and there are more important things to think of."

His hand pressed gently onto my belly. He laughed softly at our daughter's answering ripple.

"This one," he said, his voice husky. "This one is the most important of all."

"I know," I said. "She is who I'm going back for. She, and all the children who would have come after her, are worth the risk, whatever that proves to be."

I rolled onto my side, pressing myself against his length, so I could see his face. The sharp planes and angles were softened by the lamplight. In the semi-darkness, his eyes were reduced to pupils, the almost-colourless blue washed away.

"I was always going to do this," I said. "Long before the chance of having you with me, do you see? I made my choice as soon as I knew she was here; evidence of our love growing inside me. Even when I doubted my own strength, I knew what I had to do."

He reached up to stroke my face, glancing towards the window.

"The moon is at her peak," he said. "She'll turn from us soon."

I leaned up to kiss him; slowly and thoroughly, wanting to savour every last touch of him.

"Then let's not waste our time talking over what's already been decided," I whispered.

He took me in his arms and answered with a kiss of his own.

Chapter 39

The days passed quickly. I filled them with walking in the woods around the cottage, gathering posies of flowers and daydreaming by the stream. I scrubbed the floors and washed the windows. Linens were laundered and hung out to dry in the fragrant spring breezes. I cooked simple soups and picked fresh greens; I gathered early strawberries, foraged from the wild edges of the meadow, which I ate by the heaping handful, until my fingers and lips were stained with juice. Every morning, I awoke to a basket of bread and fruit, jars of preserves and bottles of fresh milk and the sweet, honey wine that the faeries brewed at midsummer. There were tangy cheeses and savoury pies, delicious bowls of nuts and dried berries. I never saw my benefactor but was sure to leave offerings in return for the kindness shown me. I sewed tiny bundles of pressed flowers into charms and strung the dried berries into garlands, leaving them in the place where the food appeared as gifts for my unseen friends.

In my mind, I'd be returning here after having birthed our child. While she had to be born in my world, there was no provision about how long we had to stay there once she'd arrived. As long as I could get there and get back within the span of nine days, then we would be safe from the clutches of the villagers and their intention to hand her over to be raised by the sea-folk. I couldn't imagine a more magical childhood than that of growing up in my little glade in the woods, even if it couldn't be for always. Cernach said she had to be raised in my world, but that didn't mean I had to start right away. If the faery-folk could manipulate the terms of bargains, then so could I. If nine days of my world could stretch into months, entire seasons — long enough to fall in love —- then it could easily be years, enough to let my child get her start.

In the evenings, I sat by the fire, sipping the sweet, honeyed wine, and making my little presents. I sang to the baby and told her stories - tales of my childhood, although not the unpleasant parts, only the parts that involved Callum and Hetty. I told her everything I knew of her grandmother and always, I told her of her father and how much we both loved her.

As the days wore on and my belly grew even larger and my breasts began to swell, I started to worry. My plan was to travel through the corridor of trees, to the place where I'd had to leave Fingal at the end of our first time together. The corridor opened up into the cave, hidden in behind the rocky outcropping, and was where I'd originally intended to go when I left Callum. My worry lay in the fact I knew I'd be alone.

The truth was, I was frightened. I had no experience of birth other than what I'd overheard other women saying - and none of it was encouraging. Even Hetty's assurances of it being the most natural thing in the world and something my body would just know how to do hadn't really comforted me much. The simple, generally uncomplicated efforts of ewes at lambing time had given me a false impression and Isabelle Dunn had been only too happy to disavow me of my naive notions. The idea of bringing my baby into the world without the support of other women was terrifying.

One morning I woke up to a dull ache in my lower back. It wasn't unusual, I'd had an aching back off and on for several months and simply took it to be a symptom of my expanding girth. I got out of bed and made my way into the living area to prod the fire and make my morning cup of tea, as was my usual routine. Also part of my routine, was opening the door of the cottage to see what surprises had been left on my doorstep. It wasn't quite the surprise I'd been envisioning when I turned the doorknob, but I was met with a surprise all the same. A small, wizened faery-woman stood on my step with a large basket over her arm. She was about waist-high and had long grey hair that hung in many plaits around her face. She had a red and white spotted kerchief tied over them and large, silver earrings, studded with sparkling gemstones, which dangled and clicked at her ears.

"Oh!" I said, "Hello! Are you the lovely person who's been leaving me food parcels all this time?"

She smiled and bobbed a curtsy. "Aye, milady. And thank ye for the gifts in return. 'Tis a fine thing to have the work o' the hands given ye. 'Tis an honor indeed."

She curtsied again.

I couldn't help but smile back, despite the sudden wave of pain that rippled across my lower abdomen. I winced slightly, trying not to show my discomfort.

"Would you like to come in and have some tea with me?" I asked. "And perhaps some breakfast? I was just about to put the kettle on to boil."

The little woman nodded again and walked past me into the cottage. She turned around and looked me closely up and down. She placed a small, nut-brown hand on my belly, causing me to start in surprise. A feeling of incredible warmth had radiated from her touch.

Nodding again, she placed her basket down on the floor.

"I reckon we've time for a quick cuppa and then we must be off," she said, busying herself with filling the kettle.

I gasped as another pain rolled through me, leaving me slightly breathless. I clutched the edge of the table until it passed.

"Aye, lass. 'Tis time at last."

She smiled at the look of surprise on my face. Surely she didn't mean...

"The bairn's on her way," she said. "And so must we be if we're to get ye where ye need to go in good time."

She handed me a bundle of cloth.

"Go and put this on," she said. "And I'll get the tea going. Ye'll need my special brew to get ye through what's to come. By the feel o' that belly o' yours, she won't be long in getting here."

The faery-woman had given me a long, ivory-coloured, gown to wear. I rubbed the material between my fingers - faery-cloth, of course. It was very similar to the swatch of fabric the old woman had given me for the baby. The gown was embroidered with brightly coloured thread — birds, flowers and spirals of leaves wound their way around the bottom edge and cuffs and around the yoke. It fell away in soft folds from my swollen breasts and gently over the protrusion of my belly. I felt immediately soothed, calmer and able to think more clearly.

My first thought was that we needed to leave the cottage and head for the corridor of trees before I was unable to walk. My limited views of childbirth involved screaming women lying in beds and I knew I didn't have the luxury of staying here. I wanted to be in the right place before things got too far along.

When I finished getting changed, the faery-woman was already waiting, basket over her arm and my little traveling bundle tucked under her elbow. She handed me a tall flask, and a piece of bread and honey wrapped in a blue checkered cloth.

"Ye can sip and munch as we go," she said. "It's best if ye keep moving for now. It'll slow things down a tiny bit 'til we can get ye where ye need to be."

"How do you know where I'm going?" I said, taking the food and tea that she offered, grateful beyond my wildest imagining to have someone with whom to travel.

She laughed, a cackling little chuckle. "There's naught many places ye could go, lassie. And none ye'd get to wi'out a bit o' help."

"How do you mean?" I asked, shrugging myself into my overcoat. It felt slightly too small, I wasn't able to button it over my stomach. I had no idea what season I would be facing when I returned to my own world so thought I'd better plan for every eventuality.

She looked at me sideways. Her brown face and bright eyes made me think of a sparrow or other small bird.

"D'ye think ye'd be allowed to wander, like?" she asked.

"'T'wouldn't be safe," she continued, not waiting for my answer. "No, pet. Ye wouldn't get much further than the edge of the forest afore the path turned ye around and brought ye back again."

I thought about that for a moment. True, I hadn't tried to go further than the boundary of the forest around the cottage, I hadn't any need to. Fingal and I had gone farther afield, but I suppose I'd done so under his protection.

With a twist of irony, I realized I'd been as much a prisoner in my lovely little cottage as I had been in my room at the tavern.

She eyed me closely.

"Come on, then, lambkin. We'd best get started while the pains have eased for a bit."

She set off at a quick march across the glade. I scurried after her, in my awkward, waddling gait. I barely had time to say goodbye to my little cottage. I stopped and turned to look back. Prison though it may have been, it had held and sheltered me and my love, and it felt like home.

I muttered a quick 'thank you' and 'see you soon' before turning to catch up with my companion.

* * *

The pains returned in earnest as we reached the leafy corridor of trees. The faery-woman had kept me at a quick pace and while we were walking, the pains had remained subdued, more of a dull ache than the sharp, rolling, agonies which were overtaking me when we stopped within the cool, green, tunnel. Through a haze of dull pain, I could hear the distant thunder of the ocean and the sharp tang of salt drifted along the quiet passage.

The faery-woman took her hands and placed them on my belly once again. The suffusing warmth of her touch radiated over me, sending tendrils of comfort down into my pelvis and legs.

"Aye, won't be long now," she said, a smile crinkling her small face. "Ye've all my blessings, lass. I wish ye well." She handed me the basket and turned to walk back out of the tunnel.

Panic gripped me just as another pain shot across my hips. I gasped, moaning my way through the surge until it passed, leaving me panting.

"Wait!" I said, "Where are you going?"

The faery-woman turned, smiling sadly.

"I cannae go any further wi' ye, lassie. It must be as ye do this wi'out us now."

"But you've already been helping me," I wailed, not believing myself to be abandoned at this, the most desperate time of all. "Why stop now?"

She turned without answering, disappearing into the shadows near the entrance of the tunnel.

I found myself sobbing. Tears of fright and frustration poured down my cheeks. Just then, another birth-pain wracked my body, dropping me to my knees. Groaning, I breathed hard through it then clenched my teeth and got to my feet. My daughter was coming, and I had to get back to my own world. Everything depended upon me doing this properly, and if I had to do it alone then so I would.

I hoisted the basket onto my arm and walked as swiftly as I could towards the end of the trees and the entrance of the cave. I willed myself to keep going, praying that another pain wouldn't hit until I set foot upon mortal ground as I wasn't sure I could walk through another one.

Sweat streamed down my face, plastering my hair to the side of my head. I wished I wasn't wearing my heavy coat but didn't dare stop to take it off. I reasoned I would need it once the babe was born, to keep us both warm on the journey back.

I rounded the corner at the edge of the trees, feeling the grass give way to sand under my feet and the cool, damp scent of the sea cave filled my nostrils. I was almost there. A pain shot through me again, a rising agony that tore a shriek from my throat. A wave of nausea accompanied it; I fell down on my hands and knees and vomited, retching onto the sand.

I barely noticed the warm glow of the cave, or the scent of herbs that mingled with the iron-tang of kelp and saltwater. I crawled along, feeling suddenly that I was no longer in control of my own body.

"There now, lass," said a familiar voice, soothing and welcome. A pair of small hands pressed themselves into my lower back, easing the pressure that was building. "When this one passes, let's get ye comfortable by the fire, aye?"

"Hetty?" I whispered, through a miasma of pain and sweat.

"Aye, *mo leanbh*, it's me. I've let ye down so far, lass, and for that I'll be ever sorry. But I'm here now, aye?"

I leaned against her, sobbing with pain and relief. I couldn't form the words, but I had never been so happy in all my days.

"Och, lass, I know, I know. Never mind that now. Let's get this bairn safely into the world, shall we?"

Chapter 40

I have never felt so simultaneously helpless and powerful. If ever I'd doubted that I could have birthed my baby alone, the sudden and immense way in which my body somehow knew exactly what to do, removed that doubt. Having said that, I was so very grateful for Hetty's presence. It was terrifying and exhilarating and without her gentle guidance and calm encouragement, my daughter's birth would have been tainted by my fear of the unknown.

The moment that Hetty placed her squalling, naked body, slick with blood and birth-water, onto my chest, I felt my heart was stolen. Tears of joy and relief, mingled with sweat on my cheeks. She was here! She was a tiny thing with a shock of black hair and already I could see the shape of the high, angular, cheek bones of her father.

"She's a grand set o' lungs on her," said Hetty, smiling through tears of her own. "And I reckon she'll take after her mother for temper."

I grinned like a fool, wrapping my arms around her, marveling at the miracle that she surely was.

"Right, let's get her dried off a bit and wrapped up, lest she catch a chill," said Hetty, reaching up to take her from me.

Panic gripped me and I tightened my arms around my daughter, who flailed in protest as I pulled her away from Hetty's hands.

A look of shock flashed across Hetty's face, then shame and embarrassment. She hung her head so that I couldn't see her face. Immediately, I was sorry. I reached out a hand to touch her arm.

"I'm so sorry, Hetty. I didn't mean..."

"It's alright, lass. Ye'd be mad to trust me, I ken. I've let Isabelle Dunn's poison trickle into me own mind. I've no excuse, I've been a silly fool feeling sorry for meself." She paused, looking up and reaching out to smooth a wet, strand of hair back from my face. "Ye've been like a daughter to me, lass, all these years. It's been such a joy to watch ye grow up. I know yer mam would be so proud to see what a strong and brave lassie ye've become. Please believe me, I'd never hurt ye, or that wee bairn, not for all the world."

I gripped Hetty's hand in my own, squeezing it tightly, unable to speak for the flood of emotion. I nodded, blinking away the tears. I'd felt so alone for so long, to hear her say those words filled the hollow place in my heart that I hadn't even realized was there.

"Thank you, Hetty. I'm sorry I reacted that way. It's been such a long and lonely road, and I've never been sure who I could trust. Please, do take her. I trust you, absolutely."

I held out my arms and Hetty gently took my daughter from

me. I watched as she wiped down her little body with a warm cloth, and then wrapped her in a soft blanket of lamb's wool.

"There's a wrap in my bundle," I said. "It was given to me for her. Would you mind fetching it?"

Hetty handed back the baby and then rummaged in my pack for the piece of cloth. She held it in her hands for a moment, a strange expression on her face, before handing it to me.

"It's beautiful," she said. "Faery-craft, aye?"

I nodded but said nothing more, tucking it carefully around the outside of the lamb's wool swaddling.

Hetty cleared her throat.

"Right then. I think the wee one would like a bit of a nurse, and then I'll get the water boiling for a cup of tea, aye? I think we've all earned it!"

***

The next few days passed in a blur of happy discovery. I learned about my daughter, and she about me. I spent hours gazing at her sleeping face, watching her blow milky bubbles, inhaling deeply the rich, baby scent of her.

In between sleeping and nursing the baby, I told Hetty all that had passed since last we'd had a proper conversation. She shook her head in disbelief when I told her of Cernach.

"I'd never believe it, meself," she said. "I wouldn't warrant it were possible if anyone but ye had told me. The lord of the forest himself? The old stories allus have a ring o' truth to them, but I'd never imagine he'd walk among us, plain as day, like. I allus thought that lot had disappeared into the hills and woods for good once the churchmen came around."

"And ye think it were your mam's pendant that let ye hold the memories of yer one? What was it? Fingal?"

I nodded, shifting the baby over to my other breast. She snuffled contentedly and settled in to suck. The absolute rightness of her felt like a magic all its own.

"That's what Callum said. And it seems reasonable, I suppose." I paused for a moment, wondering if I ought to bring it up. Having just got Hetty back, I hesitated to do or say anything that would send her retreating into the darkness of her own experience.

"Do you really not remember him?" I asked, deciding to avoid the topic of her own baby. "Your faery bridegroom?"

Hetty shook her head, a small, wistful smile on her face.

"No, pet. I sometimes have flashes, like. Impressions, really, like something flickering at the corner of your eye that disappears if ye turn to look. I remember how I felt, though; it were a warm feeling, like great happiness and contentment, aye?"

"Would you have loved him, do you think?"

She shrugged. "I suppose I must've," she replied. "From what ye've told me of yer Fingal, he was probably a devilishly handsome lad and a real gentleman. What's to stop a young lass falling in love?"

I blushed deeply.

Hetty laughed softly, so as not to startle the babe. "Dinna get all bashful, lass. It's common knowledge that there's nowt like a faery-man to set a lass's heart afire." She nodded towards the baby. "And it's not like I dinna ken what ye've been up to!"

I grinned widely, quite suddenly overcome with immense happiness. I'd managed the first, and, I thought, most difficult hurdle. My baby had been born in the mortal world. Now all I had to do was travel back through the cave and corridor to our cottage where, I was sure, my beloved Fingal would be waiting to welcome his little family home.

As if she could read my thoughts, Hetty said,

"Have ye given much thought to what we're going to do next? It's been three days since the bairn was born. Ye'd likely be fit to travel in another day or so."

I nodded.

"I have, actually. All I needed was to make sure she was born in the mortal world. I think it'll be safer for all of us if I just take her back through the portal. I think that's the safest option."

I stroked the tiny head, running my fingers through the spiky, black tufts of hair.

"It'll be best to raise her away from the village-folk for a little while, I think." I said, avoiding Hetty's eye. "If I could, I'd spare her the...difficulty...of living among folk who'd rather have given her to the sea."

I raised my eyes, setting my jaw defiantly, expecting Hetty to protest.

Instead, all I saw was an acute sadness in her expression; her eyes were filled with sorrow that I assumed was for her lost babe.

"Oh, lass," she whispered. "Didn't they tell ye?"

"Tell me what?" Instinctively, I held the baby closer.

"The portal," she said, nodding her head towards the back of the cave. "It only goes the one way - out. Ye cannae get back that way. Ye'll *have* to take her into our world."

***

I couldn't believe what Hetty was telling me.

I stood up, the baby still cradled against me, and stumbled to the back of the cave, back to where I'd entered it only days ago. Sure enough, all that was there was a solid wall of rock. I spun around, frantic.

"What will I do, Hetty?" I cried. "I can't take her through! They'll find me and take her from me! I'd have to go up the cliff path and back to the hollow. How will I get there without them seeing me?"

I railed at the circumstance in which I found myself, yet again. Always so close and yet always so far away. As soon as I started to allow myself a bit of comfort and happiness, it seemed to be yanked cruelly away. I cursed the faery-folk and their changeable, confounding natures. Why did they show me the way, only to change course again?

"There now, pet," soothed Hetty, coming to lead me back. "Ye'll do no good leaping around like that. Ye need to rest and heal afore ye can think o' going anywhere. Let me brew ye another mug o' my Mother's Tea, will I?"

"How can I sit drinking tea?" I wailed, dramatically. "I've got to sort out how I'm going to get us home!"

Hetty sighed.

"Is that what ye think, lass? That yon faery cottage is a home? Did ye not tell me yer own self that ye couldn't wander, that it kept ye a prisoner of a sort?"

"Well, yes, but..."

"What kind o' life is that for the bairn, eh? D'ye want her growing up wi'out other bairns to play with, wi'out other folk who'd love 'er as their own?"

"Like who?" I exploded, fury displacing my panic. "Who among that lot would see her as anything but a burden, a living reminder of something more important that was denied them? You heard what they all said, the giving of the child is supposed to guarantee prosperity and safety and all that nonsense. Every time a net breaks loose or someone's sheep gets the scours it'll be her fault. They'll never believe it's just been a cruel trick all this time..."

"What did ye say?"

Hetty's face was drained of colour.

"A trick..." I faltered, realizing the implications of what I was telling her. "Oh, Hetty, I'm so sorry." I reached out to squeeze her hand, hardly bearing to see the expression of utter desolation on her face.

"The only thing that's ever been binding is the custom of the sea bride," I said. "The giving up of the child was a separate agreement, full of trickery and deceit on both sides of the bargain. It was made long after the original pact between men and the Old Ones."

"But why didn't it stop?" whispered Hetty. "Surely folk'd known..."

I shook my head.

"Nobody ever questioned it. The whole thing is steeped in fear and greed, and it was always to the benefit of that horrible Lira, so she wasn't likely to draw anybody's attention to it, would she? And the islanders are so terrified of what might happen they just go along with it. That's why I can't let them take her, don't you see? If I can break the cycle, no other woman need go through this."

Hetty blinked away her tears and offered a small smile.

"Well, then, lass. We'd best sort out how we're going to end it then, hadn't we?"

Chapter 41

At Hetty's insistence, I stayed in the cave for two more days. She fussed over me and the baby, bringing me mug after mug of Mother's Tea and delicious soups and stews to help me regain my strength. The baby nursed well and voraciously and was getting stronger by the minute.

On the morning of the sixth day Hetty announced that she would leave the cave so as to get an idea of how things stood in the outside world.

"They all think I've been across the island tending to a poorly relative," she explained. "I hadn't told them when I'd be back so nothing will seem amiss. I'll just tell them I'm stopping in to stock up on some herbs and to make sure our John hasn't starved to death."

Seeing the look of worry cross my face, she smiled fondly at me, smoothing back my hair and resting a hand on the baby's head where she lay in the crook of my arm. I'd fashioned the faery cloth into a sling so that I could have my hands free while she slept against me. The familiar weight and warmth of her did more to embolden me than anything else.

"Dinna worry, pet. I'll be back in the morning, aye? Promise me ye'll stay here and not get any foolish notions about striking off on yer own?"

I forced a smile.

"I'm going to see our Callum, alright? We're going to need someone else to help us and he'll be mad wi' worry. He's the only one who knew where I was really going and it's only fair I let him know he's an uncle, aye?"

"Of course!" I said, filled with guilt and shame for not having given him a thought. My entire world had shrunk to the size of a baby girl. "Give him my love, will you?"

Hetty nodded. She packed herself a small bundle. "I have to look the part, aye?" she said with a grin. She stood at the bend in the cave, where it turned the corner that led out to the beach. "What ye said before," she began, "about no-one out there who'd love her?"

I bowed my head, biting my lip in yet another wave of shame.

"I already love her like she's my own grand-bairn. And she'll have the love of her three uncles as well. Which is no small thing at all."

"I know, Hetty. I'm sorry I was so awful," I said, still hiding my face.

"Never mind that, pet. Ye've had a hard go of things, ye allus have. So I know where the upset came from. All that matters is that ye remember who ye are and what ye've become. There's a grand power in that, lassie. A grander one than the spite of a few small-minded folk."

I laughed softly, looking up.

"It's funny, you saying that," I said. "About remembering who I am - or what I am - it seems to be a recurring theme these days."

I smiled brightly, making a point of looking brave and unconcerned.

"Go on, then," I said. "Be off with you. The sooner you go, the sooner you'll be back, isn't that right? And don't worry about us. We girls will be just fine on our own. And we promise to stay out of mischief until you get back!"

I watched her round the corner towards the cave entrance before I sat down and let myself cry.

Chapter 42

Hetty didn't come back the next morning. Nor the morning after that.

I filled the time caring for the baby, reasoning that it was likely she'd been delayed by some business with the tavern or some other soul needing her ministrations. By the evening of the second day, I began to worry.

My daughter was almost eight days old, and time had started to press in on me. The islanders wouldn't risk the nine days passing, the point beyond where the child could be taken to the sea. Nor did I want to risk her bonding so fully to the land that she wouldn't be safe in the Otherworld. No-one had said as much, but I had an inkling that it made a difference. I kept myself moving by walking up and down the length of the cave, venturing as far as the corner leading outwards, so that I could roughly judge the time of day, but I daren't go any further for fear of what might be waiting on the beach. The cave was extremely well-concealed – I even suspected a glamour of sorts – but once I left the shelter of the rocks, I would be exposed to the wide world.

I needed to get myself back to the faery grove before the ninth day. Hetty had explained to me that on the ninth day, Lira and the water horses would come ashore. I had no idea of the dangers that might come with refusing to give up my baby, but I suspected the worst. What I hoped to do was get myself and the baby back up to the hollow before the ninth day, thereby making it pointless for the village folk to be anywhere near the water horses. At least then, no-one would be down at the water's edge and would thereby avoid the immediate danger of the creatures. I shuddered to think of the consequences of incurring their wrath. As much as I loathed some of the village folk for the way they'd treated me and what they intended for my child, I couldn't bear to think of any of them being injured or even killed in such a horrible way. At least if they knew I was beyond reach, they could stay safely away from shore.

Those were the plans I made as I paced up and down. I went over and over it, rehearsing the route in my head, imagining possible obstructions, wondering when the best time of day would be. I was terribly afraid to travel at night, especially with the baby in her sling, just in case I slipped and fell. But, by all calculation, it seemed to be the best and only option.

After spending most of the day fretting and pacing, I decided that if Hetty had not returned by the following morning, I'd set off for the hollow that evening, by myself. I felt better having made the decision and busied myself gathering up the things I'd need to travel. I had only a little bit of bread left, and a small pot of honey as well as some of Hetty's cheese. I tucked that, along with some clean cloths for the baby, adding a flask of fresh water to make it a slightly larger bundle than I'd arrived with. I needed to drink to keep my milk flowing so even though it was heavy, I included it in the pack.

I spent a lot of time talking to the baby. I told her my plan and why I had to make sure we got to the hollow in good time; I told her again about Fingal - and that he'd be waiting for us - and about Cernach and the strange woman who had given me the wrap in which she was safely snuggled. Of course, I also told her about Callum and Morag and how both of them had made it possible that she'd arrived safely. I reminded her about her grandmother, my own mother, who, even though I'd never known her myself, I had the knowledge of from those who had loved and cherished her, which was the next best thing. Whenever I felt my confidence starting to wane, I would hold tightly to the pendant and will myself to be worthy of her gift. What I couldn't do for myself, I knew I could do for my mother and for my daughter.

I thought a lot about what the old woman had said to me, about how all I needed to do was remember what I was. As much as I was now used to the faery-folk penchant for speaking in riddles, this was the most exasperating one of all. They'd kept repeating to me that I wasn't allowed any help, and yet, time and again, one or another of them had stepped in to help me. The reason Hetty had been in the cave at exactly the right time was down to a message she'd found tucked under a bowl of rising dough in the tavern kitchen. That could only mean there was an even bigger task ahead of me, for which I would most definitely be alone. The thought of that was terrifying, especially since my only clue on how to be successful with this particular task, was vague and rife with all manner of possibilities.

My last trip around the cave showed me that night was beginning to fall and still, no sign of Hetty. I resigned myself to having to strike out on my own. Which, all things considered, was probably how it was supposed to be anyway.

I nursed the baby to sleep and settled myself in for what would be my last night in the relative safety of the cave. The light from the small fire flickered on the walls, casting a comforting orange glow. Even the fire, seemingly without the need for additional fuel and without the tell-tale smoke which would be seen from outside, was an example of how I was somehow still under the care and protection of faery folk. That, in itself, made me feel slightly less alone and so I fell into a deep, dreamless sleep.

* * *

I woke with a start. I checked the baby, but she was still nestled beside me, fast asleep. The fire still glowed, emitting warmth and light and now, because it was still dark outside, a great deal of shadow.

I sat up, gently, so as not to disturb my daughter and strained my ears. The sound of the nearby ocean had become such a regular noise as to hardly be noticeable, but there was something else, something that I couldn't quite identify that was drifting along the corridor from outside the cave. Suddenly, the flickering light of a torch became visible.

I stifled a gasp and bent down to scoop up my baby, willing her not to awaken and begin to cry. I settled her, with her blankets, in a shadowy recess, out of range of the revealing light of the fire. My heart thudded so loudly, I was sure that whoever was coming would be able to hear it. I retreated into the shadows beside her and waited.

"Aibhlinn!" came a panting whisper. "It's alright, lass. It's me, Callum. I'm with Hetty."

Callum!

I almost shouted with joy. I emerged from my hiding place and ran over to where he stood, bewildered and looking quite disheveled, a boat lantern held aloft. Behind him, Hetty slipped around the corner and into the cave itself. She, too, looked wild-eyed and ragged.

I threw my arms around Callum, tears of relief running down my face. With his one free arm, he hugged me back, fiercely and without reservation.

"Are ye alright, pet?" he said, stepping back to observe me at arm's length. In the light of his lantern, his face was deeply lined and there were dark smudges under his eyes. He looked as if he hadn't slept for days.

I nodded, emotion making it difficult to speak.

"Where is she, then?" he asked, looking beyond where I stood. "Let's have a look at the wee lass."

I took him by the hand and led him over to where she was nestled in the recess of the cave. I picked her up and handed her to my brother, taking the lantern from him that he might hold his niece in his arms.

"Aw, Leeny," he said, gazing down at the sleeping face of the baby. "She looks just like Mam, I warrant." He looked up at me, smiling through happy tears. I grinned in reply. He reached out a thick, work-roughened finger to touch the tiny, clenched fist. Immediately, she opened her hand and gripped Callum's finger.

He laughed softly. "Well, she's got her mother's grip, that's for certain. She's a feisty wee thing, isn't she?"

Hetty moved to interrupt us.

"I'm sorry, lass. I couldn't get back any sooner. It were all I could do to get to Callum and get away when we did. They've got a watch on everywhere. Morag, the poor lass, she's been through hell and back wi' her mother..."

"Oh no!" I said, my hand flying up to my mouth. "Poor Morag! She didn't..."

Callum shook his head.

"Nay, she's been a rock, that one. She's put up wi' some bloody awful stick from that auld harpy but she didn't give ye away."

A feeling of great affection for Morag washed over me. Even to the last, I wasn't sure if she'd stay the course and defy her mother. I wouldn't have blamed her. I knew only too well the price of being the pariah.

"Good old Morag," I said. "She'll be an honorary Auntie when all this is over with."

"Aye well, that's the next bit o' bad news," said Callum, glancing at Hetty whose face was a mask of fear and worry.

"I'm terrible sorry, lass," said Hetty, her voice trembling. "But we've been followed. I caught sight of a light flashing at the top of the cliff path, just as we got to the bottom. Me and Callum had to find our way here in the dark, but I think they know where we've come to."

Callum nodded, reaching out to squeeze my arm.

"It's true, pet. It's only a matter of time afore they get here."

I think I somehow knew that it would come to this; that confronting the island folk was part of the plan all along. I have no doubts, either, that much of it had all been planned out, engineered by hands not my own. It couldn't have been a coincidence that I was visited by the old woman - or, *an Cailleach*, as Hetty seemed to think it was. Why ever would a being so ancient and powerful appear to an impertinent upstart such as myself, if not for a purpose grander than my own trials and woes? And Cernach, the lord of the forest, the horned god - what possible interest could he have in the trifling affairs of mortals? All of the old tales told of the relative indifference towards mortals that otherworldly creatures such as Cernach possessed. The only time they ever expressed an interest was if there were some benefit to be gained for themselves.

My reasonable assuredness of the truth of these matters had seeped quietly into my mind, trickling in around all of my frantic planning and strategizing. It wasn't until I was faced with the inevitability of having to take my daughter out to the water's edge to confront those who would take her from me, that it all slid into place. Over and over again, the repeated refrain of not offering me aid, and yet, over and over again, at every turn, I was safely delivered. It was all to a purpose; all to ensure that I would reach this place and this time.

The place where I truly *was* to be alone.

Chapter 43

Samhain

The sound of drums drifted in through the corridor of the tunnel. They were summoning the water horses. Hetty and Callum stood, side by side, arms linked together in front of me. Callum held his lantern high, the light casting a sickly glow over the strain on their faces. He turned back to look at me; I stood about ten paces behind them, my daughter, nestled in her sling, held snugly against my breast. I still wore the gown I'd been given by the old faery woman, right before I left my little cottage in the grove. Hetty had taken it out to the sea and washed it for me, under the cover of darkness, three days after my baby was born. It just seemed the right thing to do, to put it on again. If nothing else, it gave me a connection to happier, more secure, times.

I gave Callum my brightest, bravest, smile. He looked ill.

He'd begged me to let him speak for me – then, when I wouldn't budge on that, to let him take the baby himself and just run - and while it was sorely tempting, just for a moment, I knew that wasn't how it was meant to be.

"Are ye ready, lass?" he asked, his voice hoarse.

I nodded, not trusting myself with words just then.

Hetty had also turned, giving me her own version of a bright, brave, smile. Oh, how I admired her! For a person who thought herself alone and bereft of female companionship and guidance, I had such great treasures in Hetty and, funnily enough, Morag. I sorely regretted the willful disregard I'd had for them until now. I'd taken one for granted and, incorrectly assumed I knew the soul of the other.

"Ye'll be alright, pet," said Hetty, stating it, not asking it. "Ye've all the blessings of every sea bride as came afore ye. And all the ones who let the bairns go from them, not knowing they had a choice."

I felt tears pricking the backs of my eyes and a lump rising in my throat. I blinked and swallowed and put my hands, protectively, against the back of my sleeping daughter.

Nodding again, I squared my shoulders and said,

"Let's get it over with, then, shall we? The babe's going to want a feed shortly."

* * *

The sun was just beginning to appear above the horizon when

we stepped out onto the beach. It was cold, much colder than when I'd left the hollow with Cernach. The last of the stars were barely visible and the pink and orange glow of sunrise tinged the clear blue of the autumn sky. Samhain, Hetty had told me. Time had moved so strangely for me over the past few months, extending and shrinking and turning back on itself, and now here we were at the change of the year. So much had transpired and so much yet to happen.

There was a shout. I saw a group of people standing around a small bonfire. One of them raised an arm and pointed; several separated from the group and came striding quickly towards us, holding their own lanterns high in the dim early light.

"Here we are, then," muttered Callum under his breath. "Who would've guessed it'd be that auld cow leading the charge?"

Sure enough, the ominous, bustling figure of Isabelle Dunn led the group towards us. I patted the baby gently, despite the fact she hadn't woken. I think perhaps I was simply bolstering myself against the verbal tirade that I knew was coming.

"Aibhlinn MacFinlay!" she shouted, still twenty paces away. She was dressed in her usual high-buttoned silk embroidered gown, but with now with a thick, woolen shawl pinned around her shoulders. Breathing heavily, she reached us where we stood, just outside the cluster of boulders that marked the entrance to the faery's cave.

Her pinched face was red - with rage or the cold, I wasn't sure which. But her tightly pressed lips and scowl indicated the former more than the latter.

"How dare you?" she spat. "How dare you flaunt the generosity and indulgence of this community? How dare you defy the very order upon which our safety and livelihoods exist? What do you have to say for yourself? Have we, at last, reached the limits of your impertinence?"

I looked around at her companions. Her husband, Frederick, was nowhere to be seen. Nor was Morag. I hoped desperately that she wasn't on the beach at all. I recognized a couple of the women who'd been present when they took me from my washing that day. They were all staring, unabashedly, at the tiny bundle I had strapped to my body. Her black hair was only just visible above the white of the faery-cloth I'd used for her sling.

I cleared my throat, not wanting any wobbles of fear to betray me.

"That's an awful lot of questions, Isabelle. Which would you like me to answer first? Although," I added, "I'm inclined to answer the last one and to tell you that no, indeed, we have not reached the limits of my impertinence. In fact, I've only just begun."

The look of shock on her face might have been comical, were the circumstances not so terribly dire. The women who stood behind her stifled gasps and squeaks, turning into themselves to whisper furiously.

"You should probably know," I continued, "Before you go any further with your accusations and demands, that I have no intention of giving up my baby. Not to you, not to the sea, not to anyone," I raised my voice so it would carry to the gathered crowd. "This so-called custom is one based in deceit and trickery. There is no need, nor has there ever been a need, to hand the children of the marriage back to the sea-folk. I have it on very good information that our safety and livelihoods, as you so clearly state it, are not beholden to the sea-folk in any way. The rite of the sea-bride was created in goodwill and mutual respect between folk of our world and of the Otherworld. It's been twisted, over time, by greedy and power-hungry people - and faeries - into something hurtful and cruel."

By now, the rest of the group had joined us beside the boulders. I saw Alfie, John Avis, my father - of course - Duncan and Alexander. No other women besides Isabelle's cronies. The men had gathered behind the women and heard everything I'd said.

"That's a load of nonsense!" shouted someone from the back. Other voices were raised in agreement. I did my best to not even look at any of them. Instead, I focused on Isabelle.

"How long have you been bribing John?" I asked her, gambling on something that I'd begun to suspect months earlier.

It was quite satisfying to see her blanch. To her credit, she recovered quickly; quickly enough that anyone not standing close to her wouldn't have noticed her immediate reaction.

"Morag is quite a few years older than me. And your husband has had her name down since she was eighteen - that much she told me," I added, in case Isabelle tried to deny that part. "It just seems ever so strange that someone of your... influence, in the community, would leave it all to chance. If you'd wanted Morag to be a sea bride, I imagine you'd have made it happen. Instead, though, you've bribed John all this time to keep her name out of the draw, haven't you?"

Isabelle drew herself up to her considerable height and bulk.

"Poisonous lies," she rasped, spittle flying from between her gritted teeth. "Nothing but poison and slander. But what else would we expect, from someone such as yourself, eh? Vicious little half-breed that you are. Nothing but a dirty little upstart, spawn of faery filth and a good-for-nothing, drink-sodden, fisherman."

Her words cut me to my very bones, but I didn't let it show. I heard Callum draw his breath sharply, but I raised my hand slightly, staying his retort.

I shook back my hair – my mother's hair – as fair as she was with curls as wild as the waves that rolled and spun onto the shore.

"Ah, Mr. Dunn, too, I suppose?" I said, tilting my head and smiling sweetly. "I heard she had that way about her. Everyone loved her, my mother. How could they not? She was beautiful and kind; gentle and soft-spoken. A generous spirit, I think, is how I've heard her most often described."

Isabelle's face twisted into an ugly grimace.

"Everything that you're not, Isabelle Dunn."

Hetty spoke up from where she'd come to stand, beside me.

"If anyone is guilty of spreading poison and slander, it's ye, ye pinch-faced harpy. How long did I let ye string me along, playing on me own grief? How long did I let ye convince me it were the right thing t'do? Well, I own that's a debt I'll be payin' for the rest o' my days but let me tell ye this: I'll not stand by and watch ye do to this lass what ye and the likes o' ye, have done to the women o' this island all these years. This ends here."

Hetty was left breathless by her speech. I reached out a hand and squeezed her elbow. She nodded imperceptibly and then crossed her arms in front of her chest.

"Alfie!" screeched Isabelle, turning sharply away from us. "Get those drums going. We've a summoning to do this day and no-one, with their wild stories and vicious lies, is going to stand in our way. Do we want the wrath of the sea-folk descending upon us? Do we want to be cringing under the force of deadly winter storms? Storms that wreck our boats and claim our menfolk? Storms that blow the roofs from over our heads? And what of the water horses? What of their hunting grounds? Would we allow them back among us - slaughtering our sheep, our children?"

She was raising them into a frenzy of pumped fists and shouts. The men all had rowan staffs, tied about with ribbon and hung with charms. They started thumping them into the sand, solid, muffled thuds that reverberated under our feet. The drums rose again, in earnest, and the menfolk turned, including my father, began to walk back to the bonfire.

Isabelle turned back to us, smiling thinly.

"You'll find it's all without avail, my dear. Once the beasts come ashore, you'll have no choice whatsoever. And after they have what they've come for? It will only get worse for you. You can't expect to be welcomed back into the fold after this performance."

"I somehow doubt I'll want to be," I replied, softly so that no-one could hear.

Not everyone walked back to the fire.

Three of the women stayed. As did Alexander and Duncan.

"Aw, lassie," said Alexander, walking towards me with his hands outstretched. Duncan hung back, grinning like a fool.

I let myself be folded into my eldest brother's arms, placing a hand over my baby's head so that she wouldn't be crushed between us. He stepped back and looked down with wonder at his niece.

"She's a grand head o' hair, hasn't she?" he said, his eyes brimming. He looked back at me, searching my face. "I warrant I haven't a clue what's gone on wi' ye, but it's clear to me that things are terribly amiss. I trust ye, that ye know what ye're about," he glanced at Hetty. "And I trust our Callum and Hetty as well, to see ye alright." He gestured with his head towards Duncan. "And that grinning eejit does an' all!"

We all laughed, then. Softly and with a measure of restraint, but it was a welcome relief from all the hatred and nastiness that had been thrown around in the last minutes.

"Now," he said, looking back towards the group at the fire. "Is there aught we can do to help?"

I shook my head.

"Nothing," I said. "Your trust is everything. Promise me you'll just let me do what needs doing, no matter how it looks, and that you'll trust it'll all be right in the end?"

He narrowed his eyes, looking, again, at Callum and Hetty. Callum nodded, silently.

"Right you are, then," said Alexander. "I'll take ye at yer word. Come on, you lot," he gestured at the three women.

"No," I said, putting out a hand to stop them. "Can you wait a minute. Callum?"

He nodded and walked to stand with Alexander and Duncan.

"Just the womenfolk now," he explained to Alexander's questioning glance. "That's the way it has to be, so I'm told." He frowned, briefly, in our direction then put an arm around each of our brothers. "Besides," he said. "I reckon we might be needed after all, once this lot gets wind o' what our wee lass is up to." The three of them grinned mischievously and headed off towards the fire.

I turned to the three women.

"If you're willing," I said. "I'd have you to stand with me. At the last, I'll need to be alone, but in the meantime, I'd draw strength from your presence."

The three women glanced at each other, nervously and with an air of indecision.

"There'll be no ill will between us, if you decide not to stay. But you should know that you'll not be in any danger. It's the child they want, not any of us."

My voice broke as I said it, but it was the truth. Inwardly, I hoped that they'd stay but I knew I couldn't compel them against their will.

Maggie Stuart nodded.

"Aye, lass," she said. "We'll stay. We've not been happy wi' how things've gone on this past while. There's a feel o' truth in what ye said, and I reckon it's time the womenfolk took back what was ours from long ago."

I reached out my hand and briefly squeezed hers. She smiled widely.

"Can I see the bairn?" she asked.

I nodded and soon all three women were gathered around, cooing softly at my sleeping daughter. I looked over their heads to Hetty, who stood facing the water's edge, her hands twisting in her skirts.

She turned back to me, fear written plainly on her face.

"They're coming, lass."

"I know," I said. "I can feel them."

The three women turned from their admiration of the baby to stand, hands held fast together, beside me. Hetty walked back and stood on my other side. We were all trembling, none of us without fear, but we stood our ground and watched.

The sea was a churning mass of black and brown bodies. From time to time, a head and neck would be visible above the foaming surf. Massive and deadly, with long, pointed heads and rows of vicious, snapping teeth. Lured by the sound of

Alfie's summoning drums, the water horses came ashore.

<h1 style="text-align:center">Chapter 44</h1>

There were three of them. Tall, heavily muscled, long of limb, their coats streaming with water, they stood at the very edge of the ocean; the place where the sea met the sand. The undulating waves washed forwards and backwards over their feathered hooves. Fingal had told me that, as long as the treaty held, they could come no further onto land. Despite this, John Avis and the other men of the gathered group seemed disinclined to get too close.

"We've called ye here, on the eve of the year's turning, to offer a great gift!" intoned John, his arms held aloft. "Let it be known that the people of Glencarragh have long upheld the traditions and bargains of our ancestors, acknowledging our place – and yours – in the continued prosperity of this land."

He paused, as if expecting a reaction. One of the water horses stepped slightly forwards. It was the tallest of the three, black as midnight, the long, tangled mane woven through with shell and bone. It scanned the group over by the fire, then turned its gaze towards us. It cocked its head in a strangely familiar gesture.

My breath caught in my throat.

Could it be him? I wondered. Could it be my Fingal?

I made to step towards the creatures, but Hetty caught my arm and shook her head, her eyes pleading with me. I placed my hand on hers and held it there, willing her not to object, willing her to let me do what needed to be done. I hadn't known, until that very moment, what it was I had to do. But now it seemed so very clear. Seeing the black water horse standing there on the threshold of the ocean, I was reminded of the day I first met Fingal – the day I became a sea bride. And, suddenly, but with a quiet surety, all of the pieces fell into place.

"Today marks a momentous occasion," continued John, warming up to his role, "'Tis a day not often occurring, but when it does, we must all give thanks for the great good fortune and the bounty of the union between land and sea!"

He turned towards me, beckoning me forwards with his arm. I suppose he imagined me to refuse, because his face registered great surprise when I quietly walked towards them, my hands resting lightly on the back of my sleeping babe. A murmur shot through the crowd. I couldn't help but notice the smug expression of Isabelle Dunn as she moved herself closer to the front of the group, until she was just behind John. She folded her hands in front of her and smiled a beatific smile. I imagine she felt herself the victor.

That's the way, lassie, said a familiar voice from inside my head. I turned to look behind me. There, just visible around the edge of one of the largest boulders, stood the old woman. She nodded slightly.

Ye remember rightly, my girl. Trust what ye are and from whence ye've come. Them who tend will be cared for in their turn.

And then she was gone.

I stood, facing the three water horses, and I was alone.

* * *

"Give them the child," ordered Isabelle, striding towards me.

The water horses hissed and snapped, and she took a startled step backwards. John Avis grabbed her arm and pulled her further away.

"Are ye mad, woman?" he said, his eyes wide. "The bastards'll tear ye limb from limb if ye get too close. Dinna think for a minute that they wouldn't."

"But she needs to hand over the infant," said Isabelle, her face suddenly pale with the realization of how close she'd been to an unpleasant end. "Make her give it over!"

"Yes, human," came an imperious voice. "My pets grow weary of waiting; their appetites only increase, and I fear I may lose control of them should our business take longer than necessary."

I hadn't seen her appear, but suddenly, there she stood at the water's edge, a long, pale hand caressing the muscled neck of the black water horse. She gave me a knowing glance, scorn etched clearly on her impossibly beautiful face. Lira, the queen of the sea-folk. I tore my gaze from her, not wanting her to see my fear and loathing. And something else. The suggestive way in which she touched the water horse, a proprietary gesture, made me seethe inwardly. Despite my efforts, she must have seen my reaction because she laughed, hollowly and curled her perfectly shaped lips into a sneer. My daughter shifted in her sling, and I placed a soothing hand on her back, bringing me back to myself.

"Aibhlinn, lass," said John. "Ye know what ye must do, so, please, wi'out a fuss." He smiled, kindly and lowered his voice. "It's yer own fault that ye've to be the one to do it, pet. Usually, the bairn is taken from its dam afore now."

"I'm her mother," I said, stiffly. "And I will not hand her over."

Isabelle lunged forwards, apparently heedless of the danger.

I stepped back, stumbling in the wet sand. I spun around to steady myself and when I regained my balance a great commotion erupted. There was a shout from somewhere beyond the fire and a figure came hurtling towards us. Even the water horses seemed momentarily surprised, as they, too, moved back into the sea as the person came running towards us, holding high a flaming torch and something else held aloft in the other hand. Then, if that weren't enough, yet another figure came labouring up behind them, breath coming in heavy gasps.

"Morag!"

"Father Ewan!" she shouted, for it was, indeed Morag. A very disheveled and out of breath Morag. "No!!!"

Just then, I realized what was happening.

Father Ewan had slowed to a walk but was marching steadily towards the water's edge where Lira and the water horses waited. He held the torch high, so I could see his face. It was stark white, and his eyes were wide and wild. There was a strange light in them, and his expression was one of grim determination. He held a large, wooden, cross in the other hand and raised his voice to speak aloud what seemed to be a prayer of some kind, although not one I'd ever heard. His words were lost in the shouts and roar of the men from beside the fire, several of them broke from the group and came running towards us. The wind had picked up and the waves offshore became choppier.

Still, the water horses stood their ground. One of them pawed the surf, sending a spray of water outwards. Lira simply stood there, her face expressionless. Father Ewan kept on marching.

Too late, I realized his true intent.

"No!" I shouted, echoing Morag's plea.

She stood, weeping, beside her mother, who had intercepted her, holding Morag's arm in a vice-like grip.

I darted forwards to intercept the old priest, but he barely acknowledged me. He spared me a glance and paused in his prayer to smile, although his eyes, I'm sure, weren't seeing me.

"Forgive me, dearest Anwen," he said, and walked into the sea.

I cannot speak of what took place then. There was an inhuman shriek, followed by a scream, as the water erupted into a mass of churning foam. I heard other people screaming, but I turned away until the sounds abated. Turning back, the only signs of what had taken place was the extinguished torch bobbing on the blood-tinged tide.

Lira smiled, a cold, mirthless, smile, and shrugged. "Once a fool, always a fool. Now, I believe we have matters to attend. I see no reason to delay. My pets have whetted their appetites now; I would hate for this to get any... messier." She gave me a calculating look, then lowered her gaze to my daughter, bound tightly to my breast. "I believe you have something of mine?"

I was still trying to reconcile what had just happened when Isabelle charged up to me, gripping me by the shoulders.

"You!" she screamed, spittle flying from her lips. "You have done this! You wretched, wretched child! Do you see now, the price of your selfishness?" She reached up and slapped me, hard, across the face. I reeled backwards, my face stinging. The shouting and the staggering impact of the slap woke the baby who began to cry loudly.

"Give me that!" Isabelle reached out and attempted to pull the sling loose from my body. I staggered backwards again, trying to wrench myself from her clawing grip.

"They're coming back!" came a shout. "Get away from the edge!"

"Let me go!" I shrieked, shoving hard, but Isabelle was a large woman, tall and strong and she outweighed me by at least half. I could feel the binding of the sling giving way. My daughter wailed, frightened, no doubt, by all of the noise and rough treatment. I couldn't lose her now, not when we'd come so close!

"Aibhlinn!" Morag's voice was in my ear. "Go," she said, panting heavily. "Now!"

Isabelle's grip suddenly slackened, and she staggered backward. I could see Morag, her fists twisted into her mother's hair and dress, hauling her away.

I looked wildly around me; everything was in confusion. Back towards the shoreline, the three horses had returned, blood-flecked muzzles champing. The black one regarded me with its wicked red eye.

"I won't know you," Fingal had said.

"It won't matter, my love," I said, under my breath as I approached the water. "Because I will know you, and I will remember."

I held my wailing daughter tightly to my chest and stepped into the ocean.

Chapter 45

I am my mother's daughter. She, in turn, was daughter and mother, both. Maiden, mother, crone. Over and again, it spirals through the generations, each becoming the other - one reborn into the next. If we remember that, we know we are never lost, never truly alone, never truly gone.

* * *

My baby stopped screaming once the water closed over her head. I held firm, pressing my hands against her back, my eyes ahead, on the horizon. The cold water clung to my dress and pulled the loose wrapping of the sling downward, but still I walked, wading through the surging tide.

All around me was chaos. The water foamed and spat with the churning bodies of the water horses. They charged past and around, sending up salty spray that stung my eyes and blurred my vision. They shrieked and hissed and spat, all snapping teeth and the stink of rot on their breath. If it was Fingal among them, then he truly did not know me, for that one, of all of them was most bold and most savage. His tail whipped against my bare legs. I felt myself pushed off balance and sought to stay upright, not certain why it mattered, but somehow it did.

The birthing gown, woven from the same faery cloth as my bride's dress, and that of the sling which held my babe close to my breast, kept them from me.

* * *

I remembered the fear on Fingal's face when I wanted to take off my dirty, ragged, gown.

I remembered the way the old woman had left the length of cloth, to keep the babe safe.

I remembered the charm that hung around my neck and how it held my memories against the faery spell.

Most of all, I remembered that I was not alone, that there was a lineage of women who'd tended the soul of the land, walking beside me.

* * *

The water had risen to my chin. I found it hard to keep walking and knew I'd have to strike off and swim.

My daughter was still, nestled snug against me.

The water horses were swimming now, circling around me, up ahead and behind.

I took one final breath and sank beneath the surface.

Chapter 46

While I'd every faith in the faery cloth to protect us from the water horses, my faith in our ultimate survival was not so absolute. I'd been required to put a great deal of trust in the forces which I was sure had led me to the choices I was making, and trust in others isn't something I've had much practice in.

Help is allus there, Hetty had been fond of saying, *for those as pay close mind to it.*

The help that did come, though, wasn't at all what I'd expected.

***

Even though I'd experienced it once before, the ability to breathe, with ease, underwater, still came as a shock. It was easier, I suppose, for my baby, having not long ago been suspended in her birth brine. Perhaps that's why she didn't struggle or fuss when she went below the surface; perhaps that's why she settled so easily. Whatever the reason, she lay, nestled and content against me as I swam, awkwardly, down.

The water horses were following us. They kept their distance, passing closely only on occasion. It was as if the protection of the cloth also weakened them, as their initial savagery seemed to be waning slightly. Or perhaps, like other predators, once the ease of the catch was gone, they became disinterested.

It was dim under the surface. The light was that of twilight, or the threshold moment just before the sun begins to climb; the point where familiar shapes are still blurred outlines and only the memory of them makes them real. It's as if remembering them holds them in place amid the swallowing blackness of night. In the grey gloom of the sea, it was only the memory of the water horses that swam around me. I half-wondered that if I forgot them, would they leave us alone.

I had only a vague notion of where I was going and even less idea how long I would have the strength to carry both of us through the constant tug and pull of the tide.

The water horses kept pace, circling widely, their outlines emerging and retreating in the murk. They were waiting, I'm sure, in the other way that predators do, for me to weaken.

All along, I kept up a steady stream of invocation in my mind. I called on my mother and her mother before her, and every other woman of Glencarragh who had watched over and cared for the land and its creatures - human and not; on every sea bride and mother of children lost to a wicked bargain. It became a one-sided conversation, a plea for the strength to carry me and my child to a place of safety and it kept me from going mad with the fear that it would all end wrongly, no matter how far I'd already come.

I was trying to get us to the underwater cave to which Fingal had brought me on our first day together. If I had it sorted properly in my head, it was the exact reflection of the cave in which I'd just given birth to my daughter. If that were true, then to find the cave would be to find our way back into the enchanted grove – the underwater cave being the way in and the cave on the surface, being the way out. It seemed a clever enough plan when I thought of it. Now that I was facing fatigue, dark water and circling water horses, I began to question the wisdom of my choice.

My arms and legs ached. I swam with only one arm, not trusting the sling to hold my baby so keeping one hand on her back at all times. This meant clumsy, awkward and terribly slow progress. Ever so gradually, I felt the dullness of exhaustion taking hold.

The water horses must have sensed me getting weaker. They became bolder, sweeping brazenly past and underneath me. There were more of them now. Five or six, instead of just the original three. I wondered briefly what might be happening on shore, if my going into the water had really broken the treaty between the sea-folk and my people. The vision of Father Ewan came, unwelcome, into my mind's eye and I quickly shoved it aside. I offered up another plea to my ancestors, this time for the safety of my friends and family. If Lira, cheated of her prize, no longer bothered to control the water horses, things on land would be very dire indeed.

I couldn't think of that, I told myself. I needed to focus only on getting to safety, sure as I was, that bringing my daughter back to the glade would somehow make everything right.

Still, as much as I tried to bolster myself along, I found my thoughts drifting quietly towards defeat. It started to make sense to me that I simply give in. I wasn't going to be able to find the cave. Whatever made me think that I could? I was no longer afraid, though, just tired and wanting nothing more than to surrender to restful oblivion. I let myself stop swimming. I wrapped both arms around my baby and tucked my chin onto the top of her head. Her tousle of black hair fanned upward like reeds in a loch, the strands waving gently with the movement of the water around me. It felt so calming, so comforting, to just let myself be carried by the nudge and pull of the ocean.

I was vaguely aware of a gathering of dark shapes in the grey-green gloom of the water. I didn't care. If there were more water horses coming, then so be it. I was tired, so very tired. I'd been fighting for months. Years, even. My whole life had been a fight of one kind or another. I'd done everything I could. Surely, nothing more could be expected of me. Surely, it was time for me to finally have a much-deserved rest. I closed my eyes and stopped fighting.

Chapter 47

I don't know how long I drifted. It may have been hours, or it may have only been seconds, but I found myself being drawn back to conscious thought by the sound of faraway voices.

As the voices grew louder and closer, I realized that they weren't speaking in any tongue that I understood – in fact, it was more melody than words, an echoing ripple of song that slowly surrounded me.

I opened my eyes. The light was slightly less dim than before, and I could see the outline of dark shapes. The shapes, however, were smaller, and more numerous. They swam closer, a group of ten or more, long, sinuous shapes that slid effortlessly through the water to surround us.

They couldn't be water horses, I reasoned. They were too small. I blinked, still feeling leaden and slow, not believing what I was seeing.

Seals.

No, not seals, I thought, absently, through my fatigue. Not seals. The selkie. The selkie are here.

I smiled dreamily to myself, gently tightening my arms around my daughter as if to reassure her.

I closed my eyes again, this time to let the selkie guide me home.

Chapter 48

I was sure we would die there, in the sea. It came to me like a quiet agreement, a gentle sigh of recognition that that was how it would be and that it was alright. I think that if true dying is like that, then I shall never fear it.

I remember dreaming of seals - no, the selkie - and then nothing more until I awoke on the floor of the cave, wrapped in a dry blanket, my daughter warm and snug beside me. The fact that we were alive was less a moment of joy than one of equal acceptance as it would have been had we died.

Of what happened in between, I have only half-dreamed images. I have vague memories of a woman, a fair-haired woman, smiling down at me. But every time I try to see the finer details of her face, it slips away from me. She reached out to smooth my hair, smooth my baby's hair, and to touch the pendant at my breast with her fingertips. I can still feel the tingle of her touch if I close my eyes and concentrate. She never spoke, at least not with words, but I feel, sometimes, that she had a voice like the sea - rhythmic and soothing, a gentle caress over my tired body and aching heart.

When I awoke properly, though, she was gone. My birthing gown and my daughter's sling were clean and dry and folded neatly in a pile beside the little fire that crackled merrily in the middle of the cave. For all appearances it was the very cave to which I'd arrived, my body heaving with birthing pains, not so long ago. It was, I hoped, the cave which would lead me back to the enchanted grove, to safety and to Fingal.

"Did she give you the child's name?" came a voice from just outside the light of the fire.

I suppose there was a time when a voice emanating from the shadows would have unsettled me, but that time was a far distant memory. Besides, I would have recognized the deep, rumbling tones of the forest lord anywhere.

"Who?" I asked, impulsively wanting to dissemble. For some reason, I didn't really want to share my mysterious benefactor, but I was aware of how much I was beholden to the forest lord for Fingal's deliverance from his punishment. I thought, briefly, of the water horses then quickly shoved the memory from my mind.

He laughed. It was a pleasant sound, like the rumble of distant thunder.

"I know that you know you can't hide anything from me, lovely creature. 'Tis a fine wee lassie you've got there. Well done indeed."

I nodded, stiffly, shifting my daughter to my breast as I felt her stirring. She immediately settled again and began to nurse. I still felt terribly vulnerable, and not only because I realized I was naked underneath the blanket. Despite having slept deeply, I still hadn't entirely regained my strength and I knew I had a fair bit of traveling ahead of me. Cernach's interest in my baby didn't sit easily.

He emerged from the dimness, the improbability of his antlers casting strange, tree-like shadows as he stepped into the firelight. He was dressed as a gentleman again, wearing fine, tailored coat and trousers. He rather fancied himself, I think.

"No need to worry," he said, waving a hand dismissively. "I've no inclination towards raising a mongrel brat. I've never understood that particular preoccupation of Lira's." He paused to tug at the lace cuffs of his shirt. "Although, I suppose I can see from whence it stems." He shrugged. "Never mind, it's of no importance. She overstepped herself, again, and it needed to stop. All that really matters in this moment is that you've upheld your part of the bargain and so, as I'm an honorable sort, I shall uphold mine. Even if you're not going to tell me the child's name," he added, winking.

I think I must have looked slightly bewildered because he began to laugh again.

"Oh, I know she told you," he said "You may not have it yet, but it's in there." He pointed towards my head. "It'll come. Now - have you all of your things?"

It was my turn to laugh.

"What things?" I said, "Everything of importance to me is right here - the rest is just trappings."

"Good lass," he said, smiling widely. "Come on then, let's be off."

He held out a hand.

I shook my head.

"I'm not fit to travel," I said. "I'm exhausted and can't face carrying the baby all the way to the cottage. I'll be fine on my own for a day or two. I'll make my way there once I feel a bit more rested."

Cernach narrowed his eyes.

"You don't trust me."

It was a statement, not a question, and I couldn't stop my face from flushing. I avoided his gaze.

"I don't feel like I can really trust any of you," I said, quietly. "You - you and the old woman - you planned all this, didn't you? You let me think the choices were mine to make, but you've just been using me - us - to further your own ends. I don't see how that makes you any better than Lira."

The only sound was the snap and pop of the fire.

"You're a clever lass, Aibhlinn," said Cernach, finally breaking the silence. "But you need to understand that you're only one thread in the tapestry. A very important thread, yes, but still, only a thread."

I kept my eyes down, willing myself not to cry. Of course, he was right, putting it like that. But it still didn't make me feel any less used and I told him so, not being willing to let it go unacknowledged.

He dipped his antlers towards me.

"We forget," he said, "My kind, being what we are, that you're only here for the blink of an eye. And so these things matter to you - these trespasses upon your will and your lives - indeed, it's regretful that we must tread as roughly as we do sometimes."

I nodded, realizing how much it cost him to say that. I suppose it was as close to an apology as the lord of the forest ever comes.

"And it's just as regretful to me to occasionally complicate your well-laid...trespasses," I said, demurely.

The trace of a smile tugged at one side of his mouth. I hid my face behind my hair so that he wouldn't see my own failed attempts at suppressing a grin.

"If you would be so kind as to pass my gown and avert your eyes," I said. "I'll get dressed so that we can get going."

His eyes widened and he made no attempt to hide his amusement when he realized I hadn't any clothing. For a brief moment I panicked, being all too familiar with the tales of his... appetites. He saw the expression on my face and grinned, lasciviously, before making a show of walking past me to retrieve my gown. He peered over the top of the blanket and winked.

"Hungry little tinker, isn't she?" he asked, chuckling as he handed me my gown. He stepped to the other side of the fire and turned his back. "Hope she can hold her appetite long enough for you to get your clothes on."

A few moments later and I stood ready to travel once again. I'd retied the sling and the baby, her belly full, was content to drift back to sleep. She was getting bigger by the day, it seemed. And heavier. My back protested the weight of her, and I tried to ignore the trembling in my legs.

Cernach smiled winningly and held out his arm. I accepted it, tucking my hand in the crook of his elbow.

"As a token of my continued good will," he said, as we walked towards the back of the cave. "And with your permission, of course," he added, with a nod of his head. "I'm going to save us a bit of time – and your legs a bit of wobbling – and get us back to your wee cottage in a less, shall we say, direct, fashion."

I could have cried with relief. I suppose my leaning heavily on his arm had not escaped his notice. All the same, I wasn't about to argue. I summoned the last of my strength and bobbed a trembling curtsy.

"As you please, my lord," I said, with as much dignity as I could muster.

* * *

We rounded the corner of the passage at the back of the cave and stepped directly into the forest glade. My beloved cottage was no further than twenty paces away.

The late spring sun shone warmly, and I closed my eyes for a moment, hardly daring to breathe. I was here. We were here. I had brought my daughter safely home.

"I would offer to walk you to the door myself," said Cernach, gently disengaging himself from my grip. "But I believe there's another gentleman that would like the honour."

I looked up to see my beloved Fingal standing in the doorway of the cottage. In the space of two heartbeats, he was beside me, holding me in his arms as I sank to the grass, sobbing with relief.

We sat there for what seemed like an age until the sound of Cernach clearing his throat brought me out of my exhausted reverie.

"I shall leave you now," he said, smiling down at us. "I know you're exhausted, and I imagine you're in a hurry to get yourselves off to bed." He paused, mischief in his dancing eyes. "But before I go, there's one last thing,"

I think my heart sank then. I thought it had been too easy. Surely there must be another catch - another trespass. I was determined not to let him see my fear, though.

"Oh?" I said, quietly.

"Be well," he said, placing a hand on my shoulder. "Teach her what it means to be your daughter and a child of the land and sea. Make sure she knows the magic she carries within her."

My throat was tight with unshed tears. I hadn't expected a blessing.

"When you're ready," he added. "And not before long, mind you, you'll have to go back. You vowed to raise her in the mortal world and that vow will be upheld."

He held up a hand as I gathered my protest.

"Only when you're ready. And one day, you will be, you can be assured of that. Remember that she has her own thread in the tapestry."

He bowed then, a deep, sweeping court bow that made the tips of his antlers touch the grass, and turned to go.

"My lord Cernach," I called after him. He turned back, a question in his eyes.

"Aila," I said, looking down at my black-haired daughter where she was cradled in her father's arms. "Her name is Aila."

The old god smiled and dipped his antlers again.

"Hope," he said. "And so she is."

Chapter 49

Epilogue

Morag

"Will you go again?"

Hetty's face is hopeful and worried all at once. She asks me this every day, even though she knows the answer. I promised her I'd go every day, no matter what, and I intend to keep that promise. So, I smile and pat her arm, like I always do, exchanging a look with Callum across the room.

"Of course, Hetty. Just as soon as I've finished scrubbing these pots, I'll be away. Tide's out so it's perfectly safe."

"Aye," says Callum, bringing me a fresh stack of plates to wash. "Our Morag hasn't missed a day yet and she's not likely to start. Now, let me steep the tea and ye get on and sit yerself down and have a cup and mebbe a bit of toast, aye? Ye're looking a bit peaky and we cannae have ye wasting away to nothing. Aibhlinn'll never forgive us if she thinks we havenae looked after ye while she's been gone."

I smile gratefully at Callum. He's far better with soothing and cajoling Hetty than I am; I'm afraid I get impatient and a bit snappish sometimes. We're all worried about Aibhlinn, but seeing Hetty collapsing in on herself has only made it worse.

It's been nigh on seven months since Aibhlinn and her bairn disappeared into the sea. I don't think I've ever seen anything so terrifying as the sight of her walking into the water with all those mad-eyed water-horses thrashing about. All the screaming and carrying on, my mother being the worst offender. That nasty piece Lira was shrieking like a banshee, Alfie and his drummers banging away like their lives depended on it, and I suppose they did. All of our lives did. The men were all shouting and bellowing, trying to get the women away from the shore but there they were just standing there with tears streaming down their faces. I just left. I didn't know what to think or do or feel and it was days before it all calmed down.

I had to leave our house. My mother became unbearable, and my father wouldn't even look at me. Hetty took me in, against John's wishes but she stood up to him, telling him it was her tavern anyway and he was in no position to cross her. Anyway, here I am. I help Hetty in the kitchen for my keep and spend the rest of my time walking the shore, waiting and hoping that she'll come back.

***

"Are ye ready, lass? I'll walk ye down, if ye like?"

"You don't have to," I say, blushing. I wish I didn't act such the gormless idiot around Callum. He's been so kind to me and has stood up for me with the other islanders and truth be told, I don't quite know how to take it all. I know he's just being nice, but sometimes...well, it doesn't matter.

"Well, I know that, ye daft creature," he says, with that grin of his that's all crooked, "but I'm going that way anyway and who knows, mebbe I'll be the good luck charm and this'll be the day she comes home."

"Do you really think...." I bite the end off the sentence. I don't want to be the harbinger of doom, but it *has* been seven months since she disappeared and only slightly less than that since that strange old woman turned up on the tavern doorstep and told Hetty that Aibhlinn was safe and so was the bairn.

"I don't *think*," says Callum, his voice stern, "I *know* that she'll be back. And when she comes, one of us needs to be there waiting for her."

I nod, pulling on my coat and fastening an oilskin hat over my hair. It's wild out there still, the wind battering against the windows of the tavern. It's been this way, more or less, since she left. We ought to be having light spring breezes by now, but the winter won't let go. Just one of the many things she's being blamed for.

We don't speak as we make our way down the cliff path. Every once in a while, Callum reaches out a hand to steady me over a steep or rocky bit. He's just being a gentleman but it's a kindness I appreciate. Eventually we get to the bottom; the water's edge is a distant blur, and the sand seems to go on forever. The water horses haven't come, even though my mother was convinced we'd all be slaughtered in our beds, but still, no-one dares go down to the beach when the tide is in. The horrible sight of what happened to Father Ewan is still burned into my brain. In unspoken agreement, we start making our way towards the cave.

"How's the croft shaping up?" I ask, by way of making conversation. Callum has been doing up the little cottage that Aibhlinn found for herself over by the wood. I've been helping when I can - my mother's insistence on me learning how to embroider has come in handy. Aibhlinn has some lovely curtains and cushions to decorate her ramshackle little house.

"Grand, lass. I've put the last coat of whitewash on, and the windows are mended. It'll be ready for ye to put yer little bits and pieces in soon."

He gives me that crooked smile again and I look away.

"She's going to be so pleased to see it," I say, going along with the charade, because that's what if feels like at this point - just some fantasy we tell each other to make ourselves feel better. "You don't think she'll be cross that you showed me it, do you? I mean, it's supposed to be a secret."

The pressure of his hand is warm, even through the sleeve of my coat.

"Nay, lass. She'll be glad of yer help. After all, if it weren't for ye, she might never have got herself away."

I try not to flinch at that because I'm still not sure I did the right thing.

*****

We stand, silent again, for some minutes. I'm leaning against a large boulder, my hands stuffed in my pockets, hunched into my coat away from the bite of the wind. Callum has gone into the cave, but he won't find anything. Just an empty space and a wall of rock at the back. I should know, I've been in there countless times.

"Nothing?" I question, already knowing the answer by the look on his face as he emerges.

He shakes his head and I nod. We stand quietly for a minute or two.

"You don't have to stay," I say. "I usually just wait here for a bit then walk up and along and back again to stay warm. It's a few hours before the tide turns and I'm sure you've things to do." As much as I like his company, I feel awkward, like I should be entertaining him with my clever conversation and sparkling wit.

He looks out to the sea then back at the mouth of the cave before shrugging and clearing his throat. His eyes are shining with a sad sort of light.

"Aye, well. I should be getting on, I warrant. Will ye walk wi' me back to the path? Ye look as if ye need warming up. Hetty should send ye with a flask of something."

"Hetty has enough on her mind without worrying about me," I reply, falling into step beside him. "I'm fine. I can look after myself." I don't mean it to sound so defensive, but the habits of a lifetime don't die easily.

We're walking into the wind, and it buffets and pushes insistently, making it too difficult to carry on talking, which is fine because I have nothing clever or sparkling to say.

"Eeeh, lass, this wind is a beast," he shouts, leaning in so I can hear. We stop walking and I stand huddled against him, thankful for the warmth. "Go on back to the shelter of the cliff. I can manage from here."

I nod, my face numb from the blast of the wind and turn around, thankful for the brief reprieve.

I only get about five strides away from him when I look up and see her. I know it's her, even from the distance. Her hair is billowing around her in a golden cloud and she's holding the hand of a small child.

"Callum!" My voice is hoarse, and it comes out in a barely audible croak. "Callum!"

I feel him come to stand beside me, but I don't even turn to look. I'm already running.

THE END

About the Author

Melanie Leavey was born and raised in the north-east of England before emigrating to Canada with her family at the age of nine. An aspiring hermit and passionate gardener, she likes nothing better than drinking tea and thumbing through the latest David Austin rose catalogue. A country mouse turned town mouse, she lives with her husband, two children, a badly-behaved Jack Russell and a cat named George on the Territory of the Haudenosaunee Confederacy, Fort Erie, Ontario.

You can connect with me on:

🌐 http://www.threeravens.ca

Subscribe to my newsletter:

✉ https://landing.mailerlite.com/webforms/landing/a6v1h6

Also by Melanie Leavey

Tales of Glencarragh

Skelly - Book One of the Sea Glass Trilogy

Wind Singer - Book Two of the Sea Glass Trilogy

Soul of the Sea - Book Three of the Sea Glass Trilogy